A LEAP OF FAITH AT THE VINEYARD IN ALSACE

BOOK 3, DOMAINE DES MONTAGNES

JULIE STOCK

CLUED UP PUBLISHING

Cover Design: Fully Booked Cover Design
Editing: Helena Fairfax
Proofreading: Perfect Prose Services

To the Kirzdorf line of my family,
who inspired this trilogy of books

CHAPTER ONE

Sunday, 25 November 2018

Ellie

Ellie woke early that morning and slipped out of bed, leaving Henri snoring gently behind her. She put a jumper over her pyjamas, pulled on some warm socks and, careful not to make any noise, padded out of the bedroom, through the living area and out onto the balcony. They'd been in Crete for almost a month, but this was only the second morning she'd got up in time to see the sunrise. There hadn't been too many seven o'clock starts on this whole trip, thank goodness.

Wrapping her arms around her against the late November chill, she gazed out across the inky sea. The salty tang filled the air even from this far away, so strong she could almost taste it. She could just about make out the mountains in the distance – they already had a sprinkling of snow on them – and the sky was changing colour from black to navy, and shades of lighter blue, as well as hints of orange and yellow. This sunrise was as stunning as the last one they'd watched together just after they'd arrived.

She'd already made up her mind to return to Crete when the weather was a bit warmer. They'd loved the island so much, they'd stayed longer than the two weeks they'd originally planned. They'd meant to go on to Athens to finish their trip, but that would also have to wait until another day. She sighed as she thought about this being the final day of their trip. If it was up to her, they would keep on travelling and never return to 'normal' life.

But there was also the not-so-small matter of money. Hers had pretty much run out, so even if she didn't have the dreaded responsibilities to return to, she would still need to work to pay for more travelling. But she was determined to do it. The little voice in her head that had been nagging her whenever she had such thoughts immediately started up again. *What are you going to do about Henri? Could you bring yourself to leave him behind for a life of travel? Isn't it time you put down roots and stayed in one place for the rest of your life?*

She still had no answers to these questions. Henri wouldn't want to keep travelling; he'd been clear about that. Ever since she'd first met him back at the vineyard in Alsace, she'd found herself falling for him, so much so that when her friend Fran offered her a job, she hadn't had to think twice about accepting it. It had been so much fun working with her best friend, but now things had changed, and she had no idea how she and Henri could both get what they wanted in the future.

The sky was now a mixture of glorious oranges, yellows and blues, and she could make out some tiny boats dotted about on the sea, as well as the unusual churches with their rounded rooftops on the hillside leading down to the nearby village. She would miss Crete so much – the people, the food, the countryside, the sights. She longed to return to Italy, Croatia and the South of France, as well, after the wonderful times they'd had there.

From behind her, Henri emerged blinking into the daylight.

'*Bonjour, chérie. Tu as bien dormi?*' he asked, bending down to give her a kiss.

'I did sleep well. I just woke up early,' she said with a smile. 'At least I was able to catch the sunrise.'

Henri glanced out at the now pale blue sky and shrugged. 'I'd better jump in the shower. We're going to need to get going soon.' He rubbed his hands together. 'I can't wait to go home.'

Ellie's face fell. 'Aren't you going to miss all this? Not even a little bit?'

'I've had a wonderful time, you know I have, but I love my home and we've been away for five months now. I know it's not as long as we planned, but I do want to get back to the vineyard, my job and our friends. I miss all of that more, even though travelling with you has been fabulous.'

She smiled again, remembering how reluctant Henri had been to travel at first. She was pleased that he'd enjoyed himself, despite all his fears, but travelling wasn't in his blood like it was in hers. 'I'm sorry but I can't say I feel the same about going home, going back to normal. I've loved not being tied down, being free to go where we want and when we want. I'm looking forward to seeing Fran and everyone else, of course, but apart from that, all that's waiting for us at home is the same old routine, day after day until we die.'

Henri pulled a face. 'I love my routine. I'm sure you'll get back into it in no time.' He ruffled her hair and kissed her cheek lightly before going off to have his shower.

Ellie went into the kitchen to make some breakfast for them both before they set off on their journey to the airport. She'd saved some thick Greek yoghurt and the last remains of a pot of local honey for them to have on their final day. Lifting the little jar to her nose, she took in a deep breath, savouring the fragrant smell of the local thyme that would now always remind her of Crete. She put the coffee machine on, as well, before laying the dishes on the table and taking her favourite seat looking out to the sea.

She and Henri were so different, she thought not for the first time, and yet they'd fallen in love. But how were they ever going to reconcile these differences? After all that had happened in her past, settling down, getting married and starting a family would never be top of her list of priorities. She couldn't bring herself to believe in that particular dream. And yet, for Henri, that dream meant everything, making her the last person on earth to be able to give him what he wanted.

Henri

'*Salut*, Didier, *comment ça va?*' Henri could hardly keep the excitement from his voice as he paced up and down the small departure lounge at Chania airport.

'We're all fine, Henri, but looking forward to seeing you and Ellie again.'

'How has everything been? I can't wait to get back and catch up properly.'

'I've got lots to tell you, but mostly, everything's fine.'

'What do you mean, mostly? Fran's okay, isn't she?' The only check-ins that Henri had been able to make while they were away were about Didier's partner Fran's progress through her pregnancy, as Ellie had insisted they needed a break from work.

'She's absolutely fine. She's just very tired, that's all, and looking forward to you coming back and helping with the workload.' Didier chuckled.

'I'll be back in the office tomorrow and you can tell me everything then. In the meantime, send our love to everyone, won't you?'

Henri rang off but carried on pacing, unable to control the nervous energy he felt about returning home at last. He'd also heard by text that morning from his friend Thierry, the winemaker on the estate. He'd repeated that everything was fine, but a little niggle of doubt was starting to creep into Henri's mind. Didier hadn't sounded his usual positive self on the phone, and now Henri wondered whether everything wasn't fine at all.

'Henri!' Ellie waved at him as he went by for what must have been the hundredth time, and he finally gave in and went to join her on the bank of hard plastic seats provided for passengers about to depart.

'Sorry. I just can't seem to sit still. I spoke to Didier and he told me that things are *mostly* fine, and now I can't stop worrying that they've been keeping something from us.'

Ellie patted his hand. 'Don't be silly. They're our friends. They would have let us know if there was a real problem.'

Henri admired Ellie's confidence. She never worried about anything, unlike him. He'd always been a worrier right since he was a child, but it had got worse since his parents had died. 'I just want to get home now so I can be sure.'

They boarded the plane shortly afterwards. They had a long day ahead of them. First a short hop to Athens and a brief stopover before they boarded their next plane to Paris. Then finally, they would take the TGV to Strasbourg and catch a taxi back to the vineyard. It would be late when they got home, and they would have to wait until tomorrow to see everyone, but it wouldn't be long now.

Ellie was quiet on the plane to Athens. She'd wanted to visit there so much, but they'd both liked Crete and made a joint decision to leave Athens for another time. Henri wasn't that bothered about it, but he knew Ellie was.

'Are you okay?' he asked once they were in the air.

She turned away from the window to give him her attention. 'It's only that I've had such a wonderful time, and I'm going to miss travelling and exploring new places with you.'

'If we did it all the time, though, it wouldn't be as much fun, would it? And you must be looking forward to seeing Fran and Lottie? Lottie's baby must be crawling by now.'

Lottie was Fran's younger sister, and the partner of Henri's friend Thierry. Ellie nodded but didn't say anything.

'Didier said that Fran's really tired now,' Henri continued. 'She must be coming up to five months pregnant, I think. Didier said she can't wait for me to get back and take some of the workload away from her.'

'But Lottie was helping her with that, wasn't she?' Ellie asked, getting drawn into the conversation.

'She was, although I'm not sure whether admin's her sort of thing. Thierry's texts have said that she's been working more and more in the Visitors' Centre and developing her idea of having a café there.'

'You're right, that does sound more like her sort of thing, doing something practical. It will be good to see her and little Marie, and to see how they've settled into life together with Thierry.' Ellie smiled at the thought, and Henri relaxed a little, hoping that she would feel better once they were home again.

He was looking forward to getting back to his house, as well, after months in hotels of varying degrees of comfort. He liked his own things and his own comforts around him. After years spent moving from one house to another, as his dad's job in the army dictated, he craved the stability of his own home and staying in the same place for the rest of his life.

By the time they reached home, it was ten o'clock. Henri paid the taxi driver and hauled their largest rucksack into the hallway of his little house before going back to fetch Ellie's bag from the pavement. He studied the bright orange façade and the traditional Alsatian timber struts and expelled a large sigh of satisfaction. Everything was as it should be and he could now get back to normal.

He dumped the second bag next to the first and followed Ellie down the corridor to the galley kitchen at the back of the house. Ellie was sorting through some of the post on the kitchen table. Didier's mum, Sylvie, had been keeping an eye on the house for them while they were away.

'Anything interesting?'

'No. Just the usual stuff. I think I'm going to start planning our next trip to try and cheer myself up.'

'You don't mean now? I need to get an early night before we go into work tomorrow.'

'Please, don't mention the w-word yet. It's far too soon for that. I'm still in holiday mode, and yes, I'm going to get straight onto it. There's no better time than the present.'

Henri watched Ellie disappear into their little office and close the door behind her. He sighed and went upstairs to start the unpacking.

Ellie

'Fran! Oh, it's great to see you. Come on in. You look amazing.'

Fran laughed at Ellie's enthusiasm, but immediately pulled a face. 'I don't feel amazing. I'm becoming more and more like a beached whale these days.' She stepped inside, with Ruby, her dog, close on her heels, and waited for Ellie to shut the door behind her.

'Let me give you a hug then, while I still can. It's so good to see you after all these months.'

They made their way through to the kitchen and Ellie directed Fran towards a chair while she made them both a drink. Fran eased herself onto a chair at the table and sighed with relief. Ruby settled on the floor and closed her eyes.

'So, how are you? How was your trip?' Fran asked when Ellie turned back to face her.

Ellie beamed at her friend. 'It was every bit as wonderful as I was expecting. Visiting all the places I've dreamed of – Biarritz, Seville, Barcelona, Rome and so many places in between. And then there was Crete. Lottie was right about that – I didn't want to leave. I can't wait to be able to travel again.'

Fran frowned. 'Don't say that when you've only just come back. I've missed you too much. I need you here for a while before you go gallivanting off again.'

Ellie put two cups of tea down on the table and sat down. 'I've missed you, too, but I've got the travelling bug now.' She paused, knowing that she shouldn't go on when, as Fran said, she'd not long come back. 'Anyway, how have things been here? It's been great to get your messages, but it's not the same as seeing you.'

Fran glanced away for a moment and then back at Ellie. She took a breath as if she was about to say something but then changed her mind.

'What is it?' Ellie asked, reaching for Fran's hand across the table.

'It's nothing. Everything's fine. I'm fine and so is the baby. Chlöe's doing well at school, and Sylvie and Frédéric are settled together now. So it's all good.'

Although Ellie was grateful for the update on the whole family, she was sure there was something Fran was keeping from her.

'I'm glad that everyone's okay. Chlöe must be getting very excited about her new brother or sister coming along soon.' Didier's daughter by his first wife lived with him and Fran.

'Oh, yes, even more excited than when you last saw her if you can imagine that. She's been helping us decorate the baby's room and choose all the furniture, and she's counting down the days now. So am I, to be fair. It's felt like the longest five months of my life.'

'And how's everything been going at the vineyard?' Ellie took a sip of her tea.

'We had a busy summer and, of course, the harvest was hectic, as always. The Visitors' Centre has got off to a good start – Lottie and Thierry have taken charge of that. And the great news is that Lottie's set up a café in the Centre, too. She's in her element, which has been great to see. And Thierry has been wonderful with little Marie. I'm so happy for my sister that she met such a good man. I don't think it will be long before he proposes to her, you know.'

Ellie's eyebrows shot up. 'It feels like I've missed out on such a lot in these past five months.' For the first time since coming home, Ellie felt the stirrings of regret. She had missed her friends and knowing in detail what was going on in their lives.

'But you're back now. I have to admit that I'm looking forward to having Henri take the pressure off for me a bit. Lottie has been spending more and more time at the café, which is understandable, but it has left me with all the estate admin to manage, and there just seems to be so much of it these days.'

'As you'll have seen, Henri couldn't wait to get back to the office today. He'll probably have everything sorted out and tidied up by the end of the day.' They both laughed, but Ellie was only half joking.

'Lottie was halfway out the door as I was leaving to come here until I reminded her that she needed to hand over to Henri. She has confessed to hating admin, and I can see she's not cut out for it. She's more of a hands-on person like Thierry is. That's another reason why they get on so well together, I suppose.'

'And I have to ask, what's the position with the restoration of the château now? Any news on funds for me to continue my work?' She had committed to restoring Didier's family château when she'd moved to the vineyard after being made redundant from her job in London. The plan had been to open the château up to visitors, and she'd loved doing it, but when the funds had run out, it had seemed a good time for her and Henri to go travelling.

Fran's face fell. 'I have been trying hard to find a new source of finance for the work when I've had the time, but I haven't found anything yet. But Didier and I are just as committed to finishing the work and to renting the rooms out as another source of income. I'm hoping that you and Henri might have some good ideas about how we can raise that money.'

Ellie chewed on her lip. This news didn't sound good, and worst of all, it meant that she had no work to be getting on with, which would only lead her to daydream about her next travel destination. And that was the last thing she needed when she was supposed to be settling back down into normal life and committing to her future with Henri.

Henri

Henri sat down at his desk with a sigh, glad to be back where he belonged at last. There were several neat piles of papers in the middle of the desk, and his in-tray was empty. Lottie had shown herself to be very organised before he'd left, but this was even tidier than he'd been expecting. He itched to spread his things out around him, to mess it up in his own personal way, but first he'd have to pay attention while Lottie handed everything over to him.

'It's great to have you back, Henri, it really is. I hope you had a great time away.' Lottie smiled and passed him a document. 'I've been spending more time at the Visitors' Centre this past couple of months and only popping in here to help out when Fran was overwhelmed. So I've put everything in this document instead to help you get up to speed more quickly, as I need to get over to the café. I hope that's okay and that everything makes sense. If there's anything that doesn't, you can ask Didier. He'll be in soon.'

She went to get her coat, leaving Henri to stare at the contents of the document and to try to work out what had been happening in his absence.

'I'm sorry to have to rush off,' she said. 'Will you be okay?'

Henri looked up. 'I'll be fine,' he replied, although he wasn't too sure of that just yet.

'Okay, see you later.' And with that, she was gone.

Henri had expected more of a thorough handover from Lottie, but he understood how busy she was. He would just have to get on with it and ask questions later. He stood up and went to put the coffee machine on. Coffee always helped to focus his mind. While he waited for the machine to do its work, he picked up the first set of papers – they were all invoices to be paid. He leafed through them, surprised by how overdue some of them were. He narrowed his eyes as he considered what might have caused this. Surely Lottie had kept on top of paying the bills? Or were their finances not as good as they'd been when he left? He tutted at the thought of the disorder he was going to find when he logged in to the vineyard's bank account.

An hour later, Henri stood up again and started to pace around the small office. On his third time round, he almost bumped into Didier coming through the door.

'Henri, good to see you! God, it's cold out there.' Didier went straight to the coffee machine and lined up two cups for them. 'It's great to have you back. I've missed seeing you every day. Did you have a good time? It sounded like it from your texts.'

When Henri didn't reply, Didier finally turned round to look at his old friend.

Henri held up the pile of unpaid bills. 'What's going on, Didier? This pile of bills hasn't been paid, and the bank account looks terrible. I think we need to talk.'

Didier's shoulders fell. Henri took the cup of coffee Didier handed him and sat down at his desk to wait while his friend composed himself.

'This year's harvest wasn't as good as we were expecting after some unexpected and terrible frosts earlier in the year. The quality's great, but there's not so much of it, so we haven't had the pre-sales we were hoping for to set us up for the winter as usual. On top of that, we've been trying to get the Visitors' Centre off the ground, which has cost a lot of money, and we're just about managing to break even at the moment. Lottie assured me that she would contact everyone we owed money to and negotiate longer payment terms wherever possible.'

'I can't find any record of that in the document she gave me this morning,' Henri confessed.

'Didn't she do a handover with you?' Didier tutted softly. 'I asked her to cover for me while I took Chlöe to school.'

'She just gave me this document and left me to sort it out for myself.' Henri suspected that she didn't want to be the one to tell him about the state of the vineyard's finances. He couldn't blame her for that.

'If we could just get people in through the door of the Centre, then they'd spend money in the café and the shop, as well, but it costs more money to advertise, as well, of course, and it's not the best time of year for it either.' Didier downed the rest of his coffee before looking back at Henri.

'Have you got any plans for what you can do about this?' Henri asked.

'The four of us have talked it over many times, and *Maman* has tried to help, too, but all possible solutions require more investment, and I'm worried about doing that for obvious reasons. Having you back to keep everything in check, and to talk to, will definitely help me though.' Didier gave Henri a rueful smile. 'It's been a lot for Fran to deal with on her own while Lottie's been trying to get the café going. We've all been stretched to our limits.'

Henri felt guilty then. He'd been away enjoying himself when they needed him most. But there was no point dwelling on it now. He needed to get on and sort things out. He'd always been proud of the good job he did for the vineyard and he wasn't about to let that change now. 'Right. I'm going to work my way through these piles of paper and I'll make a note of any questions I have for you by the end of the day. Then I'll catch up with Lottie and Fran tomorrow. We should try to come up with a plan then to sort things out.' Henri paused. 'I take it this means that you still haven't found any money to pay for the château restoration.'

Didier shook his head. 'Fran's been doing some research when things have been quiet, but still hasn't managed to come up with any funds for it. I've been dreading telling Ellie to be honest. I know this is going to hit her hard.'

Henri had an idea how she would respond to the news – if she was free to go travelling again because there was no work for her to do, as long as she could find the money to pay for it, she would jump at the chance regardless of whether he could come with her or not.

CHAPTER TWO

Ellie

'How was Fran when you saw her today? I only spoke to her briefly before she left the office, but she looked well.' Henri laid the table for dinner while Ellie served their pasta and creamy mushroom sauce into warmed bowls.

'She seemed in good spirits to me, too. I think she's particularly glad to have you back to share the workload. It sounds like Lottie hasn't been available to help her much.'

Ellie brought the plates to the table and they sat down. Henri poured out a glass of Pinot Blanc for them both.

'No, that's the impression I picked up from Lottie as well. She hardly even stopped to talk to me this morning before she was off to the café. My desk was so tidy I had to wonder when she'd last done any work in the office.'

Ellie swallowed her mouthful of tagliatelle and pondered Henri's words. 'It all seems very different from when we left, doesn't it? There wasn't even talk of a café five months ago, and now it's taken over all Lottie's time. How was the paperwork when you got back into it? Did she do a good job in your absence?'

Henri groaned. 'All the paperwork was neatly organised, but that was hiding the complete mess the finances are in.' He told Ellie about the pile of bills still waiting to be paid. 'I'm so meticulous about paying everyone on time, you know how I pride myself on it, and now in one fell swoop, our reputation will have been ruined.'

'God, that sounds awful. What are you going to do about it?'

'I went straight to the bank accounts to check what the current financial situation is, and that confirmed what I thought – we just don't have the money to pay those bills.'

'What? How can that have happened?' Ellie was distraught at the mere thought of it.

'Didier came in just after I worked all that out, so I asked him straight out what was going on. I couldn't believe it when he said Lottie had assured him she would get in contact with all our suppliers to negotiate more time to pay.' Henri rubbed at his temples to try and relieve the pressure. 'I felt ashamed at the thought of her having to do that. The Domaine des Montagnes has always prided itself on paying its bills on time – it affects all small businesses in the area if someone doesn't do their bit.'

'Did Lottie manage to negotiate with them though?' Ellie understood Henri's feelings, but if times were hard, then needs must.

'That was the next problem. This afternoon I started ringing round the suppliers who were waiting to be paid and found she hadn't been in touch with any of them. Some of them were angry when I spoke to them.'

'Have you told Didier?'

'Not about that yet. The trouble is they've all been under a lot of strain while we've been away, and I can't be too critical when they've been working so hard to keep everything afloat.'

'This is my fault for taking you away from the vineyard when you could have been helping them avoid this crisis.'

Henri shook his head. 'I did feel guilty about being away earlier, but it's not our fault that all this has happened while we were travelling. It could have happened at any time.'

Ellie took a steadying breath before asking the next question on her mind. 'And what did you pick up from Didier about the château restoration?'

Henri threw up his hands. 'They still haven't found any more money for that either, although from the sounds of it, Fran has been trying hard.'

'That's what she told me, as well, and she did sound like she still wants to make a go of things. I have to say that I'm disappointed, though, to have come back and found there's still no work for me to do. Mind you, I don't know how they'd pay me if there was.' She pushed her bowl away.

'I'm sure there's plenty of other work you could help with,' Henri said, reaching out to take her hand. 'And I will do my best to find a source of money now I'm back. You could help me with that, as well, if you like.'

Ellie turned to face him. 'I do want to help, but I'm just finding it so hard to settle back in when, in my heart, I still want to be travelling.'

Henri pursed his lips and she hated herself for upsetting him. 'It's bound to be hard at first, but I think you need to give it some time, Ellie. You need to give us some time to be here together again, as well, and to get back into our routine. You could even make a start on your travel blog idea, as it looks like you're going to have some time on your hands.'

'That's true. I must admit I'd forgotten about that. Still, I have to be honest and say that I don't relish the idea of getting back into a routine like you do.'

'Try to be patient, Ellie. We've only been back a day, so it's going to take you a while to settle back into life here on the vineyard. Setting up your blog might be just the thing you need to take your mind off everything else.'

She let him pull her towards him for a hug, but there was no denying that this was going to be even more difficult than she'd thought.

Henri

Henri strode away from his house the next morning towards the vineyard, feeling more conflicted than ever about where his relationship with Ellie was going. Even though they'd only been together for just over a year, for him there was no doubt that he wanted to spend the rest of his life with her, and he had expected her to feel the same when they got back from their trip. But she still didn't seem ready to settle down with him. She had promised to get started on her blog idea today, but despite what he'd said, he wasn't sure that would really be enough to help with her restlessness.

He turned onto the track that led to the vineyard estate. Just making this journey was usually enough to lift his spirits, even in the depths of winter as it was now when everything was dormant and almost all the leaves had fallen from the vines, but his mood was just too low today. The sky was dark and imposing, and it threatened to overwhelm him. He took in a deep breath and released it slowly, trying not to let his problems defeat him.

He was on his way to meet Thierry to catch up with him and to get his take on the situation with Ellie before going into the office. Thierry had been a good friend to him and he trusted his judgment. Surely he would know what to do?

Lottie answered the door to him a few minutes later. It was the first time he'd seen her since finding out about the finances, but he couldn't bring himself to say anything to her about it outside of work. As it was, she had Marie balanced on her hip and looked flustered.

'Hi, Henri, come on in. It's lovely to see you.' They exchanged kisses. 'Sorry, I've been trying to get Marie to eat something all morning, but she's playing hard to get today.' She laughed but Henri could see how worn out she was.

'Do you want me to try? It probably won't work but it would give you a break at least.'

Lottie handed Marie over with a look of relief.

'*Ça alors*, haven't you grown?' Henri said as Marie settled into his arms. 'I'm not sure I can still call you *ma petite* any more.' He sat down at the table with Marie on his lap and pulled a bowl of what looked like porridge towards him. He didn't fancy it much himself so he sympathised with little Marie. But he played the game of wanting to eat it, taking the spoon Lottie offered him.

'Mmm, this looks delicious. Shall I try it first?'

The little girl studied him with big, round eyes. He popped a tiny spoonful in his mouth and was surprised to find it quite tasty. To his delight, Marie picked up her spoon from the bowl and helped herself to a spoonful as well.

'Mmm,' she copied, and they both laughed.

'Isn't that just typical?' Lottie muttered. 'Can I get you a drink, Henri? Thierry should be back from his inspection soon.'

'Yes, please.' He carried on eating alongside Marie, although trying to encourage her to eat more than him. She was soon bored though and fidgeting to get down. He set her down on the floor and watched as she crawled towards her toys. 'She must be getting around a lot on her own now.'

'Yes, she's managing a few steps, so it won't be too much longer before she's fully walking. It's a full-time job keeping our eyes on her at the moment.'

Thierry arrived back then, and at the sound of the door closing, Marie started crawling towards the hallway. Lottie followed behind her to alert Thierry.

'*Bonjour, ma petite*,' he cried as he came into the lounge, swooping down to pick her up for a cuddle. He rubbed his beard gently against her cheek and she giggled.

'*Salut*, Thierry,' Henri said when his friend came into view.

'Hey, good to see you. You've caught the sun, *mon ami*.' Thierry smiled as they exchanged a quick hug. 'Is everything okay?'

'Yes, yes. Just fancied a chat before work if you've got time.'

'I was about to take Marie for a walk so I'll leave you to it,' Lottie said.

Thierry helped her to gather her things and to pop Marie into the pushchair before kissing them both goodbye and closing the door.

'So, how are things really? Are you settling back in okay?' Thierry asked as he made another cup of coffee for himself.

Henri filled him in on the latest with him and Ellie since their return. 'And with there being no money to pay for the work to be finished on the château, I'm worried she's going to disappear off on her travels again, and if she does that, I'm sure that will be the end of everything between us.'

'It's true there's no money for that as yet, but if she loves you, she won't just go. You need to find a way of working this out so you're both happy.'

'Exactly, but I was hoping you might know what that is.'

Thierry groaned. 'I have no idea. You do seem to want different things right now, but I know Ellie loves you, so she must be struggling to know what's the right thing to do.'

'I think the only thing stopping her from going is that she has no money left after the last trip. If she had the money, she'd have gone by now.'

'Why does she want to go again so soon? I don't understand that at all.'

'I don't know either. It's as if she feels trapped by life here. She doesn't want the routine, while I crave it.'

'Perhaps she's searching for something but maybe even she doesn't know what that is.'

'What could she be searching for? She's already been with me for over a year.'

'Her mum died recently, didn't she? Maybe that's unsettled her and made her restless.'

Henri pondered Thierry's words. The idea for travelling did come up shortly after her mum passed away, and Ellie did tell him she wanted to travel while she still had the chance.

'You're right,' he said at last. 'Maybe there's more to this than just travelling. She wasn't close to her mum, and I don't know much about her relationship with the rest of the family. So it's time I found out.'

Henri made his way back through the vineyard and up to the office, all the while thinking about how to encourage Ellie to tell him what was really on her mind.

Ellie

Ellie opened the door to Lottie about ten minutes later.

'Henri just arrived at ours for a chat with Thierry, so I thought I'd take the chance to come and see you and find out how you are,' Lottie said, handing Marie over to Ellie as she stepped into the hallway.

'What a big girl you are now, Marie.' Ellie smiled at Lottie's daughter, marvelling at the change in her during the five months they'd been away. She led the way down to the kitchen, jiggling Marie up and down as she went.

'Would you like a drink, Lottie? And have you got something with you for Marie?'

'I'm fine, thanks. And yes, I've got a drink for her.' She took a seat at the table and smiled as Marie played with Ellie's curly red hair. 'So, how are things? Are you settling back in after your trip?'

'To tell the truth, I'm finding it hard being back here. I miss the freedom of just being able to go wherever and whenever we want. If I'd had the money, I don't think I would have come back just yet.'

'Really? I know you wanted to go but I would have thought you'd have had enough by now.'

'You of all people know what it's like when you have that travelling bug. It's hard to get it out of your system, isn't it?' Ellie leaned towards Lottie, sure that she would sympathise with how she was feeling.

Lottie pulled a face. 'I did feel like that once, when I was young and carefree with no responsibilities. But once I became pregnant, everything changed, especially because I knew that Marie's dad wouldn't be in the picture. And while I had a lot to learn, and a lot of growing up to do if I'm honest, it's been the making of me, becoming a mum. And now Thierry's a part of our lives, I don't have that restlessness any more. I do like travelling, but the chance of the odd weekend away would be more than good enough for me these days.'

Ellie set Marie down on the floor and sat back, surprised by her friend's change of attitude since the last time they'd spoken of their shared love for travelling. 'I do have some responsibilities, or at least I thought I did. You know there's no money to continue with the restoration of the château?' Lottie nodded. 'That was one of my main reasons for coming back, but now there's no work for me to do. Henri's been encouraging me to get started on a travel blog idea I have, but that's not quite the same thing.'

'There's plenty of work that needs doing around the estate, even if that job isn't available right now. And there's also Fran's wedding to plan, don't forget. She's been desperate for you to come back and help with the organising.' Lottie reached over to guide Marie away from the fireplace, giving her some toys to play with instead.

Ellie went out to the kitchen to make a drink and to give herself a moment to try to understand why Lottie seemed so unsympathetic towards her. She returned a few minutes later with a tray and a pot of coffee.

'The thing is, Lottie,' Ellie continued, desperate to confide in someone, 'I do want to go travelling again, particularly if my old job is still in the same situation. But Henri is delighted to be back and there's no way he'll come with me if I go off again. So I just don't know what to do.'

Lottie rolled her eyes. 'Look, I think this is just the usual post-travel anticlimax. You'll get over that soon. You just need to get stuck into something here, either this blog idea, which I think is a good one, or helping out with something else on the estate. I'm not joking about the workload, Ellie. We've had so much to do without you and Henri around, especially with Fran being pregnant as well. I could always do with some help at the Centre if you'd be up for it.'

For a moment, Ellie was speechless. 'You seem to be missing the point I'm trying to make here, Lottie. I don't want to stay and "get stuck in". I want to continue travelling, which I'd need to do to get material for a travel blog anyway.'

'And where will that leave Henri and Fran? And what about the rest of us who've kept everything going while you've both been away? Doesn't what we want count for anything? You do have a responsibility – most of all to Henri – but also to the vineyard that you've made your home.'

'I would have thought you'd be more understanding, but you've made yourself pretty clear. I can't believe how much you've changed since I've been away.' Ellie shook her head at her old friend.

Lottie stood up and her face softened. 'I have changed, Ellie, because I've had to. I've matured a bit and understood that it's not all about me any more. I don't mean to be unsympathetic, but I'm thinking of everyone here, not just you. And I think it would be helpful if you could step outside of your own bubble for a moment and do the same. Have you thought about what it would do to Henri if you just upped and left without him? And what about the promise you made to be Fran's maid of honour at her wedding to Didier, and to be here for the birth of their baby? You'll be letting all of us down if you don't stay and honour that commitment.' She picked up her bag and then lifted Marie up into her arms. She gave Ellie one last look. 'I'll see myself out.'

Ellie remained rooted to the spot for several minutes after Lottie left, unable to believe what her friend had said to her. Was she being selfish as Lottie had suggested? She went out to the kitchen to put the cups and coffee pot in the sink. She knew she'd been concentrating on what she wanted, for the most part, even though it would upset Henri if she left. But she hadn't given much thought to the estate – that much was true. And as for the wedding, it hadn't even crossed her mind. She was ashamed of herself for that.

She stared out the window at their little courtyard garden, thinking about the transformation that had taken place in Lottie in the past few months. It was as if Lottie had been a child herself when Ellie had left, and now she had become a woman. Ellie wondered if she had been thoughtless towards her friend, inadvertently criticising the life that Lottie had made for herself and her daughter on the vineyard. If so, she would have to apologise to Lottie and to tread more carefully where their friendship was concerned. And maybe it was time for her to stop thinking about travelling and to try to focus on settling back into life at the vineyard alongside her friends, and that meant helping Fran to plan her wedding, as well as talking to Didier about the château and maybe getting started on a blog.

Henri

Henri had wanted to talk things over with Ellie the night before but she'd gone to bed early, and this morning, she had a meeting with Didier about the château. He supposed he should be glad that she was thinking about the château and focusing on what she could do to get things moving again. He hoped that between them, she and Didier could come up with a plan.

In the meantime, he wanted to finish speaking to all the vineyard suppliers today and to negotiate how to pay their outstanding bills as soon as possible. It hadn't been an easy job so far, but he would feel much better once that was done.

'Morning, Fran. How are you feeling today?' He closed the door behind him and wiped his boots carefully on the mat before hanging up his jacket. He bent down to stroke Ruby, who was snoring gently on the floor next to Fran, before making his way over to his desk.

Fran gave him a bright smile. 'I'm fine, thanks, Henri, and all the better for seeing you. It's so good to have you back in the office with me again. I've missed you, you know.'

'I've missed being here, too. I did enjoy travelling with Ellie, but it's easy to lose your hold on reality if you're away too long.'

Henri switched on his computer while he made a drink and then sat down with the remaining list of suppliers to call in front of him. The first call of the day went quite well, with the supplier sounding glad to hear from him again so soon, and he negotiated their payment quite easily. He put the phone down hoping that the other calls he had to make would go as well.

'Who was that you were speaking to, Henri?' Fran asked with a frown. 'It sounded like we hadn't paid their bill.'

Henri was nervous all of a sudden, not wanting to drop Lottie in it but still needing to let Fran know what was going on. 'I found a number of unpaid bills when I went through the paperwork on Monday. Didier told me that he'd asked Lottie to negotiate more time to pay the bills with our suppliers, but when I contacted them, most of them said they hadn't heard from us for some time. So I started ringing them all again yesterday to organise payment schedules.'

Fran rubbed her eyes. 'Does Didier know about this?'

'No, I haven't seen him since Monday.'

'And do we have the money to pay those outstanding payments?'

'Not at the moment. But my plan is to pay them each a regular amount until the bills are paid off. They've all been very happy with that approach so far.'

Fran heaved a sigh of relief. 'Thank you, Henri. It's good to have you on top of everything. I'm sorry Lottie didn't make those calls. She must have forgotten with everything else that was going on. And we should have checked ourselves.'

'I know you've had a lot to deal with, what with setting up the Visitors' Centre and café. Have we had many customers coming in since it opened officially?'

'Visitors were still coming in the autumn, but as it's got colder, they've dropped off.'

'And what about online sales? Has there been any progress there?'

Fran leaned forward, a gleam of interest in her eye. 'Apart from setting up our website when I first came here, I haven't ever done much else with it, mainly because I haven't had the time, or the skills if I'm honest. We don't even have an online shop function.'

Henri sat up and pressed the space bar to wake up his computer. 'We could sell all kinds of goods from our online shop if we could get one set up, which might help us deal with the slump in our sales over the winter.'

'Absolutely,' Fran agreed. 'Do you know anything about websites, though, Henri? As I say, I only know the basics and wouldn't have the first idea how to set up a shop. And we can't afford to pay anyone to do it.'

'I'm sure that this is something I could do with Ellie's help. If it's okay with you, Fran, I'm going to dash home and talk it over with her.'

'Of course. I'll see you after lunch.'

Henri grabbed his coat and set off back to the village, almost running the whole way in his excitement to get home and tell Ellie of their idea about the online shop. And he'd had another idea about her blog, too, which, if she was up for it, would also give her something to do to make her feel more a part of things. If these ideas worked and sales started to come in, everything would feel a bit easier for everyone, and they could maybe even start work on the château again in the near future.

'Ellie?' he called as he took off his coat in the hallway.

'Hello. I wasn't expecting you to come home for lunch. It's a nice surprise to see you.' She put her arms out towards him and drew him closer.

'I had to talk to you about an idea Fran and I had this morning. But first, how did you get on with Didier?' He pulled back so he could see her face.

'He confirmed that there's no money for the work we still want to do, but he also said that he's open to ideas as to how to get the work done gradually. So I agreed to come away and give it some more thought before we meet again to discuss it in more detail. We only talked for about ten minutes today because he needed to get off and do his inspection, so I'm hoping he'll have more time when we meet next.'

Henri told her then about his conversation with Fran. 'Would you be able to help me set up an online shop, do you think?'

'Definitely. If the website's already there, it won't be difficult to add on a shop function. You'll need to speak to Thierry about adding the stock though and you should speak to Lottie as well.'

'Why would I need to speak to Lottie?' Henri already felt like his brain was going to be frazzled by all these new activities.

'We can put the café menu on to the site, as well, and even take bookings.'

'This is all brilliant, if a bit overwhelming. I had another idea, as well, which I think could be great for you.' He looked hesitantly at her hoping she would be able to keep an open mind.

'Go on,' she said with a smile.

'I was wondering if, instead of setting up a travel blog, you could create one all about the vineyard and the surrounding area to encourage people to come and visit.'

Ellie's face lit up as she glanced over at her open laptop on the kitchen table. 'Now, that is a brilliant idea. I could blog about the château and our plans to open rooms for people to stay in, about the café, about the tastings and the shop. I might even be able to generate some income from advertising.'

'And there's so much to do in the local area, both in the village and further afield, like in Strasbourg, especially with Christmas coming up.'

'If you can ask Fran to send me the details of the website this afternoon, we can talk about it some more this evening.'

'You haven't already started work on a travel blog, have you? I wouldn't want your work to go to waste,' Henri said.

Ellie looked shamefaced. 'No, I did plan to get started this morning, but instead I got drawn in by some travel sites and was looking up places to go to next.'

Henri's face fell at the thought that Ellie was still thinking about her next travel destination rather than about settling back into the vineyard like he was. He hoped this new blog idea and the challenge of setting up the online shop would be what she needed to distract her and give her a new focus.

CHAPTER THREE

Ellie

Ellie had got straight to work on the website as soon as Henri had sent the details through to her the previous day. The bare bones were all there with Fran having created a static home page and an About the Vineyard page, but although she'd obviously made a start on listing their products, that job had never been finished. Fran's original role as marketing manager for the estate had grown to include so much more, and Ellie understood how easily the website must have fallen to the bottom of her friend's to-do list.

After spending the previous afternoon tidying everything up and creating a page for her new blog, she was now ready to go. She began by writing a short piece detailing all the work done so far to restore the downstairs of the château, including a namecheck for each of the companies that had been involved. She planned to email them all once she'd finished writing to let them know that they would be getting free advertising for the first month after she published her article in the hope that they would pay for more after that once word got round.

She dug out some photos of the magnificent staircase work, as well as the decorative mouldings around the ceilings in the down-stairs rooms. After adding these to the post, she reviewed her work one last time before publishing it to the blog. She then turned her attention to how she would generate interest in the website and her blog, which made her wonder if there was a village magazine to help spread the word. There was only one person who would know that kind of information, and that was Sylvie.

After emailing all the tradespeople who had worked with her on the first phase of restoring the château, she threw on her coat and scarf to set off for the village. It wasn't far from Henri's house to the market square, but this time, she paid more attention to the shops and other businesses she passed on the way. She stopped in at the florist's to pick up a bouquet for Sylvie as a thank you for looking after the house during their absence. Although she'd been in many times before, to her embarrassment, she'd never really engaged much with the owner.

'*Bonjour, Madame.*'

'*Mademoiselle.*' The woman nodded and smiled.

Ellie placed her order and was about to go when, on impulse, she decided to take a chance. 'I'm sorry I've not introduced myself before, but I'm Ellie. I work up at the vineyard.'

'Yes, I know. You're Henri's girlfriend, *n'est-ce pas?*'

Ellie relaxed a little then. 'Would you be interested in being interviewed for a feature on the vineyard's blog about the local area? We're trying to attract visitors.' All her words came out in a rush as she gathered her confidence to make her request.

'*Oui, certainement.*'

Ellie was delighted by her first success, and after arranging a time to come back and interview Madame Gastaud, she made her way to Sylvie's house with an extra spring in her step.

A few minutes later, Ellie knocked on the door of the house that Sylvie now shared with her partner, Frédéric, admiring the neatly tended front garden while she waited for her to come to the door.

'Ellie! *Quelle bonne surprise.*' Sylvie's face lit up as Ellie handed over the pretty bouquet of flowers she'd bought. They kissed affectionately before going inside.

'Thank you so much for looking after the house while we've been away, Sylvie.'

'It was my pleasure, *chérie*.' Sylvie led the way to the kitchen and put the kettle on before gathering the cups. 'Did you have a wonderful time?'

'We really did. Even Henri enjoyed himself.' Ellie laughed and Sylvie joined in, knowing that Henri hadn't really wanted to go travelling at first.

'I'm sure he's glad to be back home again though.' Sylvie made the drinks and passed a cup over to Ellie. They both took a seat at the kitchen table.

'He couldn't wait to come back.'

'How about you? Are you glad to be back?' Sylvie asked perceptively.

Ellie frowned. 'I wasn't looking forward to coming back, and I'm still finding it hard to settle, and when I found out that there's no money to complete the restoration of the château, that only made things more difficult. But Henri and I are working on a new idea to help raise funds, and that's given me something to keep me busy.'

She proceeded to tell Sylvie about the blog and online shop idea.

'That sounds wonderful, and just the input we need to get things going again.'

'I wondered if you knew about a village magazine I could contact, Sylvie. I need to get some interviews arranged to help spread the word.'

Before long, Sylvie had provided Ellie with a list of her contacts within the village.

'This is such a wonderful idea, Ellie, and it will help you to get more involved in the community. I will tell everyone I know about your plans, as well, when I go to the market on Saturday.'

'That's an excellent idea. I hadn't even thought of that.' Ellie finished her tea. 'I must get off. I need to see Fran to talk about the wedding as well.'

Sylvie clasped her hands together. 'Ooh, yes, I'm so looking forward to seeing them both get married at last, and to welcoming another grandchild.'

As Ellie made her way back to the house for some lunch, she had to admit that she was beginning to feel glad to be home, at last. Maybe all she needed was something to focus on, as Henri had said, and that would be enough to take her mind off the draw of travelling, at least for the short term.

Henri

Henri had spent all morning adding their wines to the newly created online shop after a crash course in how to use the shop function with Ellie the night before. He'd been nervous about adding products at first, but now he'd added so many, it had grown easier. They would also have to add photos for every item and that was the next job on his list. He finished adding the last product and stood up to stretch out his back.

'I'm off to find Thierry now so that he can check the listings and help me make sure I have photos of all the wines,' he told Fran as he grabbed his coat and scarf.

'Great. Thank you for getting onto this idea so quickly. I can't wait to see what it all looks like. I noticed that Ellie's already uploaded her first blog post.'

'Yes, it's good to see that she's been busy as well.'

Henri made his way down to the Visitors' Centre in search of Thierry. There was no-one in the shop and Henri's heart sank at the lack of interest in the vineyard during these winter months. At least it gave them time to get things done on the website.

'Hey, Thierry. I've come to show you the new online shop we've set up.'

'Have you set it up already?' Thierry raised his eyebrows with a smile. 'You two don't waste any time.'

Henri took him through the new product pages, showing him how to find the pages and how to edit them where needed. 'Can you check that I've got everything there and that all the prices and details are correct, please? I know that's going to take some time, so don't worry if you can't get it all done today. I'm going to take some photos while you do that. Do we have any photos already that I can use or should I just take new ones? They need to be high quality for the website.'

'You're best to start again then. The only ones we have are quite old now.'

Henri took his printed list of wines and went out to the back of the shop to find the individual wine bottles for his photos. He found a well-lit spot in front of the tasting area and set up one bottle at a time for its photo.

'Hey, Henri, I didn't know you were here,' Lottie said as he appeared with the final wine bottle an hour or so later.

'I've been taking photos of all the wines for the online shop. This is the last one to do.'

Lottie watched as he snapped his final photo. 'That must have taken ages – we have so many different wines now.'

'It has taken a while but I really wanted to get this done today. We need to make the pages live as soon as possible. With Christmas coming, I'd like to really start pushing the website and the shop particularly. Ellie also suggested that we could put the café menu on the site if that would be okay with you.'

'That would be fantastic. It doesn't change that often, but it would be good for people to see what we do before they visit.'

'Ellie wondered if it would be useful for people to be able to book via the website as well. What do you think?'

'It would be great if we could set it up. Do you know how?'

'I have no idea, but I'm sure Ellie does.'

They laughed.

'If we could add online bookings for tours and tastings, as well, and maybe offer a free drink in the café when booking for them, that would be a real incentive to encourage people to visit,' Lottie suggested.

'Okay, I'll speak to Ellie about it. I know she'll want to talk to you and discuss these ideas.'

'Have you spoken to Thierry about his gift ideas for Christmas? He was going to put together some two-bottle cases and some food-and-wine pairings if he could find a supplier.'

Henri found Thierry in front of the laptop in his office.

'You've done a great job in setting up these pages, Henri. I can't believe you've done it so quickly. I've checked all the listings and I worked out how to add stock, as well, so now all we need are the photos.'

'Fabulous. I'll get Ellie to help me with that tonight. And then you have some ideas for Christmas gifts, I hear. I'd like to organise some more photos once you have those ready and we can get those on the shop then too.'

Henri packed his digital camera away and set off home for lunch with a renewed sense of enthusiasm. He had every confidence that setting up the online shop would be of great benefit to the vineyard estate, and he was relieved to have something to do to try and turn their fortunes around. With Ellie's help, they had already managed to achieve such a lot in no time at all, and he could sense that everyone was feeling more hopeful about the future.

From his personal point of view, he was sure that Ellie would be feeling more settled as a result of something to sink all her energy into, and he hoped that would help her forget about wanting to continue travelling. He still hadn't got round to asking her about whether the reason for her restlessness was also something to do with her mum's death – there never seemed to be a good time to ask a question like that – and he didn't want to upset the fragile balance they'd established since starting work on the shop and the blog. He was just going to keep working and hope that everything else would sort itself out along the way.

Ellie

After lunch, Ellie set off for the château where she'd arranged to meet Fran to talk about her wedding. She'd felt terrible for not asking her how the wedding plans were coming along when she'd seen her the other day. Now that Lottie had reminded her about her promise to be Fran's maid of honour, she was keen to find out what needed doing.

'Come on in,' Fran said when she opened the door a few minutes later. 'I've only just got back myself. I wanted to make sure Henri was there before I left.'

Didier and Fran had been living in the château with Chlöe since she and Henri had gone on their travels, so Ellie was expecting the downstairs to look quite different now. She shut the heavy front door behind her and followed Fran towards the kitchen.

Aside from coats and shoes, the hallway looked much the same. She glanced up the stairs as she walked past and was relieved to see that the beauty of the balustrade was still intact. It had been a labour of love finishing it off, but it had been worth it.

She took a seat at the table while Fran made them both a drink. 'I'm sorry I didn't ask you about the wedding planning the other day. I'm sure you're already quite well-organised by now with only a couple of months to go.'

'I didn't want to mention it the other day – you already had enough on your mind having only just come back – but we really aren't at all organised. We've both just been so busy, and so has Lottie.'

Ellie didn't know whether to be pleased or nervous about what that meant for her in her maid of honour role. 'What have you done so far then?' she asked with trepidation.

'Once we knew the château wouldn't be finished in time, and that there was no way we'd be ready before Christmas either, we asked Lottie to book a venue near my parents' house for late January. They'll do the catering, as well, so that will make life easier all round. But that's all, so there's still quite a long list of jobs to be done.'

Ellie relaxed a little then, knowing that she could still help Fran. 'Are you looking forward to it though?'

'I am, although costs are an issue, of course, so we're trying to keep it as low-key as we can, but still make it a lovely day.'

'What's on your list of things that still need to be done? I'd like to do my bit now that I'm back.' Even as she said it, Ellie worried about her complete lack of experience on the wedding-planning front.

'I still need to get my wedding dress – that's the biggest job that's on the list, but Mum will help me with that. And I haven't sorted out the flowers yet. It's only a small group of friends and family coming, so that's been easy. Do you think I should have a hen do? I haven't thought about that either.' Fran sighed as she listed all the remaining things to do.

'You're not really in a fit state for a party,' Ellie said. 'I think a nice get-together for all the female guests would be good. Maybe I can speak to Lottie about organising that if that's all right with you. She knows more about that sort of thing than I do.'

Fran nodded. 'That's fine with me,' she said.

'The only thing I wanted to ask is whether you're sure it wouldn't make more sense for Lottie to be maid of honour instead of me, especially as she's done all the hard work so far, and she is your sister after all.' Ellie didn't want to be stepping on anyone's toes.

'No, no, it's your job, and Lottie understands that. She's only been helping out while you've been away. I think she'll be quite happy to hand everything over to you now you're back.'

'Okay, well I'll speak to Lottie about some of these things and I'll give your mum a ring, as well, and then we can meet again soon for an update. Is it all right if I just pop upstairs before I go, to have another look at the rooms and remind myself what needs doing?'

'Of course. I loved your blog post today by the way. It was lovely to be able to celebrate what you've done already.'

'It fired me up again about the whole project actually. I might take some photos now and use those for the next piece. Then I'll have to get off to this interview with the lady from the village magazine. No sooner had I asked Sylvie about it this morning than it was all arranged!'

'I'll have to go and collect Chlöe from school now so I'll leave you to it,' Fran said. They kissed goodbye and after calling Ruby to join her on her walk, Fran went on her way.

Ellie slowly walked upstairs, admiring the balustrade on the way up, and went into Chlöe's bedroom first. She used her phone to take a few photos and then made some notes about the remaining work to be done. It was mainly replastering of the walls and ceilings, but it would also be good to repaint the walls once that work was done to brighten up the little girl's room after all this time. She'd have to ask Chlöe what colour she would like.

She went on to what was obviously being prepared as the new baby's room. So far there was a cot and a rocking chair but not much else. Fortunately, this room didn't need as much work doing to it. She popped quickly in and out of Fran and Didier's room, feeling awkward in their private space, noting only what needed doing and taking a couple of critical photos, before moving on to the three further unused bedrooms. Some of the floorboards needed replacing in these rooms, as well, which was hardly surprising given their age. Finally, she made her way to the family bathroom, which needed by far the most work doing to it. It wasn't just the walls and the ceiling in here – it was the tiling, some damp patches and the whole suite needed replacing, too. It must have been awful for the family to have to make do with this bathroom all this time.

She was much more dejected on her way downstairs than she'd been on the way up at the thought of all there was still to do. The whole bathroom needed tearing out really, and if they were going to let the rooms, guests would probably prefer, even expect, to have en suites, and that was only going to add to the cost. And she hadn't even looked at the outside of the building or the gardens.

As Ellie wended her way back into the village for her interview, her need to get the website working for the estate was greater than ever.

Henri

Sylvie had called that afternoon to ask Henri to come over after work so she could hear all about his travels. He was looking forward to catching up with his old friend. Having known Sylvie for a large part of his adult life, since she'd taken him in with her husband when his parents had died, he'd missed seeing her while they were away.

It was a bit of a walk to Sylvie's new place, but he relished the thought of some fresh air after being in the office all afternoon. It had grown chilly as he left the office and was starting to get dark, but he was wrapped up against it. He tucked his chin down into his woollen scarf as he walked back through the village. He nodded hello to several people he knew on the way, enjoying being back in the community he had lived in for so long. After all the years he'd spent moving around from place to place as a child, it had been such a relief to call somewhere home, and he was experiencing the same strength of feeling now. This community was where he belonged, and though he'd enjoyed travelling with Ellie, he couldn't deny how much happier he felt to be back again.

But her sense of adventure had been good for him while they'd been travelling, and despite his fears, he'd enjoyed himself. If only he could do the same for her and show her that the things that were important to him could be good for her as well.

'Ah, Henri, *mon cher. Que c'est bon de te revoir.*' Sylvie pulled him into her arms and kissed him three times to emphasise how much she'd missed him.

'It's good to see you, too, Sylvie,' he replied, hugging her back.

He followed her down the hallway to the kitchen where they always seemed to settle.

'How's everything with you and Frédéric?' he asked, taking a seat at the kitchen counter while Sylvie bustled about, making drinks and taking a couple of sweet tarts from the oven, which she'd bought from the *boulangerie*.

'Things are good, Henri. I'm enjoying sharing my life with someone else again even though I thought I'd miss my old cottage and all the things I did there.' She smiled at him and he was glad to see her so happy. 'He's out meeting a friend so we can have a good old chat. I've missed you while you've been away. Ellie said you had a wonderful time though.'

'It was amazing,' Henri said. 'I didn't ever expect to enjoy it so much, but the places we saw, and all the experiences that Ellie introduced me to, were so different to my normal life that I couldn't help but have a good time. Still, I'm happy to be back. I missed home and all of you, too.'

Sylvie reached out and patted his hand. 'It's great to have you back, my boy, but you've had an experience you will never forget, thanks to Ellie. She seemed really well when I saw her earlier.'

Henri hesitated, not knowing what to say to that, but when Sylvie looked worried, he plunged in. 'She's fine now she's got something to focus on, but she's not as happy as I am to be back here.'

Sylvie put a cup of coffee down in front of him and took a seat opposite. 'She did mention that to me, but she didn't dwell on it. This blog will help her to get out and about in the village and to see why we all love it here so much.'

'I hope so, but it's going to take time for her to fit back in and to stop feeling so restless.'

'Ellie's a free spirit, Henri. I have no doubt she loves you, though, and wants to be with you.'

'And that's part of the problem. We do love each other, but we want different things. She's already started talking about where she'd like to travel to next.'

'Try not to worry about it too much, Henri. She's just different to you and she's going to need time to get used to being here again after the freedom she's had for the last five months. She'll get there eventually.'

Henri sighed. 'I know you're right, and that's what I've said to her myself, but you know me, I can't help worrying about everything.' He paused, unsure whether to talk to Sylvie about the estate's finances, but she sensed his concern anyway.

'Have you looked through the books since you've been back?' she asked quietly.

'I have, and I can't tell you how upset I was when I realised the full extent of the situation. I'm so sorry, Sylvie, that things have come to this.'

'We haven't had such a bad harvest for many years. It's devastating when it happens both for cash flow and for morale. But we've come back from such disasters before and we'll do so again.' Sylvie's wise, old face had taken on a determined look that Henri had seen many times before.

'We'll all do our best. I hope you know that. I've been setting up an online shop with Ellie's help, and Thierry was checking everything for me today, so it shouldn't be too long before we get it all set up and working.'

Sylvie shook her head. 'Everything is "online" in this modern world. I don't really understand how it all works, but if it will help the vineyard to keep going, then I'm all for it. As long as you young people are in charge and not me.' She laughed then.

'I must be going but it's been lovely to see you. Let's make sure to catch up again soon.'

CHAPTER FOUR

Ellie

'Oh my God,' Ellie said the next morning as she stared at the text she'd received.

'Is everything okay?' Henri asked on his way back in from a trip to the *boulangerie* for breakfast.

'Yes, sorry, it's just that I've had a text from my brother. He's coming here to visit.'

'That's good news, isn't it?' Henri smiled as he put the bag of croissants down on the table. 'It might cheer you up a little to have Chris around. Did he say how long he'll be here?'

'No. But he said he has some news that he wants to tell me in person.'

'That sounds intriguing. When's he arriving?'

'He hasn't told me yet. Hang on, I'll ask.' She sent back a quick reply and waited to see what he would say.

They sat down at the table to eat their breakfast.

'How are you feeling about everything now we've been back a few days?' Henri asked tentatively.

Ellie smiled at him. 'I'm okay. I'm sorry I've been so difficult to live with since we came back, but I'm slowly getting used to life here again now. I've loved setting up the shop and the vineyard blog. And now it will be great to see Chris again. He's just like me, a real free spirit. That's why we've always got on so well, I suppose.'

'So he's not with anyone yet? I don't remember seeing a girlfriend at your mum's funeral.'

'Oh no. He's a love-'em-and-leave-'em type. I can't see him ever settling down.'

Henri's face fell. Her phone pinged with a message, so she grabbed it to avoid having to deal with Henri's reaction.

'Crikey. He says that since we're back, he'll be arriving later today. Typical of Chris to give me no warning!' She looked up at Henri in alarm. 'I'll have to get my skates on to tidy up and sort out the spare room for him.'

'That's okay. I can help, too. I'll let Fran know I'll be coming in late today so I can give you a hand.'

They spent the rest of the morning cleaning the house and tidying the last remaining things away from their travels. They'd just made the bed up in the spare room when the doorbell sounded. Ellie looked surprised even though she was expecting him. She rushed downstairs to let him in and Henri followed behind.

She flung open the door to find not only Chris but an unfamiliar and beautiful young woman with him.

'Hello, sis! Meet Michelle, my fiancée.' Chris put his arm around Michelle and beamed at her while Ellie tried to find the right words.

'Goodness. Well... lovely to meet you, Michelle. Come in, both of you. Henri, you remember Chris, and this is Michelle.'

'Hello. I'm so sorry for the short notice. I hope we're not putting you out.' Michelle gave them both a smile. 'Chris was determined to come and tell you the news in person.' She laughed as she put her case down in the hallway.

'Meeting Michelle's been the making of me,' Chris told Ellie and Henri with a look at each of them. He pulled Michelle in for a hug.

Ellie couldn't get over the change in her brother. He'd always been such a player, and she'd thought he'd be a bachelor for life.

'Have you set a date?' asked Henri as they made their way into the kitchen.

'We have. It's two weeks tomorrow and we want you both to come,' said Michelle.

'That's what we've come to tell you because it's so soon. I'm sorry we've sprung it on you, but I wanted to invite you both over to London for the wedding. Do you think you'll be able to make it? It would mean a lot to us both,' Chris finished.

'Definitely,' Ellie confirmed without a moment's hesitation. The idea of a trip away to London was the best news she'd had for days.

'I'll have to check with Fran and Didier as we've only just got back, but I'm sure it will be okay if it's just for a few days,' said Henri.

'I hope you'll tell me all about your travels,' Michelle said to Ellie, eyes gleaming. 'We're going to South America for our honeymoon. We'll be away for two weeks just travelling round from place to place, wherever the fancy takes us.'

Ellie's heart sank at her words. Why did people have to keep talking about their upcoming travels when she was trying so hard to stop thinking about going anywhere?

'That sounds amazing. I've always wanted to go to South America. We only travelled around Europe but we had a fantastic time. We ended up in Crete and I could have stayed there forever.'

'The best cure is to start planning where you'll go next,' Chris said this time. 'That's what they say, isn't it?'

'That's right, but we have responsibilities here, so we won't be going anywhere for a while.'

Ellie looked at Henri and he raised his eyebrows at her words. She'd changed her tune because she knew she had to, but it wasn't easy listening to her brother and his new fiancée wax lyrical about their plans. And hearing that Chris had decided to settle down only put more pressure on her to do the same.

'Will you show us the vineyard estate then? We'd love to know more about it.' Michelle smiled at them both, and Ellie was glad that her brother had managed to find such a lovely person to settle down with, even though it did all seem to be a bit of a whirlwind romance.

'Of course. We can go now if you like, and I'll have to get back to the office anyway,' Henri said. 'I'll just let Didier know that we're bringing you round.' He went to get his phone.

'Henri seems great, Ellie, and it's so good to meet you, as well, after all Chris has told me about you.'

'I wish Chris had told me about you!' Ellie scolded her brother. 'When did you two meet?'

'Not long after you'd gone away, but we knew almost straight away that this was it.' Chris looked apologetic. 'I should have told you, I know, but I wanted it to be a surprise. I knew you'd never believe me if I'd told you over the phone.'

'I am surprised, but I'm also very happy for you both. I'm looking forward to the wedding already.' And Ellie realised that she really was.

Henri

After a busy weekend with Chris and Michelle, Henri was almost relieved to get back to the office on the Monday morning. He and Ellie had discovered a problem with the online shop not allowing shoppers to add items to their basket, and despite their efforts to try to correct the issue, it still wasn't working now. It had been awkward to work on it when they had guests, so Henri intended to devote all his time to it this morning instead.

He stamped the mud off his boots before unlocking the office door and going inside. After putting on the coffee machine as a matter of priority, he took a seat at his desk and switched everything on to save time when he was ready to get down to work.

'Morning, Henri. It's wintry out there today. Did you have a good weekend?' Fran was bundled up in a padded burgundy-coloured parka, with a woollen hat pulled down over her ears, and even Ruby had a little coat on this morning.

Henri dragged his eyes away from the computer. 'Yes, it was busy, but good, thanks. How about you?'

'Ours was good, too.'

'Can I get you a drink to warm you up?' Henri asked, smiling at her glowing face.

'I'll have a raspberry tea, please,' she said, pulling a face. 'I'd rather have coffee, but I need to be careful how much I drink, so I save it for my first drink of the day.' She laughed.

'How are you feeling now?'

'I'm okay, just a bit tired sometimes. And carrying all the weight around all the time is exhausting. I'm not sleeping that well now, but I have a lot of naps, which helps.'

'So how much longer will you keep working?' Henri put Fran's tea down on her desk and sat down at his own again to drink his coffee.

'I want to work as long as I can, but I'll just have to see how things go. As long as I'm healthy, I'll carry on. I don't want to leave you alone for any longer than I have to.'

'You managed without me for five months. It's the least I owe you to do the same for you, and longer if you need it.'

'I feel so much better already with you around to help me and to discuss things with.' She smiled at him. 'Anyway, I have some news. Thierry asked if he could have some time off to take Lottie to Paris, so we're all going to have to pitch in and cover their work for the next few days. They've not had any time off for ages, certainly not since Marie was born, so we could hardly say no.'

'Of course. It will be lovely for them to get away. Who's going to look after Marie though?'

'My mum's going to come and stay at Thierry's while they're away.' Fran beamed then. 'It will be so good to see her.'

'Excellent. When are they off?'

'When the shop closes today. I was wondering if Ellie would be able to cover the shop for us while they're away. Do you think she'd be up for that?'

'I'm sure she will.' Henri had a feeling that Ellie would hate the very idea of working in the shop, but she would have to grin and bear it and do her bit for the vineyard. 'Is there anything you need me to do?'

'Not specifically. Didier will cover the inspection work, and if Ellie can manage the shop, we should be all right. We'll close the café while they're away to make it easier on her.'

Didier came into the office then.

'Ooh, it's nice and warm in here. It's arctic down in the vineyard. The temperature has plummeted overnight.' He hung his jacket up and went straight to the coffee machine, rubbing his hands together on the way.

'Is everything okay down there?' Fran asked.

'Yes, Thierry has it all in hand. He made sure that the team was ready to start pruning this week if frosts were forecast, but I think it's a good idea to get started on it anyway.'

'As we're all here, would it be a good time to talk about the finances and particularly the funding for the restoration work on the château?' Henri asked a few minutes later.

Didier grimaced. 'I wish there was some good news on that front, but as I said to Ellie last week, Fran's not managed to find any other sources of funding, and we just don't have anything spare to spend on the château right now. We do have plenty of work that needs doing, though, if Ellie wants to muck in. Otherwise, I'm not sure we'd be able to justify paying her.' Didier looked embarrassed to even have to say the words.

'We've made a good start on setting up the online shop on the website and Ellie's already published a couple of blog posts.'

'I really appreciate what you're both doing, but it will be a while before that starts yielding any money, won't it?' asked Didier.

'Probably, yes, in all fairness. I'll have a chat with Ellie and see if she can come up with any other ideas for funding apart from the ones you've already tried, Fran.'

'I'm open to any suggestions, Henri.' Didier glanced at Fran and she sent him a look full of understanding.

'I'm sorry to have to ask this when we've only just come back and with Lottie and Thierry now away for a few days, but we'd like to go to London for Ellie's brother's wedding next week, if that's okay.'

'Of course it's fine for you to go,' said Didier. 'I'd love it if we could get away for a couple of days, but it's just impossible right now.' Didier looked weary, and Henri worried about the stress his friend was under, what with the estate and Fran's pregnancy as well.

'Have you considered getting some investment in from somewhere to pay to finish the work on the château?' Henri asked.

Didier nodded. 'We have, but we're quite nervous about giving any share of the estate away to complete strangers. But we have thought about it. What we'd like is a way of doing it that works for us and our family, and for all of you. Fundamentally, we want things to stay the same for all of us who work and live here, and that's not an easy task.'

'I think it's something we might have to consider, and soon, because we need an injection of cash more than ever if we're to be able to pay our bills and to keep paying the staff for the foreseeable future.' The vineyard meant as much to Henri as to Didier and his family, and he was as committed as they were to resolving their problems. He turned back to his work, wishing he had all the answers and fearing that without some soon, things were only going to get worse.

Ellie

When Fran had first asked Ellie to fill in at the shop while Lottie and Thierry went away for a few days, she'd regretted not being able to spend the time with Chris and Michelle, but they'd been happy to be left to their own devices. And she really didn't feel she could refuse when she and Henri had been away for five months, and Lottie and Thierry had been happy to help in their absence.

Still, her envy of Lottie and Thierry escaping to Paris was off the scale, especially after hearing about Chris and Michelle's honeymoon plans as well. She had at least persuaded Lottie to write her a post for her new blog about their trip when they got back.

Paris was perfect for a stop on the way to Alsace at less than two hours away from Strasbourg, and she really wanted to encourage people to come and explore France, via the blog and other social media. She was loving writing her blog posts and had already got another one lined up from Madame Gastaud, the florist, after her interview with her yesterday. She had to admit to herself that her initial reluctance to return to the vineyard had started to fade, and she was beginning to feel more at home in the community.

She had to hand it to Lottie in setting up the shop in such a short time. Not only that but she ran the café as well. Thankfully, they hadn't asked her to cover in there – she was rubbish at cooking and would have made a complete disaster of it. It had taken her almost the whole day in the shop to get to grips with the till, let alone restocking any of the shelves. She gathered that Thierry was in charge of restocking most of the time, and with the two of them away, it was now going to fall to her to understand how everything worked.

She'd expected it to be a long, boring day, but it had turned out to be quite the opposite. She'd found herself enjoying chatting with customers and putting out the wines and other items on the shelves. In fact, it was turning out to be quite useful to know how everything fitted together, and her mind was full of ideas for future blog posts.

She glanced up to see a customer waiting to be served and made her way over. '*Bonjour, Madame.*'

'*Bonjour.* I've heard lots of good things about this wine. I can't wait to try it.'

'That's great to hear. Where have you heard about the wine from?' Ellie was intrigued.

'From friends and in local restaurants. Even at the market, I think. Everyone sings the praises of Domaine des Montagnes.' The woman smiled as she handed the bottle to Ellie.

Ellie scanned the wine bottle and waited for the price to show on the till before asking the woman for payment.

'Enjoy your wine. Thank you. See you again soon.' She passed the customer her bottle, said goodbye and, noting that the shop was now empty, returned to finish putting out the new stock on the shelves, marvelling at what the woman had said. She needed to try and build on this word-of-mouth reputation that the vineyard had already established.

She checked the bottle of wine she lifted out of the box against the wine label on the shelf and started filling the empty space. By the time she'd finished loading the bottles from the box onto the shelf, it was time to close up the shop for the day. There hadn't been any customers on the final tasting of the day, so she was free to go home.

After locking up, she decided to go in search of Henri to see if they could walk home together. She knocked on the office door a few minutes later, having walked up the hill from the Centre to the court-yard where the vineyard estate's office was located. When she went in, though, Fran was on her own.

'Hello, has Henri gone for the day?' she asked as Fran looked up.

'Yes, you've just missed him. He was in early this morning so I didn't want him staying too late. How's your day been?'

'Great, actually,' Ellie replied with a grin. 'Better than I expected anyway.'

Fran laughed. 'So you'll be back tomorrow?'

'Yes, of course. Did your mum get here all right?' Ellie asked.

'She did, and we're all having dinner together tonight.'

'Have a good evening then.' Ellie nodded at her friend and then set off for home.

She followed the path back towards the village, pulling her coat tighter around her against the biting wind that had built up since this morning. She really didn't like winter. She preferred warmer weather and beaches, too, if she was honest, not cold winds and rain, or worse, snow, as Alsace was prone to in the winter months. It was pretty sometimes, but most of the time, it was just annoying and made her want to hide under the duvet all day.

'Hello,' she called as she arrived back home.

'In here,' came Henri's reply from the living room.

She sat down next to him on the sofa and leaned towards him for a kiss.

'How has your day been? Did you get anywhere with the website issue?' she asked, rubbing her tired feet.

'Not yet, but I think I might have worked out how to resolve it. I'll have another go at it tomorrow. How about you at the shop?'

'I really enjoyed it, you know, and I'm looking forward to going back tomorrow.'

Henri laughed out loud. 'I never thought I would hear you say that. I'm so glad you're settling in,' he said.

'I am, and feeling less restless about the travelling, although I'm so jealous of Lottie and Thierry. And Chris and Michelle's plans sound amazing, don't they?'

'They do, but we have a trip to London to look forward to, which will be fun and will allow you to get your travel fix.'

Ellie sighed wistfully. 'I do miss the freedom of travelling and exploring, and the sense of adventure that comes with that, but I also love you and want to be with you, which means being where you are.'

'I love you, too, but I also want you to be happy.'

'Right now, food would make me happy. I hope Chris and Michelle will be back soon so we can go out for something to eat.'

Ellie had taken her usual route of avoiding talking too seriously about the opposing feelings she was experiencing, not wanting to upset Henri any further. For now, she was managing to keep her longing to travel at bay, and that would have to do.

Henri

As it was Chris and Michelle's last night before going home, Henri and Ellie decided to take them to the bistro in the village. The food was always excellent and they'd been stocking the Domaine's wines for years.

'This is a beautiful place,' Michelle said after they'd been shown to their table.

'It's where we first met, you know,' Henri told them.

'Oh, that's a lovely memory, you two. Surely it must be time for you to settle down together by now?' Michelle asked with a wiggle of her eyebrows.

'Leave them alone, Michelle,' Chris scolded. 'They'll get there in their own time.'

'And what about you?' Henri said to Chris. 'Ellie told me you were a confirmed bachelor.'

'Yes, that was definitely me, but all it took was the love of a good woman to persuade me to mend my ways.' He grinned at Henri. 'Come on now, what should we drink?'

Henri glanced at Ellie across the table, worried by how quiet she was being. Sensing his eyes on her, she looked up and gave him a smile.

'What would you recommend, Ellie?' Henri asked, trying to draw her into the conversation.

They settled on a bottle of the Domaine's Pinot Noir, which the waiter served to them shortly afterwards. They placed their orders and sat back to wait for their food to come.

'Fran and Didier are getting married in January, and I'm going to be the maid of honour, so I hope I'll be able to pick up some tips from you to give to Fran,' Ellie said to Michelle.

'Of course. I have had some help from my family, but it all seems to have gone like clockwork, hasn't it, Chris?'

'We have been lucky. You hear all these stories about people planning their weddings years in advance, but we were able to book the church and the venue without too much hassle at all. It probably helped that we were happy to get married midweek as well.'

'We had hoped to get the château finished in time for them to get married and have the reception there, but there's just no funding to complete the restoration work at the moment.'

'Oh, the château would be an amazing wedding venue,' Michelle said. 'The turrets are so romantic.'

'We hadn't planned for it to be a wedding venue as such. We just thought it would be special for Fran and Didier to be married in his childhood home,' Ellie replied.

'But we are planning to let the rooms once it's fully restored,' said Henri.

'It would make a fantastic wedding venue, though, and would enable you to sort out your finances in no time,' Chris chimed in.

'What do you think, Henri? Should we look at that?' Ellie asked.

'I know nothing about arranging weddings,' Henri said, 'but I can imagine that it would appeal to a lot of people as a setting for their wedding day. Their guests could stay over and we could even do the catering if we talked to everyone else about it. We know other suppliers now, as well, who we could talk to about providing things, like flowers, for example.'

Ellie's eyes lit up, telling Henri just how much she liked this idea. The waiter arrived with their food then, causing a break in the conversation.

'Changing the subject, Ellie, I did want to tell you that I've almost finished wrapping up Mum's estate now,' Chris said after their food had been served. 'It took ages to get all the paperwork together before the solicitor could apply for probate, but they've let me know it shouldn't be much longer before it's all sorted out.'

'I'm grateful to you for doing it, Chris, but I don't want to know about her estate, such as it is. I can't imagine there's anything important for me to hear now she's gone. Surely it's just a question of ticking a box and getting it out of the way?' She glanced up at her brother briefly before returning to eating her pork dish again. Henri was surprised at her lack of interest in her mother's affairs, although he knew they hadn't been close for a long time.

'There's always a possibility that we might inherit something. You never know.' Chris laughed but Ellie scoffed at the very idea.

'She was so tight-fisted when she was alive that there can't be any money left now, so I won't hold my breath.'

Henri glimpsed the lingering bitterness that Ellie held towards her mother and regretted once again not asking her more about their relationship and how it had gone so wrong. Whenever he tried, she always moved the conversation on quickly and he was forced to give up.

'Are you close to your family, Henri?' Michelle asked.

Ellie's head snapped up, and she reached for his hand across the table.

'It's okay, Ellie. Michelle's not to know.'

Michelle looked pained. 'Have I put my foot in it?'

'No, it's all right. My parents passed away in a car crash when I'd just turned eighteen. I was very close to them so it was hard for a long time. But I found a job on the vineyard, and Sylvie's family took me under their wing, and I've been here ever since.' Henri smiled, trying to hide the ache he still had for the loss of his parents even now. That's why he hardly ever talked about it, not even with Ellie.

'I'm so sorry, Henri,' Michelle told him.

The waiter returned and Henri was saved from having to say any more.

'That was a fantastic meal,' Chris told the waiter.

Ellie stood up after the plates had been cleared. 'I'm going to speak to the owner about whether he'll let me interview him for the blog. I might even persuade him to buy some advertising.'

Michelle went off to the ladies, leaving Chris and Henri on their own.

'Is Ellie okay, Henri? She doesn't seem her usual bouncy self tonight.' Chris glanced over at his sister with a frown.

'She's had a lot on her mind since we came back. She misses the travelling, especially as everyone else is getting away at the moment.

And I think she's still dealing with the loss of your mum, as I'm sure you are, even though she says she doesn't want to talk about it.'

'Yes, she bottles it all up inside. She's always been a bit like that. I'll try to talk to her tomorrow before we go.'

Henri nodded, hoping that would help Ellie, and made a mental note to try and talk to her again himself very soon.

CHAPTER FIVE

Ellie

'It's been so good to see you and to meet Michelle,' Ellie told Chris as they made their way along the footpath to the vineyard estate the next morning. Michelle had shooed Chris out so she could get on with packing, and he'd offered to walk Ellie to the Visitors' Centre before she started work.

Chris tucked her arm into his and drew her closer. 'It has. From now on, we must make more of an effort to see each other regularly. I don't know why we're so bad at it.'

'Don't you?' Ellie scoffed. 'Maybe our parents might have something to do with that. I'll never forgive Mum for pushing Dad away, and I won't forgive him for not trying harder to see us after they split up.'

'Come on, that was all a long time ago now. You need to move on. I know I have.'

Ellie glanced sideways at her brother in surprise. 'How have you done it? I feel so resentful of all that happened, and it has had an impact on who I am as an adult.'

'Meeting Michelle changed my life. It's as simple as that. She showed me that you can find love and that your life is your own. We're not destined to be alone just because our parents couldn't be happy together. And yes, I agree that Mum was wrong to push Dad away, but there's no point in hanging on to that now. She's gone, and we can't let it dominate the rest of our lives. It's already done that for long enough. It's time for us to write our own stories now, Ellie.'

'It's definitely time for you to write yours anyway. Michelle is lovely, and I'll be very pleased to have her as my sister-in-law.' She leaned into Chris affectionately. 'I'm so proud of you and pleased that you've found happiness at last.'

'And what about you? You've found Henri and he loves you.'

Ellie sighed. 'I know he does, and I love him, too, but I just don't feel ready for settling down in the way he does.'

'Why not?'

Ellie bit her lip, wanting to tell the truth to her brother more than anyone else. 'I'm scared, Chris.'

'What of?' he asked gently.

'Of taking a risk of being with one person for the rest of my life, I guess.'

'But that's what love's all about. You have to take that risk if you want to be loved by someone, and Henri loves you with his whole being.'

'I just don't know if I'm ready for that.'

'I'm not sure anyone knows when they're ready. You have to make up your own mind, of course. But if you love each other as much as you obviously do, then I wouldn't have thought you have much choice about it. You'll be miserable without him if you decide against a future with him.'

'I don't want to lose him, and I feel like I'm being selfish by talking about travelling when it's not what he wants. But I don't think it's out of my system yet. And so I don't know how we can both get what we want.'

'Are you sure you're not using the travelling as an excuse though?'

Ellie frowned. 'An excuse for what?'

'For avoiding making a decision about whether to commit to life with Henri.' Ellie began to protest but Chris held up his hand. 'Let me finish,' he said. 'I used to be just like you. I had a series of relationships, and as soon as they looked like they might be getting serious, I legged it. I didn't think I deserved to be loved and to love someone in return. None of those relationships were right for me, to be fair, because when I met Michelle, I knew she was the one for me. I didn't have any doubts then and that's why I've not wasted any time.'

'Do you think that my doubts now show that Henri's not the right man for me then?'

'No, I don't think that. You're just letting other things get in the way. And judging by the way he's putting up with you through all this, I'd say he's a good man and that his love for you is real.'

Ellie gave him a playful shove. 'Putting up with me, huh? He is a good man, and that's why I don't want to say yes to him, only to go and hurt him down the line. And how can I be sure that I won't do that? How can he be sure?'

'As I said before, it's a risk, but it's one that Henri is happy to take. You just need to get yourself to the same place.'

Ellie blew out a long breath. 'If only I knew how. I can't keep Henri waiting forever, but I need to be sure that this is what I want before I make my final decision. Either way, I feel sure that he's going to end up getting hurt.'

'Have you told him honestly about all this?'

Ellie shook her head.

'That's the first thing to do. It's not fair on him to leave him in the dark about why you're feeling uncertain. It might even make him feel better to have a clearer understanding of why you're struggling with this decision.'

They'd reached the Visitors' Centre and it was time for Ellie to start work.

'I bet Michelle will have done all the packing without me by now.' Chris chuckled.

'What's her family like?' Ellie asked.

'Nothing like ours, that's for sure. She has two sisters, one older, one younger, and her parents are still happily married after thirty-odd years, I think. They're just so normal and it feels good to be a part of that for the first time.'

'Henri hasn't got any family left now. But his dad was in the army and they moved around a lot when he was young, so the only consistency he's had has been since he came here.'

'That explains a lot about him and what he wants from life, doesn't it?'

For the first time, Ellie realised that it did. She pulled her brother to her for a hug. 'Take care, both of you, and we'll see you next week.'

'You too, sis. And think about what I've said.'

Henri

While Ellie had been finishing up at the shop, Henri had prepared dinner for them both. She would be despondent about Chris and Michelle's departure when she got back so he'd wanted to do something to cheer her up. He also wanted to sit down and talk properly about some of the things that were on her mind.

His beef casserole had been bubbling away in the oven for about an hour alongside two baked potatoes. He'd just finished laying the table when the front door opened and Ellie came in.

He went out to the hall to greet her.

'Everything okay?' he asked, studying her face.

'It's fine,' she said. 'I was sorry to see them go but at least I'll be seeing them again soon. The shop kept me busy all day and took my mind off them going.'

'Come and sit down. Dinner's nearly ready, so you can just relax.'

'It smells delicious.' She smiled at him. 'Thank you for getting it all ready while I was at the shop.'

She sat down at the table and he poured the wine for them both before serving up.

'So, I was thinking,' Henri began after they'd been eating for a few minutes, 'that when we go to London for Chris and Michelle's wedding, we should make a proper trip of it.'

Ellie paused with her fork midway between her plate and her mouth. 'How do you mean?' She put the fork down on her plate.

'I thought that if we turned it into a short break, it might lift your spirits as well. Maybe stop you feeling so restless.'

Ellie gave him a hesitant smile. 'I appreciate you being so thoughtful about how I'm feeling.'

Henri waved her thanks away. 'We both need to compromise if we want our relationship to survive, and I certainly do.'

'I do, too. I just don't know how to give you what you want and to get what I want at the same time. My mum and dad weren't exactly the best role models.'

'But we're not the same as your mum and dad, are we? We're different people, so although I understand your fears about that, I don't think you need to worry.'

Ellie fell silent and he didn't know what to make of that. They carried on eating for a few minutes, until finally, Ellie spoke again.

'I do love you, Henri, but this is a big decision for me. So I really want to be sure.' She gave him a little shrug and he fell in love with her just a little bit more.

He reached out and took her hand in his. 'It is a risk, I understand that. And I appreciate that you want to be sure. But I'm prepared to wait for you to get there, Ellie. So let's take this trip away and just enjoy ourselves and see how we go from there.'

'I don't want to make things difficult for Fran and Didier by taking more time off though.'

'It's fine. I've asked them about it already. I'm looking forward to it after having met Chris and Michelle.'

He stood up and went to Ellie. He put his arms around her waist and drew her gently towards him for a kiss. She lifted her face to look into his eyes and he bent to press his lips to hers. As the kiss deepened, he drew her closer still and rubbed his hands up and down her back, trying to convey to her that everything would be all right.

Ellie pulled back first. 'I don't deserve you, you know. You love me unconditionally, and I just don't know how I got so lucky when I met you.'

He grinned at her before saying, 'I don't know how either.'

Ellie turned to the table then. 'Let me clear up as you made such a wonderful dinner.'

'No, we can do that later. Let's sit on the sofa and talk about our trip to London. Where shall we stay? You know it better than I do.'

Ellie grinned. 'The wedding's taking place just outside London, in a place called Hertford,' she told him as she joined him on the sofa. 'So we could stay somewhere near there and travel into London before and after the wedding. It wouldn't take long.'

'I'd like to visit the Tower of London this time, as we didn't get there when I visited you before. Would that be okay?'

'Of course. And we could take a boat trip down the river to Greenwich if the weather's not too bad.'

Henri marvelled at the funny-sounding English names and wondered if he would ever get the hang of the English language, but as long as he was with Ellie, he didn't care.

'Why don't we look at places to stay in Hertfordshire?' Ellie suggested.

She picked up her laptop from the coffee table and opened it. Then she went into the search engine to see what she could find. Half an hour later, they'd booked a room in a lovely country hotel just outside Hertford for four nights.

'I'm already looking forward to this getaway now we've booked somewhere special to stay. How far away did you say the wedding venue is from there?'

'It's only about ten minutes away. We'll be able to get a cab on the day of the wedding. But as we'll get there on the Sunday, we can spend some time exploring the local area if you like.'

'We've only got a few days before we'll be leaving, and there's such a lot for us to be getting on with,' Ellie said after a minute.

'I've sorted out the issue with the shop, so at least that's working now. Once Thierry's back, I thought perhaps we could do some visits to suppliers to show them the site and to encourage them to advertise with us. What do you think?'

'That's a great idea. I hope that Didier will agree to let me use the advertising revenue to start slowly working on the château. I'm going to see him tomorrow and tell him how things are going. And now that I've done the interview with the village magazine, interest will spread, I hope. Liliane from the *boulangerie* contacted me about doing a feature, as well, and I know she has her Christmas food items to promote, so she might take out an advert, too.'

'Should I still explore any other avenues for funding when things are going so well? We might not even need anything else now.'

'I think you should, just in case there is another source of income that we've overlooked. I've had some other ideas about that to suggest to Didier as well.'

'And have you heard back from any of the companies who worked on the château restoration before? It would be great if they would support us with advertising in the future.'

'The plasterer has been in touch to say that he's happy to link to our site from his, which I thought was a great idea.'

Henri released a sigh of relief. Everything was coming together slowly but surely, and he was feeling more hopeful that they'd found a solution to the vineyard's problems.

Ellie
Now that Lottie and Thierry were back from their break away, Ellie was eager to get going with the restoration of the château, and she was hoping that Didier would allow her to make a gentle start on

the remaining jobs to be done upstairs. It was a long, slow and expensive process, but so worth the effort they would put into it.

Ellie had always had the vision to turn the château into somewhere for visitors to stay and she had the motivation to make it come to fruition. She was excited, too, about the idea that the château could be used as a wedding venue in the future as well. All she needed was a regular flow of money and an assurance from Didier that he was still committed to finishing the project, which was why she'd asked if she could meet with him again this morning to discuss it in more depth.

She knocked firmly on the big oak door when she arrived. 'Ellie, come on in. It's good to see you.' Didier kissed her on both cheeks before taking her coat, shooing Ruby the dog gently out of the way.

She followed him along the hallway to the farmhouse kitchen at the end.

'Can I get you a drink?' Didier asked as they reached the kitchen.

'No, I'm fine, thanks. How have you been finding it, living here in the château these past few months?' She took a seat at the table and looked up at Didier.

'We've made the most of the fantastic job you did downstairs, and we've worked hard to keep it in the same good condition you left it in.' He laughed as she pulled a face. 'And upstairs is much the same as it was before we moved out last time to the cottage.'

'Last time we spoke, I wondered if you're still as committed to restoring the upstairs as you were before I left, even though we don't have the money for it at the moment. I know it's not going to be easy.'

Didier sat down, and she wondered whether he needed time to think about his answer to that question. 'I am definitely as committed,' he told her at last. 'But I just don't know where we'll get the money for it from when there's so much work still to be done.' He shrugged, but she was pleased with his answer.

'I just want to be sure that you haven't changed your mind, because I do have some ideas about how we could fund the rest of the work.'

'Go on.'

'We could contact the Ministry of Culture to see if we could have the château designated as a listed building. That would bring certain restrictions with it, but it would also give us access to grants to help us with the restoration.'

'That's an interesting idea and worth pursuing. Anything else?'

'I know Fran tried this one before, but I wondered about contacting the Alsace tourist board again, now that the Visitors' Centre and café are properly up and running, to see whether they might be able to help us or point us in the right direction for any grants because we want to become a tourist destination. That might also help us promote the Visitors' Centre. What do you think?'

Didier's smile told her all she needed to know. 'Those are both great ideas. We should get onto them immediately. Would you be happy to do that?'

'Of course. I'll have a look into it and come back to you.'

'I appreciate you giving it some thought. We can't even think about continuing the restoration without specific income of some kind. Our finances are just too stretched these days.'

'I understand that.' Ellie gave him a reassuring smile. 'However, I've also had some success with generating advertising revenue through the blog I've started on the website, and Michelle even suggested the château as a wedding venue. So there are plenty of other ideas we can try.'

'That does all sound hopeful, but it's maybe best to take it slowly and not get our hopes up too much, though, before we know for sure.'

Ellie's excitement dipped. 'Just to be clear, though, you do still want me to try?'

Didier sighed as if he had the weight of the world on his shoulders. 'I do, but I'm just trying to be realistic, that's all.'

Ellie had hoped that talking to Didier would give her the motivation she needed to throw herself back into the château project, but his lack of enthusiasm was putting her off.

'Let's not write these ideas off before I've even had the chance to investigate them.' She kept her voice upbeat, hoping to jolly Didier along.

'You sound very keen to get on with the work anyway, so that's great.'

'Of course. I'd like to finish what I started, but there's no denying that not having the finance is a huge obstacle. That doesn't take away from my commitment to finishing the project though. And as there is now some money coming in, not much I know, but still, would you be happy for me to use that to get started on the empty upstairs bedrooms?'

'Yes, that's fine. But you must keep within budget, and liaise with Fran about the best time for the work to be done.'

Ellie was delighted that Didier had agreed to let her make a start on the remaining renovations despite not being very positive about the project as a whole. 'Okay, thanks for seeing me, Didier. I'll get back to Fran about when to start work upstairs.'

She made her way back out to the hallway and grabbed her coat before making her way back outside. She pulled her coat on and did up the zipper, tucking her chin inside, and set off back towards the village for her next interview at the *boulangerie*. Things were starting to come together for them on the vineyard, and she also had Chris and Michelle's wedding to look forward to. For the first time since being back from their trip, she was feeling settled.

Henri

Henri went into the office with a renewed sense of purpose the following day. Following Ellie's meeting with Didier, they'd done some research overnight and he had a list of places to call this morning with regard to the funding for the restoration of the château. Ellie was also going to fire off some emails from home, as well as writing up her new blog posts.

'Morning, Henri. How are you today?' Fran arrived just after him.

'I'm fine, thanks, Fran. How about you? Did you have a good time with your mum?'

'Yes, it was lovely. It was a shame she had to get back, but it was great to see her. I need to meet with Ellie and Lottie soon and update them on the latest to do with the wedding.'

'Is everything going well on that front?'

'Mostly,' she nodded. 'It's great having Ellie back to help us now. It has been stressful trying to plan the wedding with everything else that's been going on.'

'I'm sorry about that, Fran. That's the last thing you need right now.'

'It's all fine now.' She smiled. 'What are you up to? You look like you have a long list to get through there.' She pointed at the sheet of paper on his desk as she went towards hers.

'Ellie came up with the idea of contacting the Ministry of Culture and the tourist bodies to see if they might be able to help us with funding for the château and promoting the Visitors' Centre now it's properly up and running. And this is the list of places I need to call today to see if I can get the ball rolling.'

'That sounds like a great idea. Let's keep our fingers crossed that they can help us.'

An hour later, Henri had got through his whole list, but hadn't made any progress at all. He stood up and stretched after sitting at his desk for so long.

'Any luck?' Fran asked as she came back from the toilet.

'None at all. They've all been saying the same thing. They admire what we're doing, but they just don't have any spare funds to give grants or any other form of financial support in the current climate. I can't believe it. I was sure that one of them would be able to help us. I hope Ellie has had better luck with the historic building angle.' Henri slumped down into his chair, at a loss as to what to do next.

'So none of them were interested at all?' Fran asked with a frown.

Henri shook his head again.

'That is disappointing.'

'At least Didier has approved Ellie taking things slowly with the château work, using the advertising revenue to pay for it, and she can continue with that plan, renovating it one room at a time until it's finished. But it will just take a lot longer, unless there's any to spare.' Henri gave Fran a hopeful look, but she didn't return it; instead her brow wrinkled and he felt bad for adding to her concerns.

'I have to be honest with you, Henri, and I'm sorry to have to say it, but the château is the least of our concerns at the moment.'

Henri sucked in a breath. 'What do you mean?'

'We barely have the money to pay all the staff from month to month, so we can't afford to be paying for renovation work to be done when the financial situation is so dire.'

Henri sat up, refusing to let the situation get him down. 'We need to get people in to buy our stock – that's the quickest way to improve the cash flow. The online shop is ready to go now. We just need to make it live and then get people to buy.'

'And how are we going to do that?'

Henri stood up. 'I need to speak to Thierry about going out to see our wine suppliers and encouraging them to spread the word about the shop and the tastings. And we also want their help with Christmas sales.'

Just then, the office door opened and Lottie came in.

'Hey, I was just on my way over to the Visitors' Centre to see Thierry,' Henri told her. 'How was your trip to Paris?'

Lottie beamed. 'It was fabulous. And I have great news.'

'Go on then, don't keep us in suspense,' Fran scolded her sister.

Lottie flashed her left hand in front of them, now adorned with a single diamond engagement ring. 'Thierry asked me to marry him and I said yes,' she exclaimed.

Fran and Henri gasped at the same moment and then there were hugs all round. Fran came round the desk and pulled Lottie to her.

'I'm so happy for you both, I really am. That's the best news I've had in ages. Congratulations!'

'I'll get over to see Thierry and leave you two to talk all about it. Ellie will be over the moon as well. Congratulations again, Lottie.'

Henri shrugged on his coat and scarf and made his way out into the cold courtyard for the short walk down to the Visitors' Centre. He was so pleased for Thierry and Lottie and couldn't wait to give his congratulations to his friend. There was a little part of him deep down inside that was very envious though. Everyone around him was getting engaged and married – it was now only him and Ellie who weren't – and it was the only remaining thing he wanted in his life. He loved her so much and could think of nothing better than settling down with her for the rest of their life together. But there was a way to go before Ellie felt the same, and the last thing he wanted was to push her before she was ready.

For now, he would have to be happy for his friends and hope that it would be his turn to celebrate soon.

CHAPTER SIX

Ellie

'You look beautiful, *ma chère*,' Henri told Ellie as she finished putting her earrings in.

'Thank you. I'm looking forward to hearing about Lottie's trip to Paris, and to chatting with them both about the wedding. I hope I can meet Fran's expectations for it and make it a really special day for them both.'

Henri drew her towards him and slipped his arms round her waist. 'It will be fine. You're the most organised person I know.' He kissed her lightly on the lips and then followed her downstairs.

'I shouldn't be too late back. I don't think either of them will want to stay out very late, what with Fran being pregnant and Lottie wanting to get back for Marie.'

She gave Henri a little wave as she turned right and away from the house, towards the market square where she was meeting Fran and Lottie for a drink. She'd missed them both while they'd been travelling, but it was taking a while to get back to where their friendship had been before she went away. Everything had changed so much since then, and they were all under so much pressure financially. Not only that, but she stood out now as the only one of them who wasn't getting married and starting a family. And although she was beginning to feel more settled at the vineyard, the longing to travel was still high on the list of things she wanted to do in her life. All of this made her uncertain that she would still be able to find some common ground with her two good friends tonight, or that they would welcome her back to the fold.

She arrived at their usual wine bar a couple of minutes later and found the two of them already seated at a table with drinks in front of them.

'*Salut*,' she said brightly before kissing Fran and then Lottie on both cheeks. She took off her coat and sat down. 'How are you both?' she asked, looking from one to the other.

'I'm exhausted,' said Fran with a laugh. She stroked her tummy, which Ellie was sure had grown since the last time she'd seen Fran just a couple of days ago.

'And I'm still high on my trip to Paris, and getting engaged, of course. Would you like some wine, Ellie?' Lottie's eyes sparkled as she showed off her ring.

'Yes, please, and congratulations to you both. That's such wonderful news.'

'Let's raise our glasses to both of you then. It's good to have you back, Ellie, isn't it, Lottie?' Fran clinked her glass of sparkling water against the others and smiled round at everyone.

'It is,' said Lottie. 'Thank you for covering for us while we were away as well. You did a great job.'

'I quite enjoyed looking after the Centre, although the early starts were a bit harsh.'

They all laughed, and Ellie breathed a sigh of relief. Maybe things were getting back to normal for them after all.

'So, tell us more about your trip, Ellie. It sounded like you had such a great time.' Fran beamed, but Ellie didn't want to go over it all again now for fear of stirring up her wanderlust once again.

'We did have a fantastic time, and I loved every minute of it.

Henri did, too, despite his early nerves. And we're looking forward to going to London on Sunday for my brother's wedding.'

'Oh, I didn't know about this. I must have missed it when we were away,' Lottie said.

'Yes, my brother's getting married to a lovely girl called Michelle. I never thought I'd see the day but I'm glad for them both.'

'You'll have to tell me any tips you pick up when you come back,' said Fran. 'I can't believe it's just under two months now till Didier and I get married.'

'I'll keep my eyes open and take lots of pictures at Chris and Michelle's wedding, in case there's anything you can use for yours.'

'I had a good catch-up with my mum while she was looking after Marie,' Fran said. 'We've booked a date to go and look at wedding dresses now, and she promised to double check the venue is booked and still able to do the catering. It would be great if we could get together again soon, Ellie, to go over everything else.'

'Sure. How about tomorrow? It would be good to meet before we go away next week,' Ellie said.

'Great.' Fran turned to her sister then, deftly changing the subject. 'So, tell us everything about Paris, Lottie.'

Lottie beamed as she told them all about it. 'It was so amazing and we can't wait to get away for another weekend sometime soon.' She paused for a moment. 'You were right about that, Ellie. It is a bit of a bug, the travelling thing. I'm sorry I was so hard on you about it when we spoke last.'

Tears pricked Ellie's eyes, but she blinked them away, not wanting to spoil the good atmosphere. 'It can be addictive, yes. I'm glad you both had a good time and I'd love it if you could write a post for the blog about your trip. I don't think people realise just how close Paris is to Strasbourg.'

'I'll get you something as soon as I can. It's a brilliant idea to have started the blog on the vineyard website. I've seen some of your interview posts, as well, and they've been fascinating to read. Will you be able to interview me about the café as well?'

'Of course. I've already planned to do that. Perhaps you could send me the menu over when you send the blog post. And then I just need to look into setting up the booking facility for the tastings.'

'The only problem is getting people to start using the site, isn't it?' asked Fran. 'How can we do that?'

'I'm planning to start using social media soon. I'm sure that setting up a Facebook page will help to bring some customers in.'

'That sounds good because if we still can't get people through the door, all your work will have been for nothing,' Fran said.

'The other idea I'd had was about having a wine tasting in the Centre before Christmas to show off our Christmas gifts and to show-case the wines we want to highlight for Christmas celebrations. What do you think?'

'I love that idea,' said Lottie. 'I could do canapés, as well, and Thierry would organise the gifts and the wines. It would be a great promotional event before Christmas comes.'

Ellie smiled at Lottie's enthusiasm and mentally added a few more jobs to her to-do list.

Henri

Henri was looking forward to getting out of the office for the morning to go and visit some of their suppliers with Thierry. It would be a good opportunity to meet some of them face-to-face after so long, and to apologise again for the delay in paying their bills. But first he wanted to check in at the office while Thierry was doing the morning inspection with Didier and make sure there was nothing urgent to deal with.

He decided against his normal morning coffee, wanting to get straight onto his computer before having to go out. He tapped his fingers on his desk, waiting for the computer to open up, and was surprised to see quite a few new email messages today. Perhaps he had some replies about the funding for the château. He sat down at his desk and opened up his email inbox, only to find that the new messages were all notifications of orders on the new online shop. Henri's eyes widened as he moved to check the online ordering dashboard on the website. There had been five orders overnight, and two were for quite expensive cases.

'Ready to go, Henri?' Thierry asked, coming into the office at that moment.

Henri was still speechless from receiving the new orders.

'Henri, is everything okay?'

'Yes... Yes, sorry. It's just that we've had some orders via the website and I can't quite believe it.'

'That's great news. Come on, you can tell me on the way.'

Henri climbed into the passenger seat of Thierry's car and told him all about the orders.

'We'll have to get ourselves organised to send these orders out now, won't we? Will you have time to do that?'

'I'll have to make time for it, Henri. And if we get more orders, then we might have to take someone on to help us. But let's be positive about this – the more orders we get, the better it is for the vineyard. Maybe it's just as well we're going to see our packaging supplier today, because now we can tell them that we need more stock. They might ask us to pay upfront given the situation, but again, it will be good news for them too.'

They travelled towards the autoroute and then turned north towards Haguenau where their supplier had his industrial unit. Henri worried the whole way about the reception their supplier was going to give them, and the unwelcoming look on the man's face when they pulled into the car park just over half an hour later did nothing to make him feel better.

'Monsieur Meyer. *Comment ça va?*' Henri shook hands with the man and gave him a broad smile, hoping he could win his way back into the man's good books.

The man nodded and turned to Thierry.

'Good to meet you, Monsieur Meyer,' Thierry said.

Monsieur Meyer turned and beckoned them to follow him to his office. Henri exchanged a nervous glance with Thierry, who gave him a grin. He wished he was more laid-back like his friend, rather than always worrying about everything.

Once they were sitting down in the office and coffees had been served, Henri cleared his throat. 'I wanted to say again how sorry I am that your payments were delayed for so long. Things have been tough for us this year because of the poor harvest, but we should have been in touch with you much earlier to explain. Our final payment to you is due next week, isn't it?'

'It is, and as you say, it is long overdue. But I understand the difficulties of running a business, especially when the harvest has been poor. However, we have worked together long enough for you to know the impact of a late payment on our business.' Monsieur Meyer shook his head and tsked. 'It is only because you are normally such a good customer, and have been for years, that I'm prepared to forget this mistake and move on.'

Henri breathed a sigh of relief. 'We really appreciate that, Monsieur.'

'And we would like to place another order if possible,' said Thierry.

The older man's eyes widened. 'I would have to ask for payment upfront, I'm afraid.'

Thierry nodded. 'Of course, that's understandable. We want to rebuild our reputation with you, and we hope to be sending a lot more business your way as our online shopping facility grows.'

'Ça alors,' said Monsieur Meyer, twiddling his moustache. 'Online shopping, huh? What a world we are living in today.'

The rest of the meeting went smoothly, with Monsieur Meyer even agreeing to place a free trial advert on the website, and soon they were saying goodbye and returning to the car.

'That went much better than I was expecting,' said Henri as they drove away and on to their next meeting.

'It did, but only because we have always had such a good reputation in the past. We won't let him down again,' said Thierry.

They met with the supplier of their bottles and labels next, who was more critical of their late payment, at first, but soon came around and also agreed to place an advert on their site. By the time they'd met with their cask supplier, it was nearly lunchtime and they needed to head back.

'Have you set a date for your wedding to Lottie?' Henri asked as they made the return journey.

'Not yet, no. There's no immediate rush and we don't want to steal Fran and Didier's thunder.'

'Of course. We're very pleased for you both though.'

'It must be your turn next.' Thierry glanced at Henri quickly before returning his eyes to the road.

'I'd be happy to ask Ellie now, but she's not ready to settle down just yet.'

'Is she still keen to travel?' Thierry asked.

'Yes, and she doesn't want to be tied to one place. I know she loves me, and I think she's happy here, but she still has the urge to get away.'

'To get away or to run away, do you think? Is it the commitment that frightens her?'

'I don't know, and I don't want to pressure her. She already feels left out with Fran and Lottie getting married and having children. I keep meaning to talk to her about it, but I can never seem to find the right time or the right words.'

'Maybe that will be easier when you get away to London for a few days,' said Thierry.

Henri nodded and hoped his friend was right.

Ellie

As Thierry had gone out with Henri that morning, Lottie had

asked Ellie if she would babysit for Marie until they got back. Ellie had been nervous at first, not having had much experience of looking after children, especially not one as little as Marie, but Lottie had been desperate and she wanted to help her friend out. Not only that but she loved Marie and was happy to spend more time with her. Lottie had left a long list of instructions as well as her phone number in case of emergencies.

When Lottie left, Marie was sitting in the middle of the living room floor playing with a musical penguin toy with lots of colourful buttons on it. Ellie sat down next to Marie and watched as she pressed the buttons again and again, bobbing her head along to the penguin's song. While Ellie soon grew tired of the tune, Marie loved it and even began trying to sing along. Ellie laughed then as she listened to Marie's singing.

The morning passed quickly as Marie showed Ellie all her toys. Ellie made sure never to take her eyes off the baby for too long, remembering what Lottie had said about how quickly she could crawl now and get herself into danger. Then all of a sudden, Marie started to grizzle and Ellie worked out that it was probably time for a nappy change, and then a snack. She laid Marie gently down on the changing mat, turned away to get a clean nappy and found Marie halfway across the room when she turned back.

'Oh my goodness,' Ellie cried. 'Come back here, you little scamp,' she said with a smile as she went and picked Marie up just before she escaped into the hallway. Marie snuggled into Ellie's neck with a giggle, making Ellie laugh, too. She settled her back down onto the mat, and this time, she changed her nappy without any further incidents. She picked the little girl up carefully and took her into the kitchen, settling her down into the high chair and strapping her in before giving her a drink of water and some slices of banana.

'Mmm, na-na,' Marie said, and Ellie smiled.

'That's right, banana,' she said before popping a slice into her own mouth.

The little girl's eyes widened as though Ellie wasn't allowed to have any of her fruit. Marie popped another piece from her bowl into her own mouth and then covered the bowl with her hands, making Ellie laugh out loud this time. Once snack time was over, Ellie wiped Marie's hands and lifted her out of the high chair.

She found a picture book from a pile in the corner of the living room and sat down with Marie on her lap to look at it. It was a book of animals, and Marie pointed at each one as Ellie turned the pages, and tried to say the name of the animal. Ellie marvelled at the vocabulary that Marie already had and enjoyed sharing some closeness with her. Soon though, Marie's head fell back against her shoulder as she dozed off. Ellie laid her tenderly down on the sofa and watched her chest rise and fall for a few minutes. What a beautiful little baby she was, and how lucky Lottie and Thierry were, she thought.

She'd had so little experience with children herself that the thought of having her own was enough to send her into a panic, and her own childhood had been so disrupted that she couldn't imagine ever being able to take on the role of being a mother with any success. Still, spending time with Marie this morning had been wonderful and more enjoyable than she'd ever expected.

Marie woke up half an hour later, just as the front door opened signalling Lottie's return.

'*Mama*,' Marie called as Lottie came back in. Lottie picked her daughter up with a smile and a kiss.

'Hello, little one. I missed you,' she cooed, hugging Marie to her. 'Has everything been okay?' she asked Ellie then.

'Absolutely fine. We've had a lovely time.' Ellie was delighted to find that this was true. 'Any time you need me to help, just let me know. Have you still got time for an interview with me now about the café?'

'Yes, sure. How about I make us some lunch and we can talk while we eat?'

Ellie left Lottie's after lunch, pleased that she'd got another interview sorted and that Lottie would be making a start on the plans for the wine-tasting party while she and Henri were in London. She made her way down to the château where she was going to make a start on preparing the plaster in one of the empty bedrooms to be repaired by the plasterer. There were bulges and cracks that she could clear and fill herself to save on costs, as well as assessing loose areas of plaster to see whether she could do the repairs or would need to call in their expert. It would be a slow, painstaking job, but at least she could make a start.

She put on some coveralls as soon as she arrived and made her way up to the smallest bedroom. She assessed the walls critically first and concluded that the loose plaster would have to be dealt with by the plasterer, because there was old wallpaper on top and she didn't want to run the risk of making the damage to the plaster worse by pulling at it. She made a note and took some photos to send on to the plasterer. Then she got going on the cracks, carefully filling them in as she went round the room.

'Hello! Ellie, are you up there?' Fran's voice rang up the stairs, surprising Ellie out of her concentration on her work.

'Yes, I'm here,' she called back.

Glancing at her watch, she saw that the whole afternoon had passed and it was now time for her to talk to Fran about the wedding. She stood up, groaning at the ache in her back from the awkward position she'd been sitting in for the last hour. She looked round the room quickly to see how much she'd done and was pleased to see that she'd made good progress. There was still a lot to do, though, so she would be busy working in this room for some time to come. She took a few quick photos for the blog so she could do a progress report.

She made her way downstairs to find Fran, going straight to the kitchen in the hope she would find her there.

'Hello,' Fran said. 'How have you got on?' She poured out two cups of tea for them and passed one over the counter to Ellie.

'Not too bad considering it was my first day. It just takes so long because I'm not as skilled as the plasterer.'

'Don't be too hard on yourself. You've made a start and that's the main thing. Shall we go and sit down? My feet are killing me.'

'So what else needs doing as far as the wedding is concerned?' Ellie asked after sitting down and slipping her shoes off.

'I still haven't sorted out the flowers, and after reading your interview with the florist in the village, I wondered if she might be able to do the flowers for me. What do you think? It would be good publicity for her business if we promoted it on the blog.'

'That's a great idea. I'll give her a ring and see what she says. What else came up when you met with your mum?'

'I need to sort someone out to do my hair and make-up, but as I'll be getting ready at my parents' house, I don't know anyone there these days. Mum said she could speak to her hairdresser, but I'm not sure about that. Do you think a hairdresser here would be prepared to travel?'

'Do you have one you use that you could speak to?' Ellie asked.

'I can't remember the last time I had my hair cut.' Fran looked as if she might cry and Ellie didn't want that.

'Let me chat to Sylvie and see if there's someone she can recommend.'

'Thank you. I think that's enough for now till after you get back from London.'

Ellie stood and went to give her friend a hug. 'Try not to worry about it. It will all come together and be a wonderful day for you both.'

Henri

As it was Saturday morning again, Henri and Ellie planned to get up early and go to the market in the square. Sylvie had told him how interested the stallholders had been in the new vineyard blog when she'd gone to the market the previous weekend, so they wanted to try and build on that today.

They decided to go without breakfast and to pick something up from the market instead. The air was bracing as they stepped outside the house, but the sky was clear, and Henri took Ellie's gloved hand in his as they walked along the road towards the square.

'French markets are so unique. It's one of the first things that tourists want to do when they come to France,' Ellie said as they strolled underneath the trees lining the pavement.

'I love our market. There's always a sense of excitement about what you'll find when you visit, and everyone's so supportive of each other. I can't wait to see what new foods there'll be whenever I come.'

They arrived at the square a few minutes later, passing the village fountain as they made their way into the main market area. Henri made a beeline for the *boulangerie*'s stall, keen to get a pastry as soon as possible.

'*Bonjour*, Liliane,' he said with a smile.

'*Bonjour!*' Liliane replied. 'What can I get for you both today?'

They looked at the mouth-watering produce on Liliane's stall and settled on two *pains aux raisins* for a change.

'Let me know when you're free to do that interview, Liliane, won't you?' Ellie said. 'We're off to London for a few days on Sunday, but I could fit you in before then if you'd like.'

Liliane nodded her agreement and turned to the next customer in her long queue. Ellie took a photo of the stall with Liliane hard at work before she left.

As they ate their pastries, they worked their way alongside the *Hôtel de Ville*, stopping at every stall to see what was on offer. Henri knew most of the stallholders and invariably got drawn into conversation, leaving Ellie to take colourful photos of all the fruit and vegetables, the cured meats and fish, and the delicious cakes and biscuits that were on offer.

'Henri, come and see this,' Ellie said after finally dragging him away from his latest chat. She led him over to a stall where an artist was sketching the scene in the square. His stall was covered with his designs for stationery and leaflets, as well as wedding invitations and gifts.

'*Salut*,' they said to the man when he looked up from his sketch.

Ellie introduced herself and told the man about the blog. 'Would you be interested in doing an interview with me about your business? A friend of ours is also getting married and would love to see your designs.'

She booked an interview with the designer for the following week and then they left him to get on with his work.

'This is fantastic, Henri. I've taken so many photos and booked a good few interviews as well. I'm even wondering whether some of the more established stallholders might be interested in sponsoring the blog. What do you think?'

'You've got nothing to lose by asking. And even if we can't get a grant from the Ministry of Culture or the tourist bodies, we should definitely ask them to link to our site from theirs.'

'That's a great idea. I'll do that next week as well.'

Next they wandered down a row of stalls offering soaps, lotions and perfumes before reaching the stall of the florist, Madame Gastaud, at the end.

'*Salut*, Ellie, Henri. It's good to see you again. Your friend Fran has been in touch with me now. Thank you so much for recommending me to her for her wedding. I'd love to do more weddings so this was such good luck.' The older woman beamed at them and clasped her hands together with obvious delight.

'It's my pleasure,' Ellie told her.

'It's such a shame that Fran can't get married locally, though, isn't it?'

'She did want to get married at the vineyard, but the château won't be ready in time,' Ellie explained.

'Oh, that would have been amazing. I bet lots of young couples would love to get married at your château.'

They said goodbye to Madame Gastaud to walk around the middle of the market.

'Do you think we should seriously consider the château as a wedding venue, Henri? Wouldn't it be too much like hard work?' Ellie asked.

'It would be hard work, but there's no doubt it's a beautiful setting. I'd love to get married somewhere like that.' Henri was in two minds whether to propose to Ellie right there and then after setting up the perfect opportunity, but she was too deep in thought, and he wasn't even sure she'd heard what he'd said. His sense of pride held him back from the possibility of rejection.

'The downstairs is all done, and we could make the outside and the gardens presentable if Fran did want to get married there. I'll have to ask her whether she'd want to go ahead on that basis. Then we'd have to sort out the catering, too, but maybe we could do it for them if we all pull together.'

Henri's chance had gone and his shoulders sagged in disappointment. It was probably not the best place for a proposal, though, he thought to himself as he tried to listen in to what Ellie was now saying and focus on his reply.

CHAPTER SEVEN

Ellie

'Everything will be fine, I promise. Now, off you go and have a nice time.' Ellie kissed Fran on both cheeks and gave her a quick hug before shooing her out the door and into the car where Didier was patiently waiting. They both needed a break, and now that she and Henri were back, they could babysit instead of Sylvie sometimes, so they were doing everyone a favour, Ellie reasoned.

Henri shrieked with dismay as she went back into the living room where he was sitting on the floor playing a game with Chlöe – losing it in fact.

'I can't believe how many times you've beaten me at this game now,' he told Chlöe.

'I am very good at card games, though,' she said. 'So it's to be expected.'

Henri laughed and Ellie smiled at the easy way he gave in every time.

'How about we play with your Lego now to give poor old Henri a rest?' Ellie asked.

'Poor old Henri,' Chlöe repeated with a giggle, taking Ellie's hand and leading her to a trunk full of Lego pieces.

'Less of the old, thank you very much.'

Ellie watched as Henri pulled himself up and smiled when he winked at her. He disappeared out to the kitchen with Ruby on his heels, and she gave her attention to the little girl.

'My toys are going to go on a long journey, like you and Henri did. All their friends are going to give them a party to see them off and there will be lots of tears,' Chlöe said earnestly.

Ellie was surprised by how much Chlöe must have remembered about when she and Henri left. 'Were you sad when we went away?' she asked, deciding to confront things head-on.

'Very sad, but I'm much happier now you're back. You won't go away again, will you? I'm used to seeing Henri all the time, especially, and you, too, now. I really missed you when you were away.'

Henri came back in with two cups of coffee just as Chlöe was revealing her feelings. Ellie glanced at him but answered Chlöe's question herself.

'We're going away to London next week for a few days because my brother, Chris, is getting married, but then we'll be back,' Ellie replied.

'Forever?' Chlöe asked.

Henri put the cups down and came and sat with them then. 'We will go away sometimes in the future, *mignonne*, but we'll always be planning to come back. We couldn't stay away from you or Marie for too long.'

'And there'll be a new baby soon, as well,' Chlöe reminded him.

'Yes, that's right, and we're really looking forward to meeting the new baby.'

'Me too. It's very exciting. Have you seen the new baby's room?'

'I have,' said Ellie, 'when I was here the other day. I looked at your room, too, and I was upset that there's no colour on the walls. Do you have a favourite colour, Chlöe?' Ellie gently distracted the little girl away from her sadness, wondering if she missed her real mum, too, because she hardly ever saw her these days.

'My favourite colour is yellow, like the sun. I'd love to have yellow walls. Could you do that, Ellie?' She clasped her chubby hands together and gave Ellie her biggest smile.

'I could definitely do that, and if we ask Fran, she might even let you help me do it. What do you think?'

Chlöe's eyes lit up with excitement at the prospect. 'Really? That would be fun. Come and see the baby's room, now, Henri.'

The two of them disappeared upstairs and Ellie took a seat on the sofa to drink her coffee and to consider the damage caused to little Chlöe by her parents' divorce and her mum's absence from her life. Even though Fran loved her like her own daughter, Chlöe clearly worried about being left by those she loved. She had renewed admiration for both Fran and Didier for bringing Chlöe up with such understanding. She blew out a long breath, convinced that parenting was the hardest job on earth.

'Time for a bath before bed now, little one.' Henri's voice travelled down the stairs and Ellie glanced at her watch, surprised that it was bedtime already. Soon the air was filled with the sound of splashing and squeals of enjoyment from both Chlöe and Henri, so much so that Ellie couldn't tell who was having most fun. If she was going to have a baby with Henri, he would make the best father, she was in no doubt about that. But that was an even bigger step for her to take than deciding whether to settle down with him.

Chlöe appeared at her side, forcing her to push away her thoughts and to focus on the here and now.

'Time for my story now, please,' she said, handing Ellie her book of choice.

'Absolutely.' Ellie took Chlöe's warm hand and led her back upstairs to her bedroom. They settled on the bed, side by side, and Ellie began to read. Henri popped his head in and said goodnight just as Ellie had finished reading.

'Again, again,' Chlöe cried.

'One more time, but then you must go to bed, otherwise Fran will be cross with me.'

After reading the story through one more time, Ellie tucked Chlöe into bed and kissed her goodnight, before joining Henri downstairs on the sofa.

'She really is the most precious child,' Ellie said.

'I know. I love her to bits,' Henri said.

'It was upsetting listening to her tell us how sad she was when we went away, wasn't it?' Henri nodded but didn't say anything. 'I'd hate to worry her by leaving again. It's obviously something that's on her mind, what with her mum being so absent these days.'

'She's already had a lot to deal with in her life, that's for sure.'

'Fran and Didier are such good parents, which at least makes up for Isabelle not being around much for Chlöe.'

'Do you still feel restless, Ellie?' Henri asked.

'I don't feel restless so much any more, but I would still like to travel, even though it's beginning to feel like home to me here.'

'And how are you feeling about your mum now?'

Ellie raised her eyebrows. 'My mum? What do you mean?'

'Do you miss her?'

To her surprise, Ellie's eyes filled with tears. 'I miss the relationship we could have had if she'd been a different person,' she choked out. 'And now it's too late for me to change it.'

Ellie let Henri pull her into his arms and console her as she released all the pent-up feelings she had for her mum, and at last, she sobbed for the mum she would never be able to have.

Sunday, 9 December 2018

Henri

Henri woke early the following morning, excited at the prospect of their trip to London. He slipped out of bed and went downstairs to make breakfast, looking forward to the next few days and spending time with Ellie.

He set about making some pancakes after he put the coffee on, thinking it would make a nice change for their breakfast. He whisked the eggs and milk into the flour, added a touch of sugar and salt, and then mixed in some melted butter before setting the mixture to one side while he got the pan heating. Just as he was putting out the coffees and fruit juice, Ellie appeared.

'What a wonderful surprise,' she said with a sleepy smile. She kissed him and went to the fridge to get some blueberries to garnish the pancakes with. She brought over a jar of honey, as well, before sitting down.

'Breakfast is served, *mademoiselle*,' he said, putting a plate down in front of her with a flourish. '*Bon appétit!*'

'Mmm, these are superb. Thank you. This will set us up for the journey.'

'I'm looking forward to this trip away, aren't you?' he asked her.

'I am, yes. But I'm also disappointed to have to drop everything here when we were just getting into our stride.'

That was the last thing Henri had been expecting Ellie to say. 'We can enjoy the wedding and some time away together before coming back and throwing ourselves into the pre-Christmas party and our own Christmas celebrations.'

'That's true. It will be good to have a break before everything gets really busy here. I'm looking forward to all the things we've planned though.'

An hour later, they were all packed and ready to go. The taxi they'd booked to take them to the station in Strasbourg turned up right on time, and not long after that, they were on their way to Paris.

'It sounded like Lottie and Thierry had a wonderful time in Paris,' Ellie told Henri as the train carried them through the country-side towards the city. 'She said she thought she'd got the travelling bug again herself after going and that they were already planning where to go next time.'

'Would that make you happier if we planned weekend getaways like that ourselves on a regular basis?' Henri asked, taking her hand.

'I think so.' She paused. 'I don't know, Henri. I can't explain how I feel. It's sort of about the travelling but it's also about other things.'

'What things?' he asked, willing her to open up to him.

Instead, she turned away to look out the window, and he regretted pushing her to tell him what was on her mind. Then she looked back at him. 'I can't explain it all right now, but I want you to know that it's nothing to do with you and I... I do love you and I want to be with you.'

'I sense a but...' Henri countered, disappointed that this was the way the conversation always ended.

'Let's not talk about it now. We're going to London for a few days away, and I just want to enjoy spending it with you and not worrying about the future.'

Once again, Henri had the feeling that Ellie was keeping something from him, and he wished she would just share her innermost feelings with him, rather than clamming up when he tried to talk to her. He decided to try a different tack.

'You never talk about your dad, you know. Is that deliberate? Are you angry with him for leaving?'

Ellie sucked in a breath, and he knew instinctively that this had something to do with her reluctance to settle down and commit to him.

'When my mum told me that my dad would be leaving home because he'd had an affair, I was devastated at his betrayal of our family. I was so close to him and I loved him so much. I couldn't imagine what my life would be like without him in it every day. But in time, I got used to it and I thought that I might be able to adapt to seeing him less often.'

'That must have been very hard.' Henri kept his gaze fixed on Ellie, amazed that she was revealing some of her past to him at last.

'It was hard, mainly because my mum took every opportunity to put him down to me and Chris, and to blame him for everything that had happened. At first, we saw my dad every weekend, but then it dropped off. Then the next thing we knew, we were called in to speak to a solicitor to answer questions about our dad. I didn't realise at the time that these were custody hearings. Chris explained it all to me later. Soon after that, my dad disappeared and I haven't seen him since. It's been more than ten years now, and I still haven't got over being so angry with him about it.'

At last, Henri was beginning to understand why Ellie was so afraid of commitment, having been let down by both her parents. It made Henri realise just how lucky he'd been to have his parents for so long. It was going to take a lot for Ellie to completely trust him and to let down her walls. He was determined to show her that he was worth it, but would it be enough to persuade her to stay?

Ellie

Ellie spent the rest of the journey to London trying not to worry about how much she'd told Henri about her past. He'd been very quiet since she'd told him everything and she wished she'd just kept it to herself. She was ashamed of the way she'd never bothered to make things up with her mum, and now it was too late. Even though her mum had behaved terribly, she was still her mum, and there had always been a chance that she could have retrieved some kind of relationship with her before she'd died.

She didn't know if Henri was judging her for that, but she could almost hear the cogs whirring in his brain as he processed everything she'd told him. His childhood would have been so different from hers, with two loving parents around all the time. Her sadness about not having her dad present in her life was even greater than the regret she felt about her mum, but at the same time, she harboured such anger against him for just disappearing out of their lives. And she had no idea how to come to terms with that anger. So many times she'd asked herself what she would say if she did ever see him again, but she always concluded that there was no point worrying about it because there was no way that was going to happen after all these years.

Before she knew it, the train was pulling into London St. Pancras and it was time to pull herself back to the present again.

'You've been ever so quiet since we left Paris,' Henri said as they grabbed their bags and made their way off the train and onto the platform.

A smile flickered across her face. 'A lot to think about, I guess. Anyway, let's find the platform for our next train and then we can get on with our break.'

Despite the labyrinthine nature of the station, they found their way out and across the road to King's Cross where they soon found the platform for the next part of their journey to Hertford. The train journey passed quickly with Ellie making notes for her blog about the trip so far. She'd decided to write a blog post about attending Chris and Michelle's wedding for any blog readers who might be interested in London for their honeymoon.

They caught a cab for the short trip to their hotel, and when they turned into the drive leading to the main building, Ellie could hardly contain her excitement. The gravel drive was long and passed through neatly tended gardens and an abundance of mature trees. She was delighted with her choice of accommodation.

'This is amazing, Ellie,' Henri agreed. His face was a picture of delight.

'It is, isn't it?' She laughed.

The cab pulled up outside the elegant main building, and a minute later, they stood in the marbled reception area waiting to check in.

'Ah yes, Miss Robinson and Mr Weiss, welcome to Oakley Manor. We hope you enjoy your stay with us. You're staying in our Garden Suite. If you just follow Taylor here, he'll show you the way.'

They turned and followed the young bellboy back outside and

along the pathway that led round the back of the main hotel. Just a short walk later and they arrived at the door of their suite. Once inside, it was hard to contain their pleasure at the size of the room and the seating area contained within it, as well as the view over the whole garden and the trees beyond.

Once the bellboy had gone, Henri put his arm round Ellie and she melted against him.

'Shall we have an early night so we can make the most of our day tomorrow?' he asked, stroking her back as he spoke.

Ellie nodded. 'I'll just give Chris a call to let them know we're here and that we'll see them tomorrow for dinner as agreed.'

*

Excited to make the most of their time in the capital, they set off early the next day on their way back down to central London. Ellie found she enjoyed being a tourist in her own city, making much more of all there was to see and do than she'd ever done when she lived there. When Fran had lived with her in London, they'd spent all their spare time taking in the sights, but it was fun to be doing it with Henri this time.

As they made their way out of the Tube station at Tower Hill, Ellie waited to see what his reaction would be to seeing the Tower of London. It always took her breath away and never failed to do the same for visitors. Sure enough, Henri's reaction was one of complete surprise.

'Now that's what I call a proper castle,' he exclaimed, and Ellie laughed.

'We do have quite a few, you know,' she teased.

'There can't be many that are better than this one though. It's stunning.'

They made their way along the path, past the ravens and the handsomely dressed Yeoman Warders, and into the main courtyard, where they then proceeded to explore all the outer rooms and to read all about the gruesome history of the building. Henri was most affected by the Bloody Tower, just as Ellie had been when she'd first visited as a child.

'They were so violent in the past, weren't they?' Henri said, pulling a face.

'I would have hated to live then, that's for sure,' Ellie agreed. 'We're going to have to make our way now, Henri. I'm sorry we can't stay longer, but we can come back another time.'

They were meeting Chris and Michelle, together with a small group of family and friends, at a restaurant in Shoreditch, so it didn't take them too long to get there. Ellie spotted Chris just after they'd entered the restaurant and gave him a wave. He was talking to a man who had his back to her, but Chris obviously told him that she'd arrived because he turned to look her way. All the breath went out of her lungs as she looked into the much older face of her father.

Henri

The first Henri knew of there being a problem was when Ellie stumbled in front of him, and he naturally reached out to catch her before she fell.

'Ellie, *qu'est-ce qu'il y a?* Are you okay?' he said quietly in her ear.

She turned shakily to face him, clutching at his arm. 'No, Henri, everything is not okay. We need to leave at once.'

'But, sweetheart, we've just got here. I can see Chris. Surely you don't want to leave before we've said hello?'

'Henri, he's talking to my dad,' she whispered.

Henri stilled, knowing how painful that would be for her. He glanced across to Chris, who was now walking over to join them, and back at Ellie's pale face. He took her hand and gave it a gentle squeeze. 'Chris is coming this way so you'll have to speak to him.' Henri kept eye contact with Ellie, trying to reassure her. 'You can do this. You're not on your own. I'll be here with you, but if you decide you want to go, that's fine.'

Chris appeared then looking a little sheepish. 'Hey, you two. It's lovely to see you both. Thanks for coming. Let me find Michelle so you can say hello before we sit down to dinner.'

'Actually, Chris, I'm not feeling too good. I might need to leave,' Ellie told him, her voice shaky.

'But you've just arrived, and there's someone I want you to meet.'

'No, I can't, I'm sorry.' Ellie started to back away but Chris caught her arm.

'Please stay, Ellie. Michelle will be upset if she doesn't see you.'

'And what about me, Chris? Don't you think I'm upset at what you've done?' She glared at him unable to keep her thoughts to herself any longer.

'What have I done?' He frowned at her and Henri sensed it would be up to him to find the right thing to say.

'Come on, Chris, you know what a surprise this is for Ellie to see her father after all this time.'

Chris glanced at Henri and then back at Ellie. 'I'm genuinely sorry, Ellie, if I've upset you, but I would have thought you'd be pleased to see Dad. I know I was.'

'I would have appreciated a word of warning rather than turning up to find him here,' Ellie hissed at her brother.

'You wouldn't have come if I'd told you, but now's your chance to talk to him and to put things right. So why don't you take it?'

Michelle appeared at Chris' side then. 'Is everything okay, you guys? You've still got your coats on.' A look of concern passed across her face and Henri knew that Ellie would find it hard to let Michelle down.

Ellie leaned forward to kiss Michelle hello. 'I'm sorry, I just wasn't feeling well all of a sudden, but I feel better now,' she said.

Henri marvelled at Ellie's bravery just when she needed it most.

'Let's find your seats then and get you both a drink,' Michelle said, oblivious to all that had gone before.

They followed Michelle through the milling guests to the main table, and Henri helped Ellie take off her coat before removing his jacket and taking the seat next to her. Michelle had disappeared to get them both a drink, so they had a moment to gather their wits. Ellie's dad still hadn't approached her and for that, Henri was grateful. At least he had some idea of the shock this would be for his daughter.

Henri poured them both a glass of water, and Ellie sipped at hers steadily, as if trying to get her feelings under control.

'What will I say to him, Henri, if he comes over? I want to talk to him, I really do, but I wasn't prepared for this, and I just know that all the wrong things will come out.'

Henri understood how hurt she was, and he was desperate to give her good advice, but he didn't know what to suggest either. 'I think you have to play it by ear, Ellie. Maybe he's just as nervous as you are.'

Ellie looked up at him, her eyes full of emotion. 'Do you think so?'

'It has to be difficult for him as well. He doesn't know how you're going to react to seeing him, especially under these circumstances.'

Everyone started sitting down at their places then and the meal took over for a while. Thankfully for Ellie, her dad was seated at the other end of the table with about a dozen people in between them. Ellie hardly ate anything and she kept her eyes fixed on her plate or on Henri, refusing to look elsewhere in case her dad was looking her way.

As soon as the meal was over, Ellie turned to Henri. 'I'd like to go now. I can't take any more of the tension, wondering if he's going to come over and talk to me.'

'Okay, that's fine.' Henri stood up and waited for Ellie to be ready. 'Do you want to say goodbye to Chris and Michelle before we go?'

She nodded. 'I do just want to get out of here, but I can't go without saying goodbye.'

Ellie's dad was making his way towards the bar, so Henri took her hand and led her quickly towards Chris and Michelle.

'Michelle, I'm sorry to leave early, but I really don't feel too good,' Ellie said when they reached her.

'Oh no, I'm so sorry. Thank you for coming anyway. Just take care and get better in time for the wedding.' Michelle kissed her gently goodbye and smiled at Henri.

'I'll walk you out,' Chris said, guiding them back in the direction of the exit.

'There's no need, Chris, we'll be fine,' Ellie told him with a pointed look.

Chris leaned in towards Ellie for a hug. 'I'm sorry, sis. I thought this was a good idea. I didn't mean to upset you.'

'I have to go. I'll talk to you tomorrow,' Ellie said with a quick glance around. Henri had never seen her look so haunted.

They walked quietly and inconspicuously towards the exit, with no-one noticing their departure because they were all having too good a time still. Once they were outside, they both took a deep breath of fresh air before taking off towards the Tube again at a brisk pace.

'God, Henri, I'm so sorry to have spoilt this evening. What a disaster that was.'

'You didn't spoil it. You had no idea that was going to happen.'

'No, that's true, but it's ruined everything. I'm not even sure I can go to the wedding now.'

Henri stopped in the street and she turned to face him. 'You can't mean that? Don't you want to be at Chris' wedding?'

'Of course I do, but I can't face going if my dad's going to be there as well. I don't want to have to worry about him coming up to me all the way through the wedding in the same way as I've worried tonight. I'll ask Chris to come over tomorrow so I can tell him face-to-face that we won't be attending after all.'

A knot of dread formed in the pit of Henri's stomach even as she told him of her plans. He wanted to support her in every way possible, but this was not what he'd imagined at all.

CHAPTER EIGHT

Ellie

Ellie tossed and turned all night despite sleeping in a luxurious king-size bed with crisp, cotton sheets. When she got up the next morning, it was as though she hadn't slept at all, and looking at herself in the bathroom mirror, she had the evidence in clear detail.

Henri had offered to call Chris first thing and he was talking quietly now while she was getting ready. She didn't want to hear what was said between them; she just wanted to know that Chris was coming over to talk to her.

An hour later, after nibbling her way through their room-service breakfast, Ellie jumped when there was another knock on the door. Henri nodded at her and gave her a tight smile before going to let Chris in. A minute later, her brother appeared before her, his face like thunder.

'What the hell is going on here, Ellie? You do remember that I'm getting married tomorrow, don't you? These few days are not about you, and I won't have you spoiling things for me or Michelle. She's already upset about you leaving early last night, let alone not being introduced to her family.'

Instead of dealing with all the accusations, she made one of her own. 'Why didn't you tell me that you'd made contact with Dad before last night so that I could process it in my own time? You've had plenty of time to tell me. This whole "I wanted to make it a surprise" routine is wearing thin now.' She glared at him, refusing to back down.

Chris sighed and took off his coat. He sat down and poured himself a coffee. 'It happened after Mum died, and at first, I wanted to wait and see if it would go anywhere before telling you about it. By the time I realised that he was serious about staying in touch, you and Henri had gone on your travels and I didn't feel that was the best time to tell you. In fact, there never seemed to be a good time to tell you. I meant to tell you when we visited you in Alsace but I didn't know how to begin.' He swiped his hand through his hair. 'I am sorry for the surprise last night, but I hoped it would work out and that you would talk to each other. You didn't even give him a chance.'

'Why should I after all he's done? He hasn't wanted to be a part of our lives for all these years, so why does he want to now?'

'That's for him to explain to you, but you should at least listen to what he has to say. I gave him a chance because I want to have a relationship with my dad if I can. I'm getting married and, hopefully, having children one day, and I want my wife and my children to know my father, which is why I invited him to our wedding.'

'I won't be coming if he's there, Chris, I'm sorry. I can't just wipe the slate clean after the divorce and the way it ruined our family.' She glanced at Henri, embarrassed that he was having to hear all this, but he showed no signs of feeling awkward. 'I can't forgive him for just abandoning us like that. Too much time has gone past now.' She wiped tears away from her eyes, annoyed that it still upset her after all these years.

'Look, all I can say is that there are two sides to every story and we've only ever heard Mum's. Don't you think he deserves the chance to tell you what happened from his point of view? I know you're hurt.

I was, too, don't forget. But I truly believe that it's time to move on past it all, and to have a go at forgiving him.'

'I can't do it, Chris. The hurt and the resentment are still too strong for me.' Once again, tears sprang to her eyes but she was also angry. Angry at her brother for breaking their pact never to let one of their parents hurt them again, and angry at her father for turning up now after all these years away.

'I don't want to have to choose between you, Ellie, but I want Dad to be there tomorrow, and I'm not going to change my mind on that.'

'I'm not going to change my mind either. I won't be coming if he's going to be there.'

Chris stood and put his coat back on. 'Then I'll have to accept that, Ellie, much as it pains me to do so. I want you both to be there, as well, but I'm leaving that up to the two of you.'

Ellie stared after him as he walked away and Henri shut the hotel room door behind him. He'd called her bluff on that and now she would have to make the hardest decision of her life.

'What am I going to do, Henri? I don't want to go and have to face my father, but at the same time, I do want to be there for Chris and Michelle.'

'If you want my advice, we should go to the wedding. I know it will be hard, but you'll regret it if you don't go, and Chris may not forgive you for it if you don't.'

Ellie sank down onto the sofa in the lounge area of the suite. How had everything gone so wrong? This was supposed to be a special trip away for them and now it was turning into a nightmare.

'I need to get out of here, to get away from it all and do all the things we'd planned to do today to take my mind off everything.'

'I'd love to do that, but I don't think it will be as much fun with this hanging over us. I think we should talk it through so that you can make the right decision.'

'But what about all our plans?' She'd so looked forward to everything they were going to do and now it was all in tatters. She was on the brink of tears once again with no idea how to put it all right.

Henri

Henri drew Ellie into his arms and stroked her hair to soothe her. 'We can come back to London any time, *chérie*, but we have to sort this out now, for you, for Chris and Michelle, and also for your dad.'

Ellie pulled back to look at him and her tear-stained eyes almost broke his heart. 'What do you mean, for my dad?' She pulled a face and Henri understood that this was going to be hard for her. He guided her to the sofa, composing his thoughts as they moved.

'Your dad needs closure on all that happened in the past, as well, Ellie. My gut feeling is that you don't know the whole truth of what went on before. Is there anything else you can remember, apart from what you've already told me?'

She pondered that question for a moment before replying. 'I don't think so. I mean, Mum told us he was leaving because of the affair, and that was it. We didn't question it. I didn't have the energy to; I was so heartbroken at what he'd done.'

'But you still saw him after he left home?'

'We did for a while, as I said, but it was always uncomfortable. He had a small flat with only the one bedroom so we never stayed over, and it was always difficult just spending time with him.'

'Did you ever see any sign of the woman he'd had the affair with? Do you even know who it was?'

Ellie frowned. 'No, and I don't know who it was. I don't even remember my mum saying who it was. She always referred to her as "that woman" but that was it.'

'So your dad didn't settle down with this woman then and make a new life with her. That makes it sound like it was a fling, and maybe he's always regretted that.'

'I hope he has.' Ellie's eyes flashed with the now familiar bitterness.

'And then the visits started dropping off. Why was that?'

'I don't know. Mum just said he wasn't coming one weekend and then he didn't come the next, and that seemed to be the end of that.'

'But didn't you wonder why?'

'I think Chris did. It would eat him up more than me when we thought Dad was coming to collect us but didn't turn up. That went on for several weeks. Mum would tell us to get ready for him to collect us and then he wouldn't turn up, and that hurt more than anything, to keep getting our hopes up only to be let down. In the end, I stopped believing he would come.'

'And did your mum explain why he'd stopped coming?'

'No. It was like an overnight change with her. All of a sudden, all she wanted to do was criticise him, and I soon came to hate her for that.' Ellie flushed and Henri took her hands in his.

'You were still a kid, Ellie. Everything is much harder in those kinds of circumstances.'

'I just didn't know what to believe. Even though I was so hurt by my dad leaving, I still loved him, and I didn't want to hear my mum bad-mouthing him all the time. I just wanted her to be impartial and to make us feel better.'

'And your dad didn't come to the custody hearings?'

'No. It was so weird. They asked all kinds of questions about both my parents. The hardest one was when they asked me who I wanted to live with. I wanted to go back to how things were and to be a family again, but I knew that wasn't possible, of course. So I said that I wanted to live with my mum, out of loyalty to her, but in my heart, I wasn't happy living with her and all her grudges.'

'God, Ellie. I'm so sorry you had to go through all this. I can't imagine what it was like.'

'I envy you so much for your normal family childhood,' she said quietly.

Henri didn't know what to say to that. His childhood had been great, it was true, but then both his parents had died when he was in his late teens, and he still missed them all these years later.

When he didn't say anything, Ellie looked up at him. 'Henri? Are you okay?'

'Yes, yes, I'm fine,' he said in the end, but he didn't elaborate further, not wanting to talk about his parents just then. He'd never really talked to Ellie about them much at all.

'So, you think that my dad wants to get closure by talking to me now, and that I should give him the benefit of the doubt?'

'Yes, I do. I know it's hard for you, but it might make you feel better to hear what he has to say. And more than anything, I don't think you should let it come between you and Chris. He's been your constant throughout your life, and you owe it to him, I think, to be there at his wedding.'

Ellie snuggled closer to Henri, and his heart warmed at having her by his side. 'Thanks for talking it all through with me. I feel much calmer now.'

'What would you like to do next then?'

'I suppose I ought to speak to Chris again about the wedding. Do you agree?'

'Yes, I don't think you have any choice about that unless you want to fall out with him for good.'

'And then I need to decide whether to talk to my dad before the event, so that we don't spoil the wedding.'

Henri was just about to agree with that comment when there was another knock at the hotel room door. They'd put the 'Do Not Disturb' sign up while they were talking, so Henri was unsure who it could be.

'I'll go,' Ellie said, jumping up and heading for the door.

Henri heard her gasp from the sofa and stood up to follow her. The last person he was expecting to see was her father waiting there.

'Can I come in, please, Ellie?'

Ellie

Ellie was still staring at her dad a minute later, unable to move, when she felt Henri's hand on her arm, which snapped her out of her paralysis.

'Come in,' she said despite all her instincts telling her to send him away.

'Thank you,' he said, and he stepped inside. 'I'm Bill,' he said to Henri, 'I'm sorry we didn't get the chance to meet each other last night.' He put out his hand and Henri shook it.

'Let me take your coat,' Henri said, doing all the normal things Ellie knew she should be doing. But she was still in shock, not least at how her dad had aged so much since she'd last seen him. His previously sandy-red hair was now peppered with grey.

'Thanks for letting me in, Ellie. I know that must have been hard for you to do when you haven't seen me for so long.' A flash of pain skittered across his face and then was gone again.

'It has been a long time, but I want to hear what you have to say,' she said, not admitting that she was also frightened at the thought of what he would say to her after all these years.

Ellie sat down on one sofa and Henri sat next to her, while her dad took the armchair opposite. Henri took her hand and she gripped it tight like a lifeline.

'I'd lost all hope of ever seeing you again, but your mum's death freed me to get in touch with you both.'

'What do you mean "freed you"?' Ellie asked brusquely.

'She made me promise once she got custody that I wouldn't try to get in touch with either of you. I've regretted agreeing to that ever since, but she could be very intimidating when she wanted to be.'

Ellie found herself nodding at that, but then she checked herself. 'But why didn't you want custody of us?'

'I wanted to continue sharing custody of you both as we'd been doing up till then, but she told me that you didn't want to see me any more, and I believed her. And because I didn't want to upset you any more than you already were, I gave in to her demands and left you alone. I didn't realise until much later that she'd lied to me about that. An old friend told me how she'd poisoned you both against me after I left, and I knew then that you might never know the truth of what had really happened between us.'

Ellie leaned forward. 'What did happen?'

Her dad took in a long breath, steeling himself for what he had to say next. 'It was your mum that had the affair, not me. She told me to leave, that she didn't love me any more, and then the next thing I knew, she'd told you both that it was me that had broken up our family.'

'What? How can that be true? Who could she have had an affair with? I just can't imagine her doing that.'

'It was with our next-door neighbour, Richard. And she carried on seeing him after I left.'

Ellie's thoughts exploded and she let go of Henri's hand in surprise. Could it be true? She cast her mind back to her childhood. Rich was always round their house, doing little jobs, running errands for them. And it certainly picked up after her dad left. She dragged herself back to the present day. 'But why didn't you fight her?'

Her dad wiped his hand across his eyes, looking like he had the weight of the world on his shoulders. 'If I'd told you both the truth, you would have hated both of us, me for telling you, and her, for doing what she'd done. So it was simpler for me to take the blame, and then eventually to leave. But knowing how much you must have both hated me since then has been very hard for me to live with all these years. I should have tried harder to fight her so I could continue seeing you both, and I've regretted it every single day.'

Ellie processed what her dad had said. It all made sense, but it didn't make her feel any better. Now she could clearly see her mum for the liar and manipulator she'd been, and she could see how her dad had struggled in the face of her mum's behaviour. 'What did Chris have to say about all this?' She gestured at her dad, unsure how to refer to all he'd just told her.

'He was shocked, but I had the feeling that maybe it wasn't so much of a surprise to him, about your mum and Richard, I mean.'

'He never said anything to me about having any suspicions.' Ellie was outraged about that.

'From what I've seen of Chris, he'd have been trying to protect you, Ellie.' Henri gave her a look filled with such love that her anger petered out as quickly as it had come. She'd been lucky to have first Chris, and now Henri, to look out for her, despite all the chaos of her childhood.

'And has Chris forgiven you for going away and not coming back to see us until now?' Her voice was softer now as she tried to make sense of everything that had happened. But this was the biggest obstacle for her to get over.

'Not quite, but I think he understands my reasons for doing what I did. I loved you both, love you still, so much, and it seemed the least painful way out of it all for you. I probably should have told you the truth, in your view, but I didn't have it in me to do that to you.'

'I do understand that, but my relationship with Mum was never quite the same afterwards. She never wasted an opportunity to criticise you, but instead of making me more upset with you, it made me more annoyed with her for constantly putting you down in front of us. You were our dad, and we didn't need that from her. We needed her to rise above it and to reassure us that we were loved; instead she became bitter and unkind. I left home as soon as I could and...' She was about to say she'd been on the run ever since, but that had only just occurred to her, and she didn't have the strength to admit this to either man sitting in front of her right now. Admitting it to herself had been hard enough.

***

Henri

Henri wondered what Ellie had been about to say, but he didn't push her and neither did her dad. It had been a stressful couple of hours for them all, but most of all for Ellie to have found out that so much of her life had been based on lies. Not only that, but lies told by her parents.

'What do you want to do now, Ellie? We need to make a firm decision about the wedding so that you can tell Chris and Michelle what you're going to do.'

Ellie heaved in a great breath as she gathered her hair into a ponytail. She looked so vulnerable that all Henri wanted to do was to hold her and to keep her safe from any more revelations. 'Yes, you're right. I do need to make a decision.'

'You weren't thinking of not coming, were you?' Bill asked. 'Please don't do that because of me. Chris and Michelle really want you both to be there.'

'But they want you to be there, too. I can't ruin their day. It's time for me to put them first, so I will go to the wedding. And I want you to be there for Chris as well. After all this time, and all that's happened, he deserves to have us both there for him on his special day.'

Her dad gave her a bright smile and Henri could have sworn he looked twenty years younger at that moment. 'I'm so grateful to you for that, Ellie. I would have understood if you hadn't wanted me there. I really would like us to get to know each other again and to see if we can move on from this.'

'I'd like that, too, but I'm not going to be ready to move on for some time yet, I don't think.'

Her dad's smile faded as he took in what she'd just told him, and Henri was saddened by all the hurt there was between them.

'Look, it's going to take some time, but if you both want to get past this, you can do it. I really believe that.' Henri glanced at them both and Ellie squeezed his hand.

'Thank you, Henri. I hope we can get to know each other better, too.' Bill stood up then and picked up his coat. 'I'd better go, but I look forward to seeing you both again at the wedding tomorrow.'

Henri reached out to shake his hand. There was an awkward

moment as Bill took a step towards Ellie, but she backed away, clearly not welcoming any signs of affection from her father just yet. Henri walked him to the door, leaving Ellie behind them.

'Dad?' They both turned at the sound of Ellie's voice just as Bill was about to leave. Henri was surprised that Ellie was ready to use that word again, and when he glanced at Bill, the older man had tears in his eyes.

'Thanks for coming and for telling me everything,' she continued.

Bill nodded and then he left.

Henri strode across the suite and took Ellie in his arms. 'I'm so proud of you for how you dealt with all that,' he said to her as he held her close.

'I'm quite proud of myself,' she replied. She pulled back to look into his face. 'Thank you so much for being there with me through it all. You kept me going, you really did.'

'If I helped, I'm glad, but it was all down to you and the way you handled it. And I know Chris and Michelle will be so pleased to know we're coming tomorrow. You need to let them know, and then maybe we can go out for the afternoon and make the most of the rest of the day. What do you think?'

'That sounds like a great idea.'

Henri gathered their things while he waited for Ellie to finish speaking to Chris. It sounded positive, from what he was hearing, and he was relieved that Ellie had at least managed to make everything up with Chris before the wedding.

Within half an hour, they were on their way back into London and heading for the river, where they planned to take a boat trip as the weather was good. They were both bundled up against the cold, so they sat on a bench outside, at the front of the boat, to see all the sights clearly as the boat progressed along the water. They'd boarded at Westminster and were heading back towards the Tower of London, with Ellie pointing out the sights along the way as well as taking photos and making notes for her blog. Henri had been delighted to see the London Eye, followed by the theatres along the

South Bank, and then a short while later, the magnificent Millennium Bridge and Shakespeare's Globe theatre.

'This is a fantastic way to see so many of the sights,' Henri enthused as they continued their way along the river.

'I've always loved being on the Thames. As long as it's not raining, it really is the perfect way to travel.'

'And how are you feeling about everything now?' Henri asked.

'I'm okay. This is a good distraction from thinking about it all the time, and I need that at the moment. I need some space from it all.'

As they approached the Tower of London again, Henri remembered all the things they'd done the previous day, and he was happy that they'd been able to get out and do more today despite all the difficulties of the day.

'Do you want to get off here and go for a walk around that marina you mentioned?'

'Oh, St. Katharine Docks, yes, that would be wonderful, and I think you'll like it.'

They hopped off the boat and set off along the embankment in the direction of the marina. Henri was delighted by all the food stalls there were dotted around, and they picked up some sugary churros as they went by one stand to keep them going as they went on to walk around the marina, marvelling at all the boats in the cold.

CHAPTER NINE

Wednesday, 12 December 2018

Ellie

As she got ready for her brother's wedding the following morning, Ellie's thoughts inevitably returned to everything that her dad had told her the day before. She'd worried that she wouldn't be able to sleep because of it all, but perhaps because of the intensity of all the revelations coupled with their busy afternoon, she'd fallen into a deep sleep and slept right through. But now, her mind was working overtime once again.

She tried to concentrate on her make-up and hair in an effort to stop her mind going there, but it was hard to maintain that focus. She never usually wore much make-up because of her colouring. With her red hair, she preferred to use minimal foundation and blusher, and just to go bold with her lipstick colour. She was well-practised at it by now, and she stared at her smattering of freckles when she'd finished, pleased that they could still be seen. She had the same colouring as her dad, but she'd still been surprised by just how much she looked like him when she'd seen him yesterday. They even had the same colour eyes.

She stood to give herself one final look in the mirror. She'd chosen a knee-length multi-coloured print dress that accentuated her curves, and she'd decided to wear her hair up. She popped in her drop earrings and did up her matching necklace. Finally, she picked up her handbag and, with a deep breath, went out to join Henri in the living area. He'd been waiting patiently for her for quite some time, but he never did need much time to get ready.

'Wow, Ellie, you look amazing. *Superbe!*' His eyes glowed as he took in her appearance, and her heart soared at his compliments.

'You look very handsome, too,' she told him as she fingered the lapel of his smart Italian wool suit. She took a second to straighten his tie before kissing him lightly on the lips. She breathed in his reassuring spicy scent, which calmed her with its familiarity.

'Are you ready to go then?' he asked.

'I am.'

They were soon on their way in a taxi to the little village where the wedding was to take place that morning. It was only a short drive, but Ellie enjoyed the opportunity to focus her thoughts on being there for Chris and Michelle today and making sure they had the best day possible. She was less worried about her dad being there now, although she was still dealing with everything he'd told her the previous day. She believed what he'd told her, though, and she could see how much it had hurt him to give up his children and to move away. She wondered what he'd done during those years, where he'd lived, whether he'd remarried. She gasped as she wondered if he'd had any more children.

'Are you okay, Ellie?' Henri asked as he leaned forward in the seat to look at her.

'Yes, sorry. I was just wondering whether my dad had remarried and whether he might have had more children.'

'That is possible, of course. You've got all the time in the world to get to know him better now and to ask him those questions.'

That was true, but she didn't intend to start doing that today. She wanted to watch him from afar and to see what he was like in his interactions with other people first.

The taxi pulled up outside the church, where there were already lots of people milling around. Ellie and Henri made their way up the path towards the church, saying hello to people as they passed.

'Do you know anyone here?' Henri asked.

'Not really. Some faces are familiar from the get-together the other night, but there's no-one here that I know that well.'

They went inside the porch, where they found Ellie's dad and Chris' friend, Mark, giving out buttonholes.

'Morning, Ellie, Henri,' Bill said with a smile. He picked up a cream rose and passed it to Henri for his buttonhole, then picked out one of the corsages for Ellie, as sister to the bridegroom. It was a peach rose, tied to some bright yellow freesias and gypsophila.

'Would you like me to put it on for you?' her dad asked.

She hesitated, knowing that he would be hurt if she said no, but unsure all the same. 'Thank you,' she said in the end, taking the path of least resistance. When he'd finished attaching it to her jacket, the glorious smell of the flowers wafted her way, and for a moment, she felt at peace.

'How's Chris this morning?' she asked her dad.

'He's fine. He's in the church, if you want to go in and take your places. I'll see you later.'

Ellie and Henri slipped inside, where Chris was standing on his own in front of the altar, his head down. He turned at the creak of the door.

'Hey, you two. I'm so glad to see you.' He gave them a broad smile as he walked towards them.

'How are you feeling today?' Ellie asked after giving her brother a quick hug.

'Never better. I can't wait to get married to Michelle. He glanced at his watch. 'Not long now,' he said with a grin. 'And how about you? How are you feeling?'

'I'm okay. I'm fine, actually,' she corrected, because she did feel much better than she had yesterday. She desperately wanted to talk to Chris about it all, but now wasn't the time. She was hoping to catch him later in the day before he went on his honeymoon to ask him instead; otherwise she would have to wait for him to come back to find out more.

More people started to come into the church, so she and Henri went to take their seats in the front row, leaving a seat for her dad. There was no-one else from her family there, so they were joined by Mark's parents. Not long after, her dad slipped into the pew beside her and the music that signalled the bride was on her way began.

Henri

Henri relaxed back into his seat and took a sip of the Domaine's *crémant d'Alsace*, something he had been looking forward to all day. He and Ellie had provided a case of the sparkling wine for the wedding as a gift to Chris and Michelle, and right now, Henri was very pleased about that. The wedding had gone well, and the weather had remained beautifully fine for the photos. Now he was looking forward to some lunch, although he was concerned about whether it would be up to French standards. Still, he was trying his best to keep an open mind.

'The wedding went off well, didn't it?' Ellie said, looking at him from over the rim of her own glass.

'It did. I really enjoyed it. It was quite different from the weddings I'm used to in the Catholic church. A lot simpler.' He smiled. 'I'm starving now though.' He laughed.

'It won't be much longer, I shouldn't think. Chris and Michelle are coming in now so lunch will be underway soon.' She patted his arm.

'You seem much brighter today,' Henri said.

'I am, although I've been pondering something all morning.'

'Which is?'

'How to speak to Chris about Dad before he leaves tonight. I'd like to, if I can, because otherwise I won't get the chance for a couple of weeks. But I realise that today isn't the best day for it.' She took a long sip of her drink.

Henri wanted to help Ellie, but at the same time, he didn't want to cause any upset on Chris and Michelle's wedding day. 'What do you want to talk to him about that can't wait till they come back?'

'I just want to know how he's feeling about what Dad said, how he's dealing with it all, you know.'

'That could wait till he comes back, I think, and it would give you time to form your own opinion about your dad.'

Ellie pondered that for a moment. 'Maybe you're right. It's just I'm so used to deferring to Chris about family matters and getting his take on things before making any decisions.'

They fell silent as the food started being served, but Henri was still reflecting on how difficult this all must be for Ellie. The nature of her relationship with Chris was already going to change with him getting married, and now it would change again with the reappearance of her dad in her life. After they'd finished eating, Henri stood up to visit the gents.

'Will you ask Chris to come and speak to me when he gets a moment?' She gave him one of her pleading looks, the kind that made him want to give her whatever she wanted, and he felt trapped.

'I'll try, but I'm not going to push it too hard, Ellie.'

On his way back, Henri went by the top table looking for Chris, who had disappeared in the time he'd been out of the room.

'Hey, Henri, is everything all right?'

Bill suddenly appeared before him, and he found himself telling him about Ellie's concerns. 'I don't want to drag Chris away from his big day, but Ellie wants to talk to him, so I was just looking for him.'

'Why don't I come and talk to Ellie instead? It would give us the chance to get to know each other better.'

Henri released a sigh of relief. 'Thanks, Bill. That would be great.'

They walked back to where Ellie was waiting patiently for Henri to return. Bill sat down next to her while Henri hovered in the background.

'Hi, Ellie, have you been enjoying the day?' Bill asked with a smile.

'The wedding was lovely.' She smiled back at her dad. 'I'm glad we came.'

'Henri says you have some questions for Chris, and I was hoping I could help, as he's going to have other things on his mind today.'

Ellie had the grace to look sheepish. 'I know what you said yesterday about why Chris didn't let me know that you were in touch again, but I find that hard to believe. At the very least, he could have messaged me while we were away.' She pouted at her dad, and Henri had to suppress a laugh. He'd bet money that Ellie had been a proper handful as a child.

'He could have done that, and we did talk about whether he should, but we decided it would be too much of a shock for you and that it would spoil your trip. So we decided against it. We did it with the best of intentions.' He paused for a moment to let his words sink in. 'What are you really upset about here, Ellie?'

'What do you mean? I've told you.' She hunched her shoulders defensively and Henri leaned in to hear what she would say in reply.

'There's more to this, I think, and I wish you would tell me what it is.'

She huffed for a moment, but then told him what was on her mind. 'I feel excluded from things because you and Chris have had a head start without me. I'm always going to be playing catch-up now, and I don't like being in this position.'

Bill smiled, although Henri had no idea why. 'I'm glad that you want to have a relationship with me at all, Ellie, even if you have had to wait a few months to get started. Given all the years we've missed together, a couple of months won't make a lot of difference, will it?' Bill reached out and took her hand.

'I suppose you're right,' she said. 'But I am still cross with you both for not letting me know before yesterday, especially when I saw Chris so recently.'

'I'm sorry, but as I said, we both thought it was for the best. We should have told you before yesterday, though, I accept that. Can you forgive us?'

Henri caught Ellie's eye, hoping that she would say yes. He nodded at her, trying to encourage her to do the right thing. 'I'll try,' she said, and she smiled.

Ellie

Ellie was heartened by her dad's efforts to deal with her fears. She was being irrational – in her heart, she knew that – but he was still prepared to listen to her and talk it over with her. When Henri went off to the bar to get some more drinks, she turned to her dad once again.

'How did you feel when Chris got in touch with you after all these years?'

'I was shocked, to tell you the truth. I'd lost hope of ever seeing either of you again. But I'm very glad he did get in touch. We've only met a few times since your mother died, but we've spoken on the phone and messaged a lot as well. From what he's said, Michelle has helped him turn his life around.'

Ellie laughed. 'Yes, he's been playing the young, free and single bachelor role for quite a few years now. I couldn't have been more surprised when he told me he was getting married. Again, no fore-warning. They just turned up in France and announced it to us as a fait accompli.'

'You must be pleased for him though?'

'I am, and Michelle is lovely, you're right. I just never expected him to settle down.'

'And how about you and Henri, Ellie? He seems like a decent man, and he clearly loves you.'

Ellie blushed. 'He is a decent man, and I love him, too.'

'But...' her dad pressed her.

She squirmed a little in her seat at the thought of confessing her doubts to her dad. 'I don't feel ready to settle down yet, when there's so much world out there to see and explore.'

'Can't you do that with Henri?' her dad asked.

'He's very tied to the vineyard. He works there but it's also his home and his security. I think he would travel with me, but he doesn't want to travel the world like I do.'

Bill raised his eyebrows a fraction. There was so much to tell him, but she couldn't do it all at once. 'So you're restless, and he wants to settle down. Have you talked about marriage or is that not on the cards?'

'Not directly, no. I've tried to be honest with him about how I feel though. Still, he's sticking with me through it all and being incredibly patient, which makes me love him even more.' Her heart constricted at the thought of what she was doing to Henri, albeit unintentionally.

'That is a dilemma for you, but I'm sure you'll work it all out in the end.'

Ellie was surprised that her dad hadn't attempted to tell her what to do. That was a first for her, and she appreciated him giving her space. 'Oh, there's Chris.' She gave him a small wave and watched as he and Henri made their way over together.

'Hey, you two. Good to see you both getting to know each other.' Chris smiled.

'Yes, I just wish I'd had as much as time as you have,' Ellie retorted before she could help herself.

Bill reached out and patted her hand. 'We have plenty of time, and it is thanks to Chris that we're in touch again. A little later than you would have liked, but still.'

'I have explained why I didn't get in touch with you sooner, Ellie. It's up to you whether you accept that, but I expect Dad has confirmed it, too. So, please don't spoil my wedding day by sniping at me. Try and be happy for me.'

Ellie was suitably chastened. 'I'm sorry. I didn't mean to lash out.'

'Why don't we go and dance, Ellie?' Henri intervened tactfully.

She stood up and let Henri lead her to the dance floor. He took her hands in his and drew her close. She rested her head on his shoulder and let him guide her in time to the music.

She wasn't sure if this had been a good break away for them or not. All she'd done was encounter more troubles, and however hard she tried, she never seemed able to overcome them all.

'Are you okay?' he asked after a couple of minutes had passed with them gently swaying together.

She pulled back from him to look into his eyes. 'I just hope I haven't spoilt this trip for us.'

'You haven't spoilt it at all. You mustn't think that. We had no idea what was waiting for us when we got here. It was a big shock for you, and you're doing your best to deal with it. For what it's worth, your dad seems like a lovely man, and I believe he wants to enjoy a proper relationship with both you and Chris now. I don't think either of them meant to hurt you by keeping the news from you for this long. It was just circumstances. And it must have been hard for Chris to know how to tell you.'

'I know, I know. And I agree that my dad has been nothing but kind to me. I want to get to know him so much, but I'm frightened after all that has gone before, Henri.'

He kissed her then, and the touch of his lips against hers was all the reassurance she needed at that moment in time. 'I understand your fear,' he told her, still holding her close. 'But you have such strength, as well, and you can do this, Ellie. It will all be worth it if you end up having a good relationship with your dad, despite your mum's efforts to keep you and Chris apart from him.'

'I can't believe the lengths she went to to keep him away. It's such a waste. But you're right. This is the beginning of our new life together, and I can't let anything get in the way of that from here on.'

Henri

Chris had disappeared while they'd been dancing, but Henri was pleased to see that Bill was still waiting for them to return. He hoped the worst of the discussions was behind them now, and that they could all just enjoy the rest of the evening until Chris and Michelle left for their honeymoon.

'You two dance very well together,' Bill said as they took a seat on either side of him on their return.

'Henri is an excellent dancer, so much so that he makes me look good.' Ellie grinned at him and blew her hair out of her warm face.

'Would you like a drink, Ellie?' Henri asked.

'Yes, please. A soft drink would be wonderful.'

'Bill?'

'No, nothing for me, thanks.'

Henri wandered off in the direction of the bar, glad to leave Ellie and her dad alone for a while, and to escape from all the tension around them. It had been a long day and it still wasn't over yet, and although he'd meant it when he'd told Ellie it hadn't spoilt their trip, he would be glad to go home tomorrow and to get back to normal. He placed his order for two cold drinks with the barman and turned to survey the room. He was surprised to see Chris making his way towards him.

'How's it going, Henri? Is Ellie feeling calmer now?' Chris nodded at the barman when he held up a wine bottle to see if he wanted a glass.

'She is, but it has been a long few days for us all.'

'You're right, it has. The thing is, there's still something else I need to tell her.'

Henri closed his eyes briefly at the thought of more difficult news for Ellie to digest. 'Is it likely to upset her? Can you deal with more upset on your wedding day?'

'I don't think it will, but it will come as a bit of a shock. I wanted to give you the heads-up so that you're ready to support her if she needs it. You've been so good already, and I'm grateful, but I just need your help one more time, please.'

'You'd better lead the way then.' He followed Chris back over to their table, where, to Henri's delight, Ellie was deep in conversation with her dad. He handed her one of the soft drinks.

Chris pulled a chair round and sat down next to his dad, and Henri sat next to Ellie, steeling himself for whatever was going to come next.

'Ellie, I'm sorry about this, but I have something else to tell you.' Her brother looked apologetic and Henri wondered what he could still have to say.

'Oh, Chris, no, not more bad news.'

Henri took her hand and patted it reassuringly.

'It's not bad news, but you won't be expecting this, and I don't want to leave this till we come back, in light of all we've said these past couple of days.'

'Come on then. Spit it out,' Ellie said.

Chris reached into his inside jacket pocket and pulled out a letter. He handed it to Ellie. Her name was written on the envelope in careful, neat handwriting. Henri glanced up to see Ellie had paled.

'It's from Mum,' she whispered.

'She left one for me, too,' Chris explained. 'In mine, she asked me to get in touch with Dad if she died so that he could make contact with both of us. I think it was her way of saying sorry for what she'd done, even if she never used those words.'

Ellie looked up at her brother, and Henri sensed an understanding passing between them after years spent with their mum.

'What else did she say?' Ellie asked as she turned the envelope over and over in her hands, as if she was afraid to open it.

'She told me where her will was and that she wanted me to be the executor, as you know.'

'And is everything dealt with now?'

'Yes, I've even managed to sell the house. I've paid off all her debts, not that there was much, and I now know what she meant when she told me about our inheritance.'

Ellie's head snapped up. 'Should I read this now?' she asked.

'If you want to, but I'm sure I know what it's going to say. I can tell you now if you want and you can read it in your own time later.' He looked around the hall for a moment, and Henri assumed he was looking for Michelle. It must be nearly time for them to leave.

'Okay, sure.'

'In my letter, she told me that we would be due a large sum of money each after all the bills were paid, but I didn't believe her until I saw her bank accounts.'

'Accounts?' Ellie repeated, reaching for Henri's hand to steady her. He gave hers a gentle squeeze.

'Yes, she had a good few investments and used different accounts for different things. She must have been squirrelling money away for years.'

'How... how much is it?'

Henri could almost feel Ellie holding her breath.

'We've each inherited £250,000.' Chris released a long breath as if he was glad to be rid of that information at last.

'What?' Ellie squeaked.

'I know, it's crazy, right?' Chris grinned as he stood up to go. 'Ellie, I'm sorry to have to rush off after delivering that news, but Michelle and I need to go, and I don't want to keep my new wife waiting.'

He turned to hug his dad, who had also stood to embrace him. He shook Henri's hand and then he hauled Ellie to her feet to give her an enormous hug before taking his leave of them all. Ellie swayed slightly, dazed by the magnitude of what he'd just told her, and Henri couldn't think of what to say.

CHAPTER TEN

Ellie

Ellie collapsed back onto her chair the moment Chris left. She looked from Henri to her dad and then back again, trying to find the right words.

'How is this even possible?' she said at last. 'Mum was always complaining about us being poor when we were kids, and now we're inheriting half a million pounds between us?'

'I did send money to her for both of you right up until you were eighteen,' her dad interjected.

'And Mum worked, as well, so we should never have been short. Where did all this money come from then?'

'We'll never know now, I don't think,' Henri said, 'but it's possible that she sold her house, and maybe that she had other property.'

'We'll never know for sure, you're right,' Ellie mused. 'I guess it will just be one more item to add to the list of things about my mother that will always remain a mystery.'

'Have you got any idea what you might do with it all?' her dad asked.

'Not yet,' she replied, 'although I don't think it will be a problem.'
They all laughed.

'It will make your life easier, that's for sure. You could buy a house outright yourself with that money.'

'I don't need a house, though,' Ellie replied with a quick glance at Henri. 'I live with Henri in his lovely house, and we're within walking distance of the vineyard, so I don't need a car either.'

'I'd love to come and visit you at the vineyard once you go back, if that would be possible,' her dad said.

'I'd like that, too.' Ellie was pleased at her dad's suggestion and liked the idea of getting to know him better, although she knew it wouldn't be easy.

'Do you live in London, Bill?' Henri asked.

'No, not any more. I moved out here to the countryside when I retired from my job a couple of years ago.'

Ellie was intrigued by all this information, and was grateful to Henri for asking all the questions she wanted to know the answers to but wasn't brave enough yet to ask. But then Henri fell silent as if he didn't want to pry, and she was left wondering again whether her dad had created a new family, what his job had been, what he did now... There were so many questions she wanted answers to.

'Have you been to Alsace before?' she asked him instead.

'No, although I have travelled around France a good deal over the years. I love travelling, and I'm so glad to be able to do more of it now I don't have to work any more.'

Ellie smiled. 'Henri and I had such a wonderful time when we were away, and I'd love to travel more.'

'Perhaps that's something you can spend your money on.' Her dad smiled at her, but when she looked over at Henri, his face had fallen. He'd probably worked out that there was nothing holding her back from more travelling now. While that was true, she wasn't sure what she wanted any more, especially with all they'd been doing at the vineyard before they left for London. So much had changed since they'd come for her brother's wedding, and now she had a lot to think about.

'Hello, can you all hear me?' Her brother's voice rang out across the room and everyone turned to listen. Ellie, Henri and Bill stood up to watch Chris as he gave his speech. 'I just wanted to thank you all on behalf of myself and my new wife...' Cheers sounded from all the guests as Chris referred to Michelle as his wife again. Chris chuckled. 'It's been the most amazing day, but now we have to go on our honeymoon, to which you're not invited. I'm sorry! Please come and join us outside to see us off on our new journey.'

Ellie took Henri's hand and her dad's arm, and they made their way slowly through the hall, following all the other guests outside. Chris had disappeared again, presumably to go and collect Michelle and their things before they left.

Ellie gasped as the cold night air hit her skin. Her dress was too fine to have any chance of keeping her warm. Then she felt Henri slip his jacket around her shoulders.

'That's much better, thank you. Will you be okay without it?'

'Of course.' He gave her his usual Gallic shrug and she beamed at him. This whole trip had been difficult, but Henri had been her rock throughout it, and it had made her appreciate him even more.

He drew her closer to him and put his arm round her, and she snuggled against him for more warmth. As they waited, the sound of a sports car rumbled in the distance, and Ellie instinctively knew that Chris would be the one driving it. As they watched, he came round the corner from the car park in a bright, red Jaguar E-Type, the engine reducing to a purr as he slowed down to parade the car in front of the guests. The car had been decorated with tin cans hanging from its rear bumper, and Ellie made out the words 'Just Married' written on the labels of each of them. She had no idea who had done all this, but she was sure it had all been done in good spirit, and Chris seemed fine about it.

'That car is amazing,' Henri cooed as it came to a stop a few feet away from them all.

'It's stunning, isn't it?' her dad agreed.

Ellie liked it but she would have preferred something more traditional herself. Even as the thought went through her head, she couldn't believe she'd actually considered how she might like her wedding to be. And even more surprisingly, she wasn't as afraid of the idea today as she had been just a few days ago. What was happening to her?

Henri

Despite all the drama of his few days away with Ellie, Henri experienced a true sense of calm as he stood with his arm around her shoulder waiting to see her brother and his new wife off on their honeymoon. He'd missed being part of a real family since his parents had died, but during this trip, he'd finally felt like he belonged again. Ellie's dad and brother had welcomed him in, and although he and Ellie still had a way to go before their future was decided, at that moment, he couldn't have been happier. He released a contented sigh and drew Ellie even closer.

'That was a big sigh,' she commented. 'Is everything okay?' She looked up at him, a look of concern flitting across her beautiful face, and he bent to kiss her lightly on the lips.

'Everything is good. I was just thinking how happy I am to be here with you and your family.'

She smiled then, and he savoured the moment. There was so much for them to discuss, not least whether she would use her mum's money to fund her travelling dream, but right now, none of that mattered. He just wanted to enjoy being with the woman he loved for however long it lasted. He hoped she would decide to stay with him and accept his marriage proposal when he decided the time was right to make it, but she had to make her own mind up about that. He couldn't push her to do what he wanted; he knew that.

Michelle appeared from the front of the hotel wearing her going-away outfit and carrying a small suitcase. Chris jumped out of the car and went to join her. On their way back to the car, they detoured to say goodbye first to Michelle's parents and then to Chris' family.

'Thanks so much for coming to our special day. You've all made it so wonderful for us both.' Michelle kissed and hugged them all goodbye, and Ellie wiped away a stray tear.

'Have a wonderful honeymoon, both of you,' Ellie told them.

'Oh, we will.' Chris laughed. 'And we'll look forward to seeing you when we come back.'

And then they were off, driving slowly away so that they could wave to everyone, the tin cans rattling behind them as they disappeared down the lane that led away from the hotel.

'I feel sorry to see them go now,' Ellie said as they made their way back inside the hotel to get their things.

'It's always an anticlimax at the end of a wedding,' her dad replied. 'Will you be going home tomorrow?'

'Yes, time to get back now,' Henri said. He was looking forward to going home, as always, and to life getting back to normal.

'You will let me know about coming to visit you in Alsace, won't you, Ellie? You've got all my details now, and I would like us to carry on getting to know each other better.'

'I will,' she said. 'I'd like that too.'

'We'd love to show you the vineyard, Bill. You'd be welcome any time,' Henri told him. He gave the older man a broad smile, hoping it wouldn't be long before they saw each other again.

'I'd better be on my way, it's getting late now,' Bill said. 'It's been wonderful to see you both. Take care on your journey home.' He moved to kiss Ellie goodbye and then turned to shake Henri's hand before walking away.

Ellie watched him go for a moment and then turned to Henri. 'I'm so sorry about what happened to your parents, Henri. You've spent this whole trip listening to me talk about the problems in my family, and yet you never talk about yours.'

Henri's throat tightened at Ellie's words, his emotions threatening to overwhelm him. 'I still find it hard to talk about them even after all this time. The pain of what happened is still so raw.'

Ellie took hold of his hand and squeezed it. 'Tell me something good about them.'

Henri thought for a moment. He'd spent so much time agonising over their deaths that he never really thought about the good times they'd shared. 'My dad loved football and he always joined the local team wherever we were stationed. My mum and I must have watched him play in hundreds of matches over the years. I never understood what he saw in the game myself, but I loved to watch him play.'

'And what about your mum?' Ellie asked as they went back inside the hall.

'Oh, she loved to cook. I got my love of food and wine from her, I think. She could make anything, with or without a recipe, and it always tasted delicious. I always think of her when I'm cooking.' He smiled at the memory of his mum cooking in every one of their tiny kitchens, and the ache in his heart eased just a little.

Ellie handed him back his jacket and he helped her on with her coat before they made their way towards the exit.

'Thank you for encouraging me to talk about my mum and dad, Ellie. I should do it more often,' he told her as they waited for their cab.

'I should have asked you sooner, but I hope you'll feel free to talk about them with me whenever you want to from now on,' she said.

They were both quiet in the cab on the way back to their hotel. Henri was thinking about his parents, and he imagined Ellie was processing both the shock of seeing her dad and of finding out about her inheritance. They had an early start the next morning, and it would be late when they got home in the evening, so he was looking forward to a final good night's sleep in the luxurious hotel bed before they left.

'Should we pack up our stuff tonight?' Ellie asked when they got back to their room.

Henri groaned. 'I'd forgotten that we still had that to do. I was longing for the crisp sheets and comfort of that bed one last time.'

Ellie laughed. 'I know what you mean. It has been wonderful. It won't take long to pack up and then we can sink into the bed together.'

That was all the motivation he needed. Half an hour later, they were snuggling into the sheets arms around each other. Ellie fell asleep within minutes, but despite Henri's need for sleep, it wouldn't come immediately. All he could think about was how much he loved Ellie and wanted to spend the rest of his life with her. And yet, he was no closer to persuading her to stay with him than he'd been before they'd left Alsace. With everything that had happened, she would be even more unsure about where her future lay, which made him anxious and uncertain about the road ahead.

Ellie

Ellie had fallen asleep almost as soon as the train left St. Pancras station, and when she eventually awoke, she couldn't tell if they were still in the UK or whether they'd reached France. The landscape looked much the same – endless green fields, and a dull grey sky to top it all off. She glanced at her watch and was surprised to see that almost two hours had gone by, so that meant they weren't far from Paris. She looked over at Henri to find him fast asleep as well. She gave him a gentle shake so he could wake up properly before they reached the city.

'What is it?' he asked in a sleepy voice before yawning and stretching.

'We're nearly at Paris.'

Henri straightened in his seat. 'That went quickly. I think I slept through most of the journey.'

Shortly afterwards, they pulled into the majestic Gare du Nord, a station Ellie was now very familiar with, having spent so much time travelling between London and Alsace over the past year or so. Meeting Fran in London had changed her life, and for the first time, she couldn't wait to get back to the vineyard after all that had happened during their trip to the UK.

They set off on the short walk to the Gare de l'Est where they would take their next train to Strasbourg, and although it was a crisp, sunny day, Ellie was oblivious to the draw of Paris this time.

'You're very quiet,' Henri said, interrupting her thoughts.

'I'm sorry. I've just got a lot on my mind, and I'm tired, too.'

'What are you thinking about?'

'You won't believe this, but I'm thinking about how nice it will be to get back to the vineyard, to get home.'

Henri smiled at her. 'There's some magic involved in it, I think. I always love coming back to Domaine des Montagnes.'

'I've missed the peace and quiet, and I never thought I'd hear myself say that. I used to be such a city girl at heart.'

They were soon seated on the train for the journey to Strasbourg, and Ellie sighed contentedly as she relaxed back into her chair.

'How are you coping with everything else?' Henri asked as they pulled out towards eastern France.

'I'm overwhelmed with all the decisions I have to make.'

'About what?' Henri angled his body towards her and she lifted her eyes to his.

'My dad for one thing. I just don't know if I'm ready for a full-blown relationship with him when he's missed out on so much of my life.'

'You could argue that that's a very good reason for getting to know him now, so that he doesn't miss out on any more.'

'Yes, I know. It's just that I'd want to take things slowly, but I'm not sure how he'd feel about that.'

'You can only try, but if I were you, I'd want to get to know him better. I believed him when he said he's never stopped loving you, Ellie, and he's your only parent now.'

Ellie considered that for a while without saying anything. She did want him to be a part of her life, but maybe she'd have to establish some ground rules while she got used to that idea.

'What else?' Henri prompted her after a few minutes.

'I don't know whether to accept my mum's money.'

Henri's eyebrows shot up at that. 'Why not?'

'In her letter, she said that the money was by way of apology, but I don't want an apology like that. I'd have preferred her to have told me when she was alive. If I keep the money, I can't help feeling that I'll be colluding with her manipulations in a way.'

'You know that's not true. Your mum told you things and you believed her, because she was your mum. Now you know the truth, you're going to try to put right what you can. But the money's not part of it.'

'It's all tied up together, though, don't you see? If I do take the money, I'd like to do something worthwhile with it, and I've been wondering whether to invest some of it in the vineyard.'

Henri gasped and she laughed. 'Really? That would be a very big step to take,' Henri said.

'I know, which is why I haven't completely made my mind up about it yet.'

'It is a great idea, but you'd have to be sure about it.'

'As I said to my dad, I don't have any other needs, do I? I would like to finish the work on the château and maybe take a share in the vineyard for a stake. I'm so much more involved in it now. Do you think Didier would be up for that?'

'You'll only know if you ask him, but things have obviously been really tough for them, so he'd be mad not to take you up on an offer like that.' Henri took her hand and squeezed it. 'You have been doing a lot of thinking, but you need to be really sure about this before going ahead and talking about it to Didier.'

'I know, and it is only an idea at the moment, so let's not mention it to anyone else yet until I'm definite about it.' She paused briefly.

'I've been thinking about you and me, too, just in case you were wondering.'

'I know you have. I just don't want to keep going on about it.'

'I appreciate that. And I'm sorry again for how difficult it's been while we've been away. So much has changed within the space of a few days.'

'I really enjoyed it. There were some challenging moments but it all came good in the end. It will be good to get home though.'

Ellie fell silent, trying to weigh everything up in her mind. If she loved Henri, and she saw Alsace as home, then what was stopping her from committing to him and moving on to the next phase in her life?

Henri

'What are you going to get up to today?' Henri asked Ellie at breakfast the next morning. He was due to go back to the office, but he knew she would be thinking about everything that had happened at the wedding and what she was going to do next.

'I'm going to unpack first. Then I think I'll spend some time checking the blog and planning further appointments. After that I'll maybe take a wander down to the château once I know everyone will be out of the way. Some time on my own to think about everything will do me good.'

'Will you speak to Lottie today about the wine tasting as well? I can't believe it's going to be Christmas in just over a week, which doesn't leave us much time.'

Ellie nodded and made a note on her pad. He kissed her goodbye shortly afterwards, pulled on his thick winter coat and scarf and set off for the walk to the vineyard estate office. He'd been surprised when Ellie had said she was thinking about investing her mum's money in the estate. There was no doubt it would solve a lot of their problems, but he didn't want her to feel obliged to be the one to sort them all out, just because she'd inherited a large sum of money. That money should be for her future, and he worried that she was only thinking about it out of a sense of duty. He was concerned that once Didier and the others found out about it, they would ramp up the pressure on Ellie, and she didn't need that kind of stress. He was hoping he might have received some positive emails about grants while he'd been away, which would at least give Ellie the choice about what to do.

He was on the edge of the car park when Frédéric's car turned in, and Henri stopped to wait for Sylvie to get out so they could catch up. It had been a while since he'd last seen her.

'Henri, *comment ça va, chéri?*' Sylvie beamed at him and his heart swelled with love for the woman who had become like a mother to him.

'*Très bien, Sylvie, et toi?*'

'Yes, of course, I'm fine. What I want to know is, how was the wedding? Did you both have a wonderful time?'

'It was very interesting on the whole, and not quite what we were expecting, but we did have a great time.'

They turned to wave at Frédéric as he swung the car round to leave again.

'Now I'm intrigued. "Interesting" is not the word I'd expect you to use when describing a wedding. What happened? Do tell.'

'Why don't we go in? It's far too cold to be talking out here.'

'I'm supposed to be meeting Lottie at the Visitors' Centre, but I can pop in for a minute.'

Henri unlocked the office door and stood back to let Sylvie go in first. He went straight to put on the heater and then to switch on the coffee machine. In the meantime, Sylvie had taken a seat at Fran's desk.

'So, the main reason it was interesting,' he said once he'd done everything, 'was that Ellie's dad came to the wedding as well. She didn't know he was coming and she hasn't seen him for more than ten years. It was all quite a shock for her as you can imagine, but once she'd got past her initial surprise, she was glad to see him again.'

'*Mon Dieu*, that was a surprise. That poor girl. As if she didn't have enough on her mind already.'

Henri decided not to mention the deception by Ellie's mum or the detail about her mum's money. It was up to Ellie if she wanted to share that information with anyone else, and he didn't want to put his foot in it by sharing her news without her permission.

'It was a lot for her to take in, but we did enjoy the wedding and we managed to do some sight-seeing as well. In the end, it was Ellie who couldn't wait to get back here. She even called it home.'

Sylvie's features softened into a smile. 'Ah, the vineyard weaves its magic once again. I'm glad to hear that she's feeling that way about this special place. Is there any more news about her settling down with you?'

'Hmm, well, there's no news as yet, but I don't want to push her. It has to be her decision to stay here with me.' He stood up to make some coffee and set a cup down in front of Sylvie a minute later.

'Maybe she needs a push. If you don't ask her if she's made up her mind, she might think you've lost interest. In my opinion, you need to get over your pride and take the lead. You don't want her to slip away right at the last minute, do you?'

Henri tutted softly. 'You know that's not who I am, Sylvie. She knows how I feel, I've made sure of that, but I respect her need for space and I would ask you to do the same.' He said it gently, but he wanted Sylvie to get the message. He didn't want her meddling on his behalf.

Sylvie rolled her eyes, looking just like a teenager, despite her advancing years. 'Henri, even after all these years, you still don't understand women. Sometimes we need a gentle push in the right direction.'

'I know you mean well, Sylvie, but Ellie has a lot going on right now, and I don't want to make things even harder for her. She'll make a decision when she's ready, and I'm very happy to wait till then.'

Fran came into the office just then, and Henri was grateful for her timing. Sylvie stood slowly and made her way towards Fran for a hug, and Henri sank into his chair, glad to let someone else be the focus of Sylvie's questioning for a while.

CHAPTER ELEVEN

Ellie

It took no time for Ellie to unpack after she'd showered and dressed. She emptied Henri's bags, as well, to save him the trouble later on, and then took a full basket of washing downstairs to the machine. She updated her blog and also took a minute to check for comments on Lottie's post about Paris, and she was delighted to see that quite a few had come in. She had a quick look at her emails, too, and noticed a couple from other vineyard estates in France, which intrigued her. They seemed to be interested in the work she was doing on the château. There was even one from a travel company, but she didn't have time to study all her messages in detail or to reply to them properly now. She'd have to sit down and look through everything again later.

As soon as that was done, she pulled on her coat and hat before setting off for the château. She longed to talk everything over with someone who was impartial, but the trouble was she didn't know anyone who was in that position. Everyone she knew would have an opinion, and she didn't want that. She'd gone over and over everything in her mind and still made no progress.

Before she knew it, she was standing in front of the château's main entrance, but she didn't go in straight away. She stood for a moment staring up at the 18th-century building she had come to love over the past year or so, and her heart filled with pride for all she had managed to achieve on a shoestring budget. She couldn't bear for all that to come to nothing because of a lack of funds to finish the work, and there didn't seem to be any other options available to them other than taking the work at a painstakingly slow pace. Maybe this was the easiest decision of all for her to make, and if she made this one, all the others would flow from it.

She stepped forward to unlock the big oak door.

'Ellie!'

She turned round at the sound of her name to see Sylvie making her way slowly down the hill towards her. 'Sylvie, how are you?' she asked as the older woman reached her at last.

'I'm fine, my dear, although I could do with a sit-down now. Shall we go in?'

Ellie opened the door, and taking Sylvie's arm, she led her inside.

'Oh, it is so wonderful to be back here again after all this time.'

Ellie had forgotten that Sylvie and her husband had lived here all their married life. 'Doesn't it make you sad to come back without your husband?' Ellie asked.

'In some ways, yes, but we spent so many happy years here. It was only the last months that were difficult after he became ill.' Her face fell for a moment as the memories overtook her.

Ellie took Sylvie's hand and gave it a squeeze. 'I hope the work I've done so far has restored the château to its former glory for you.'

'You've done a marvellous job, and I'm looking forward to seeing it finally complete soon.'

'I'd love to finish it, Sylvie, but without the money for it, it's going to take a long while.' She shrugged, even though she now had the solution if she wanted to take that route.

'There's always money if you know where to look.'

Ellie frowned. 'Didier doesn't seem to think so. And I understand that paying people's wages is more important than restoring old buildings. That has to take priority.'

'Of course, but you did the downstairs with hardly any budget, so maybe you could approach the upstairs work in the same way.'

Ellie led Sylvie into the kitchen so she could take a seat and catch her breath. 'I have made a start on one of the empty rooms upstairs, but there's so much work I can't do myself, and we don't have the money to pay the plasterer as yet. And there's the work outside to do as well. I have no idea how much that would cost.'

'I'm confident that you'll find a solution once you all sit down together and talk about it.' She paused. 'Anyway, I just saw Henri and he told me about your trip to London for the wedding.'

Just how much had Henri told her, she wondered. 'Yes, we had a great time and the wedding went off beautifully.'

'And what was it like seeing your father after all that time?'

That answered that question. 'It was... hard, but wonderful at the same time. I hadn't seen him for such a long time.'

'So now you can make up for all those lost years.' Sylvie nodded, as if she was sure that that's what Ellie would be planning to do.

'I hope so, but it's not going to be easy. A lot has happened that my brother and I didn't know about. Both our parents kept things from us, so it won't be easy to just forgive and forget.'

'But you must, my child. Life is so short. I know that too well. Don't let your past ruin your future.'

Ellie would have liked to talk to her honestly about Henri, but she knew how close Sylvie and Henri were, so she didn't go down that path, even though she was sure Sylvie was hinting about their relationship as well.

'I asked my dad to come and visit me here, and he said he would, but we need to take it slowly, to get to know each other before we can move on from what happened before.'

'And what about you and Henri? Have you decided what to do about your future together? I would like nothing more than to see you both happy together.'

Ellie looked away, not wanting Sylvie to see her embarrassment. 'The last thing I want to do is to hurt Henri, but I have to make my own mind up about this. It's not for anyone else to advise us.' She'd chosen her words carefully, but as she turned round again, she wasn't sure whether she might have offended the woman who was the closest Henri had to a mother.

'If you don't stop running away from your responsibilities and face the realities of your life, you will hurt Henri,' she said gently. 'Henri loves you and he wants to be with you more than anything. This vineyard could be your home, and the people who live here, your family, if you would only let them in. The rest is up to you. Now, I must be going,' she said, standing slowly and then making her way back to the front door. 'Goodbye, my dear, and promise me you'll think about what I've said.'

Sylvie was right, Ellie couldn't deny that, but she hadn't been expecting her to be quite so honest in the way she told her what she needed to do. She would be thinking about what the older woman had said for some time to come.

Henri

Henri's email inbox opened automatically and, for once, he was pleased to see that he had received a good number of emails in his absence.

He scanned his new messages, pleased there was one from the Alsace tourist board, but when he clicked on it, he was disappointed to find it was a rejection. There was no money available to support vineyards at this time, they said, but they wished them luck. Henri let out a big sigh. He clicked on each of the remaining emails, wanting to be sure he wasn't missing out on anything, but in the end, he had to accept that there was nothing else.

He looked up from his computer to find that Sylvie had left and Fran was working quietly at her desk.

'Sorry if I've been antisocial,' Henri said to Fran. 'I was just trying to see if there'd been any good news about grants while we've been away.'

'And I'm guessing that there wasn't any from all your sighing over there.' She gave him a resigned smile.

'Nothing at all. I can't believe it.'

'It's hard times for everyone, I think. We should perhaps focus on all the good things you and Ellie had set up before you went away. Lottie's planning to hold the wine tasting next Wednesday and there's been a lot of interest in it. And it's Christmas the week after so there's a lot to look forward to.'

'Perhaps you're right. That sounds great about the wine tasting. I'll have to catch up with Thierry today and check what I can do to help. How are the finances looking though? It must all be getting serious now.'

Fran drew back and looked down at her computer. 'You'll need to talk to Didier about that, Henri. It's not my place to say, I'm sorry.'

If Fran was shrinking away from discussing the situation with him, things must have become bleak, and that meant that a drastic solution would be needed if they couldn't come up with the money elsewhere.

'Where is Didier this morning?' It was late morning and Didier would usually have finished his inspection by now.

'He was going over to the Visitors' Centre after his inspection to meet with Lottie, Thierry and his mum about the wine tasting and to discuss some promotion ideas Sylvie had had for the Centre. I'm sure they'd appreciate your input if you'd like to join them.' She gave him a tired smile.

'I need to catch up here before going over, but I will do that later. It's amazing how things build up after only a few days away.'

Fran's face softened as if she had reconsidered discussing the situation with Henri. 'I do think that Didier wants to bring us all together very soon, once you've had a chance to get back into the swing of things after being away. Talking of which, you still haven't told me how the wedding went.'

Henri smiled at Fran. 'The wedding went off really well. It was a lovely venue and the ceremony and reception were perfect. Ellie will tell you all about it, but we had a great time.' He couldn't tell her about the stressful parts; that would have to be up to Ellie to explain.

'Oh good. I'm pleased you had a chance to relax.'

He was considering whether to tell her about Bill turning up when the door opened and Didier walked in with an enormous scowl on his face.

'Oh, Henri, I forgot you'd be back today,' he said, making a visible effort to banish the scowl and give his friend a smile.

'Is everything okay? You look like you've had bad news.' Henri studied his friend of many years.

'There just seems to be an endless supply of bad news these days. Anyway, how are you, and how was your trip to London?'

Henri noted how easily Didier avoided answering his question. 'It was great, thanks. I was just telling Fran how good the wedding was.'

'And Ellie? Did she have a good time?'

'She has some things on her mind now, but I'll let her tell you about that in her own time.' He paused, searching for the right words for what he wanted to say next. 'Fran said you wanted to get us all together to talk about the finances. When do you think you might want to do that?'

Didier walked over to the coffee machine, so he had his back to Henri when he replied. 'I don't know exactly, but soon, I suppose.'

'After checking my emails this morning, there's no hope of any funding coming our way from any other source, so I think we should get together sooner rather than later. Do you want me to speak to everyone about it?'

'Yes, yes, that would be helpful.' Didier sounded distracted, completely unlike his normal self.

'And what do you want me to put on the agenda?'

'I'll bring the agenda to the meeting. I need some time to think things over before then, and to speak to Fran and my mum.'

Henri felt like he'd been told to keep his nose out, and that hurt after all they'd been through together. 'I see. If you can let me know when and where you want to hold this meeting then, I'll start getting in touch with everyone.' He kept all the emotion out of his voice and concentrated on maintaining a businesslike manner.

Didier sighed, as if he knew he'd overstepped the mark, but he didn't apologise. 'I'll let you know when I'm ready for that.' And with that, he disappeared into the back office, cutting himself off from any further discussion.

Henri looked over to Fran, hoping for reassurance, but she'd buried her head in the diary and showed no signs of giving anything away either. He wanted so much to help put things right at the estate, but with no money of his own to put into the business, all he could do was look for new sources of income. He turned to look at the online shop to see how that had been going in their absence, hoping it might provide some good news in what was turning out to be a difficult day.

Ellie

It was getting dark by the time Ellie left the château to wend her way back home again. Even though the days always grew shorter at this time of year, and she should be used to it by now, it still took her by surprise every year. It was barely four o'clock when the sun set, and as she walked along the footpath towards the village, she pulled her coat in tighter around her to ward off the evening chill.

She'd been thinking all afternoon about what Sylvie had said while she worked on the minor plastering jobs in the smallest bedroom, but she was still no closer to making a decision about her future. If she accepted her mum's money, she could help the vineyard get back on its feet and she wanted to do that very much. But at the same time, she also wanted to travel, and now she would have the money to do that.

She'd tried doing a mental checklist of pros and cons. Did she love Henri? Check. Did she want to travel? Check. Could she do both things? Um, not so sure. Did she want to invest some of her mum's money in the vineyard? Check. Did she want to live the rest of her life on the vineyard? Aargh, she didn't know. How could she know for sure? But did she want to lose Henri? No, no, no.

She let herself back into the house and took off her coat before making her way down to the kitchen to see what she could make for dinner. She stared at the contents of the fridge, not feeling inspired by the lump of cheese and the dish of leftover pasta from their late return the night before. She closed the fridge door, retrieving only the chilled bottle of Pinot Blanc from inside it, and poured herself a glass of wine in the hope that it might help her think.

Deep down she knew without any doubt that she loved Henri, but she still wasn't sure about settling down for good yet. Her parents had made such a mess of their marriage and then lied to cover it up, which didn't exactly fill her with confidence about committing herself to one person. Still, Chris had found love and had believed in his relationship with Michelle enough to take that leap of faith and get married. And then there was Fran and Didier, who had grabbed their second chance together and were now on the brink of getting married, as were Lottie and Thierry.

She suddenly realised that she'd never asked her dad if he'd found love again with someone else. He'd come alone to the wedding, so did that mean that he'd stayed on his own all these years? She picked up her phone from the kitchen table. Several new emails had come in since the morning and Ellie made a mental reminder to check them later. For now, she wanted to find her dad's number. Her finger hovered over the phone icon, and then after taking a deep breath, she hit it.

'Hello, Ellie? It's great to hear from you again so soon. How are you?' His deep voice answered after just a moment's delay and now she had to follow through with her decision to call him.

'Hi, Dad. Yeah, I'm okay. How are you? Is everything back to normal for you after the wedding?'

'Pretty much. My life isn't very exciting these days. How about you?'

'I've been doing a lot of soul-searching about my future.'

'And what did you find on your search?' There was humour in his voice, but it was reassuring to talk to him all the same.

'Can I ask you a question that I should have asked you at the wedding?'

'Of course.'

'Did you meet anyone else after you and Mum split up?' She held her breath, waiting for his reply.

'I did, yes. I was very lucky. I did want to tell you at the wedding, but you had so much to take in that I didn't want to burden you with something else.'

'Tell me about her.'

'Her name's Annie and we've been married for nine years this year. She has two grown-up children as well.'

Ellie sank into one of the chairs around the kitchen table. 'You remarried? Wow, that is a surprise. And do you have a relationship with your stepchildren?'

'Yes, I do, and we get on very well together. I'd like you and Chris to meet them in time. Chris has met Annie briefly, but we decided against her coming to the wedding.'

'Because of me?'

'Because we didn't want to upset you any more than we knew we were going to already by me being there.'

'So despite everything that happened, you recovered and you married again and settled down with a new wife and family.' Tears pricked Ellie's eyes at the years that had been wasted because of her mum's behaviour.

'Yes, I did. As I said, I've been lucky. But you can have that, too, Ellie. You just have to believe in what you want and take that jump.'

'Will you come and visit me here like you said? I'd like that.' This conversation had at least helped her decide about that.

'I'd like that, too. And perhaps in the future, if you were okay with it, I could bring Annie as well. I'll have a look at my diary and see if I can come and see you before Christmas.'

Ellie rang off a few minutes later, having agreed to speak to her dad again very soon. She took a glug of her wine, trying to come to terms with all she'd just found out. She was relieved to hear Henri's key in the door shortly afterwards.

'Hello!' he called as he came in and took off his coat. His bag thudded as he dropped it on the floor, and he appeared in the kitchen a moment later. He bent down to kiss her cheek.

'How's your day been, *chérie*?' He poured himself a glass of wine and sat down opposite her at the table.

'Interesting, I suppose you could say. And yours?'

'Frustrating. I'll tell you all about it, but first, what are we doing for dinner? I'm starving.'

Henri stood and went to the fridge just as she'd done earlier. All she could think about was the way that everyone around her had found love and settled down to live happily ever after. Her dad had said that she could have that, too – and love was there for the taking – but where would she find the courage to take the leap of faith needed to find love for herself?

Henri

'As much as I love Sylvie, I couldn't wait for her to leave the office today. She really was in one of her meddling moods this morning.' Henri finished his last spoonful of pasta and leaned back in his chair, his hunger sated at last. They'd have to go shopping this weekend, though, unless they wanted to eat pasta at every meal.

'She came over to see me at the château afterwards, and I got that impression from her as well. She left me in no doubt as to what she thought I should be doing with the rest of my life. You didn't tell her about my mum's money, did you?'

'No, that's your business. I did tell her about your dad. I hope that was okay.'

'Yes, that's fine.' She paused for a moment and Henri wondered what she was going to say. 'I called my dad earlier and asked him again about coming to visit us here. It turns out that he remarried and he'd like to bring his wife with him, on a later visit perhaps.'

'*Mon dieu*. These revelations just keep coming. How did you feel about that?'

'It was me who asked about it, to be fair. I just wanted to know if he'd managed to rebuild his life after leaving my mum, and I'm happy to know that he did.' She went on to explain about his marriage to Annie and his grown-up stepchildren.

'You're taking it all very well, I must say.'

She laughed. 'I know. I've done a lot of thinking today and realised I need to try to move on.'

Henri recognised this as his cue to tell her what he'd found out earlier. 'I hate to have to tell you bad news when you seem so happy, but when I checked my emails earlier, there was one telling me there was no chance of a grant, and then nothing from any of the other organisations I contacted. So I think we have to face the fact that there's nowhere else for us to turn to now. We're going to have to make the most of what we're doing ourselves.' He braced himself for her response.

'That's what we expected, isn't it?' she said softly. 'My mum's money would make all the difference to the future of the vineyard. It's just up to me to decide whether that's how I want to spend it.' She closed her eyes briefly and he understood the pressure she was under.

He reached out and took her hand. 'Ellie, I know you want to help, but you mustn't let the vineyard's financial worries force you into making a decision that you don't want to make. You have to make your own mind up about what you want for your future.'

'I've thought about nothing else, Henri.' She paused. 'Let me ask you something. If I did want to travel from time to time in the future, after settling down here, would you be prepared to come with me again, perhaps for shorter stints rather than long trips?'

This was the question Henri had been most afraid of. 'If travelling is your priority, Ellie, then that's what you must do. It's not about me or what I want to do.' He let go of her hand, stood up from the table and started clearing the plates.

'It's one of my priorities, yes, but it's not the only one.'

He turned round then. 'What are your other priorities then?'

'You are, silly. And then there's my dad, and my mum's money. It's all been such a lot to take in, and I'm struggling with all the different decisions at the moment.'

'You've already taken the first step with your dad towards building a new relationship, so that's a good start.' He smiled, doing his best to try to understand the inner workings of her mind.

'Yes, that's true. And on Monday I'm going to meet with Didier again to put an idea to him.'

'So, have you decided about your mum's money then?'

'It's partly to do with that, but I have another idea, as well, but if you don't mind, I'm going to speak to him first to see what he says and then I'll tell you after that.'

Henri was disappointed about that, but he couldn't make her tell him her plans. 'Okay, I guess I'll have to respect your wishes then.'

He walked into the living room then, tired by the discussions and the back and forth. One minute he thought she was ready to say yes to settling down with him, the next that she was going to leave him to travel the world for the rest of her life. He sank onto the sofa and stared into the fire, not knowing what else to say.

'Please don't give up on me, Henri,' Ellie said a minute later as she joined him and rested her head on his shoulder. 'I do love you and

I want to be with you. I just have a lot of other unexpected stuff to deal with at the moment, but it doesn't take away what I feel for you.'

He put his arm around her with a sigh. 'I won't give up on you. I only want you to be happy, but I can't deny that I think you could be happy with me. There has to be a way for us to work all this out and to be together at the same time.'

'That's what I think, and I'm doing my best to find that way.'

He kissed her hair and drew her body closer to his. 'That's enough for me, and I'll give you all the help you need to find it.' For now, he had to hope that they would get there in the end.

CHAPTER TWELVE

Ellie

Ellie passed her laptop over to Fran so she could look at all the photos Ellie had taken at Chris and Michelle's wedding. Henri had gone off to get some food shopping and Didier and Chlöe were visiting Sylvie, giving Ellie a rare Saturday afternoon to spend with her friend.

'I can't believe it's only just over a week till Christmas. Are you all ready for it?' Ellie asked as she sat down next to Fran.

'Yes, I bought most of my presents early this year, knowing that I probably wouldn't feel up to it now. And Didier's in charge of cooking on Christmas Day, with some help from Sylvie, so we're pretty much ready now.' She paused, distracted by the photos. 'That's such a beautiful dress,' she cooed on seeing the first photo of Michelle ready for her wedding day. 'I love the tight bodice and the puffy sleeves. Was the skirt embroidered?' She zoomed in for a better look.

'It was, and her train was as well. It was all fairly traditional, but she looked stunning, I must say.'

'It's quite similar to my dress, minus the tight bodice, of course.'

143

They carried on looking through the photos of Michelle getting ready before moving on to the ones Ellie had taken at the church.

'Oh, what a beautiful little church that is,' Fran exclaimed. 'I love the way they decorated it, too, with the bows at the end of the pews. I must ask my mum to check with the priest to see how much decorating of our church is allowed.'

Ellie reached for her phone. She was going to make a checklist of things that still needed doing.

'Didier and I will have to go down to see my parents for a visit early in the New Year just to go over all the last-minute preparations.'

'Is there any news about the catering?'

'I asked Lottie to look into that, but I haven't asked her about it for a while. I wanted a local restaurant to do it, but because we've gone for the end of January, some of them will still be on their post-Christmas holidays, so the one I wanted may not even be available.'

'Okay, I can check that with Lottie, as well, then.'

Fran was now studying the official photos taken outside the church. Ellie had taken some of the ones she wasn't in, which hadn't been many, but there were enough for Fran to get an idea.

'We haven't booked an official photographer, Ellie. I just assumed everyone would take photos on their phones, so I didn't worry about it. But now I'm not so sure. What do you think?'

'I think it would be lovely to have a formal set of photos to look back on, and you might want to put those on display around the house. I'll chat to your mum and Lottie about it to see if we can find someone to do that for you at short notice. I might have even seen someone at the market when we were there last.'

'Thanks so much for this, Ellie. It's so good to have a different perspective on it after all these months. I feel more and more tired these days and it's hard to think about what still needs doing. And whenever I speak to Mum, she just gets all excited rather than thinking about whether we're ready for the main event.'

'It must be exciting for her, though, to see the first of her daughters getting married.'

'I know, and I'm trying hard to be patient with her because of that.'

Fran progressed through the photos until she came to one of the band who had played at Ellie's brother's wedding reception.

'That's another thing we haven't thought about. Any entertainment.' Fran swiped her hand across her forehead and Ellie could tell she was getting stressed.

'Don't worry, I'll add it to my list. That's what I'm here for, remember?' Ellie was glad there were still plenty of things for her to do. She just hoped she could sort out these remaining things for Fran in time.

Fran finished looking through the photos shortly afterwards and Ellie was able to put her computer away.

'I did contact that stationery designer you recommended to quote for the orders of service and also for the wedding gifts,' Fran said. 'That was a great recommendation, thank you.'

'Oh good, I'm glad. And did you get anywhere with that hairdresser Sylvie recommended?'

'No, she's not prepared to travel that far. I really don't know what to do about that. It's quite difficult trying to arrange the wedding in another place.'

Ellie thought for a moment, wondering whether to put another new idea to Fran when she already had so much on her mind. 'Look, tell me if this is crazy, but Michelle was encouraging us to use the château as a wedding venue when it's finished, and I know you really wanted to get married here if you could. While it's still not completely ready, no-one would need to go upstairs, would they? What if we hold the blessing here after the civil ceremony at the *Mairie* and then hold the reception at the Visitors' Centre? That would make it all a lot easier on you.'

Fran sat up and stared at Ellie, causing Ruby to sit up from her usual guard position on the floor at Fran's feet as well. 'Do you really think we could? Wouldn't it mean a lot of extra work for you?'

'I don't think it would, that's what I'm saying. As long as we can book someone to do the blessing, we can use people from the village for everything else, including your hairdresser. And I'm sure Lottie could organise the catering for us. What do you think?'

'I would really love to do it here. It would just be so much easier and then the only people travelling would be my parents and *Papi*. I'm sure they could stay over with Sylvie and Frédéric.' She clasped her hands together, looking like she could hardly believe her luck.

'I'll talk to Lottie and your mum while you check with Didier. But I really think we can make this work.'

Ellie knew it would be hard work – she'd need to get someone in to tidy the gardens outside the château too – but she was sure they could pull it off, and it would be worth it for Fran and Didier to get married at the château in the middle of their vineyard estate.

Henri

As there was now only one full week left until Christmas, and they had a busy week coming up with the wine tasting, Henri had convinced Ellie that today would be their last chance to get their Christmas-present buying finished. When he'd visited the weekly market the day before, he'd found out that there was another Christmas market taking place in the square today and he wanted to take Ellie along.

'This is a lovely way to spend our Sunday,' she said as they made their way back to the market square that morning. 'I'm so looking forward to seeing what's there and taking some more photos.'

As they approached the square, it was as if a magical transformation had happened overnight. The square was now full of what looked like traditional log cabins instead of stalls, and there was a sweet smell in the air, which Henri knew from experience was a mixture of gingerbread and *vin chaud*. The air was filled with the excited chatter of children and adults alike, and it was infectious. Right in the middle of the square was the most enormous

Christmas tree, complete with red and gold baubles from top to bottom.

Ellie gasped with delight and stopped to take a photo. They stopped first at a stall selling handmade wooden toys. While Henri studied them for something suitable for Marie, Ellie took photos and chatted to the stallholder about the vineyard blog. She must have more material than she knew what to do with by now, he thought, and he smiled as she put the stallholder's business card in her bag.

'What do you think of this one for Marie?' he asked, holding up a wooden dog with moving legs.

'That's gorgeous,' she agreed. 'Marie will love it.'

Henri paid and they said goodbye, moving on to the next stall along. Here they bought some locally made chocolates for Fran and a tin of hot chocolate for Lottie. The stall was also selling hot chocolate drinks so they bought two cups to stave off the cold.

'I'm so glad you persuaded me to come today,' Ellie told Henri. 'This is such a beautiful market. I don't remember coming to it last year.'

'It's only on every two years because it's such a big commitment for the stallholders and the village as well. It keeps it fresh, I think, when it doesn't happen year in, year out.'

'I have to warn you that we might end up being here all day, because I really want to talk to as many stallholders as possible about featuring on the blog.'

Henri laughed. 'I thought you might, but that's fine by me. I just wanted you to come and see it, and to have a good time.'

They set off again, picking up a bottle of brandy for Didier, and one of kirsch for Thierry, before turning the corner and wandering down the next side of the square.

'Hey, Henri, Ellie. I might have guessed we'd see you here.' Thierry and Lottie were red-faced from the cold, but little Marie looked warm and snug in her carrier high up on Thierry's back. Ellie reached out and took Marie's hand and the little girl smiled.

'Are you busy buying Christmas presents as well?' Ellie asked.

'Yes, very last minute, I'm ashamed to say,' said Lottie. 'We have ordered some things online, but it's nice to buy special handmade gifts, as well, isn't it?'

'How did the wedding go?' Thierry asked then.

'The wedding went well, but it was a bit crazy all in all,' said Ellie. She went on to explain about her dad being there, but said nothing about the money, Henri noted.

'Talking about weddings,' Lottie began, 'have you heard that we're getting married on the same day as Fran and Didier, making it a joint wedding?'

'Oh, that's a wonderful idea,' Henri exclaimed. 'What a great celebration that's going to be.' He beamed at his friends, filled with happiness for the two of them.

'Well, I have some news on that front, as well, which I haven't had a chance to tell you yet, Henri,' said Ellie. 'Yesterday, I asked Fran whether she'd prefer to get married at the château if we could pull it off, and she said yes.'

'Oh my goodness, that would be amazing.' Lottie's face lit up.

'Could you organise the catering, do you think?' Ellie asked.

'Hang on,' interrupted Thierry. 'I don't want you to be doing all of that for your wedding day. That would be too stressful, what with everything else that will be going on.'

Lottie patted his arm. 'I'll look into it, but I understand what you're saying. I think we can hold the wedding at the château if we do it between us, I really do.'

They chatted for a while longer and then said their goodbyes, allowing each other to continue buying presents without having to hide them. Ellie found a beautiful wooden jigsaw puzzle for Chlöe. 'It won't be too hard for her, will it?' she asked Henri.

'She's so bright that I wouldn't think so, but we can check with the stallholder.'

That led to another conversation, so Henri wandered across to another stall where they were selling glass paperweights. He picked one up for Frédéric and went on to look at a stall selling wooden cheeseboards. Sylvie loved her cheeses so he bought her one of those.

'I'd like to try to find something for my dad, but I have no idea what he'd like,' Ellie said as she returned to him. 'And I should look for something for Chris and Michelle, too. I hope we'll see them again soon.'

As Henri wanted to find a present for Ellie, he encouraged her to go off on her own to find something for Chris and Michelle, and while she was gone, he found a stall selling beautiful scarves. He picked one out in shades of green and red that would suit her colouring perfectly. The stallholder wrapped it for him and he managed to tuck it away before Ellie returned.

'What did you get then?' he asked, leading her away.

She showed him a wallet she'd bought for Chris and a colourful candle she'd found for Michelle.

'It's been a fabulous morning, Henri, but I'm absolutely starving now.' She groaned and he laughed.

'Come on then. Time for some *tarte flambée.*'

They found a stall selling slices of the traditional Alsatian thin and crispy savoury tart, and Henri's mouth watered at the sight of the lardons and onions cooking in a nearby pan. They watched as the stallholder smothered the tart base in crème fraîche before adding the caramelised onions and lardons.

'This is my favourite savoury tart of all,' Ellie said after eating her first mouthful.

'Better than any other you've had anywhere in the world?' Henri teased.

'Right now, yes,' she confirmed.

After lunch, they wandered round some more until Ellie found a photo frame for her dad, which she hoped they would soon be able to fill with a picture of the two of them together. By the time they finally left to go home, it was starting to get dark.

'Have you enjoyed today?' Henri asked as they made their way out of the square to return home.

'I've loved every minute. It was magical. I hope we get to go again when it's next here.'

Henri truly hoped that Ellie would still be here with him in two years' time and that she was beginning to fall in love with the village as well as the vineyard, just as he had.

Ellie

After a restless night tossing and turning, which led to her waking up early, Ellie slipped out of bed and texted Didier to schedule in another meeting with him. Now she'd made up her mind about what she wanted to do, she was keen to get on with it, and telling Didier about her idea was the first step. She'd have plenty of time to explain it all to Henri later, once Didier was on board with it.

She had so much catching up to do after being away for a few days, quite apart from getting all her Christmas presents wrapped, but having made up her mind about her mum's money, she wanted to speak to Didier first and foremost.

She left the house before Henri for once, wrapping herself up against the biting December air as she hurried along the footpath towards the château. Fran opened the door to her and shooed her into the warm. 'Hello. I wasn't expecting to see you this morning. Is everything okay?'

'Yes, I'm just meeting with Didier.' Ellie removed her gloves and hat, slipping them into her coat pockets before hanging her coat on the stand by the front door.

'I have to get Chlöe to school so perhaps I'll see you later.' Fran smiled before stepping forward to kiss her friend goodbye. At that moment, Chlöe came running from the kitchen.

'*Salut*, Ellie,' she cried before grabbing her coat from Fran and slipping it on.

'*Salut*, Chlöe. *Ça va?*' Ellie laughed as the little girl jumped up and down with boundless energy despite the early hour.

'Come on, sweetheart. Time for school.'

They disappeared and the house felt particularly quiet without them. Ellie wandered along to the kitchen where she found Didier clearing away breakfast things.

'Ah, I thought I heard your voice. Would you like a drink?'

'Yes, please. It's freezing out there today.'

'Yes, winter has well and truly set in now.' Didier put the coffee machine on and prepared the cups before bringing milk and sugar to the table.

Ellie sat down at the table and tried to be patient, even though she was desperate to tell him her idea.

'So,' Didier asked a minute later as he placed two cups on the table before taking a seat himself, 'what's your idea?'

'My idea is for each of us to take a financial stake in the vineyard business and for us to become partners alongside you. I found out when we were in London that my mum has left me some money in her will, which came as a surprise, of course. But since then I've been thinking it over, and I'd like to invest some of that money in the estate in exchange for a share of the profits. Obviously, I'd like to focus on restoring and then setting up the château as a business for paying guests to come and stay in, as well as a wedding venue in the future.'

Didier raised his eyebrows. 'That would be incredibly generous of you. Are you really sure you'd want to do that with that money?'

'I've given it a lot of thought and it is an investment I'd like to make, but I realise that for this to work, it would be best if we could all invest something, with the finances being in such a mess at the moment. We'd need to ask everyone else if they'd be happy to risk their own money in the same way. And you'd have to be happy with the idea of sharing the ownership of the vineyard with the rest of us.'

'It would definitely be a risk for you all. And I'd have to speak to *Maman* and ask her what she'd think about splitting the business between everyone.'

'If we could all invest something, it would take the pressure off you, Fran and Sylvie, and give us all a share in the success of the business. I know Thierry has significant savings, which I'm willing to bet he'd be happy to invest for him and Lottie to run the Visitors' Centre and café together in exchange. But I'm not jumping to any conclusions. I just wanted to put the idea to you first for you to consider.'

Didier took a sip of his coffee while he pondered what she'd said. 'And have you spoken to Henri about this?'

Ellie shook her head, wondering now if perhaps she should have discussed it with him first.

'I'm not sure that he would have any money to put in, but I couldn't exclude him from any partnership plans,' Didier said.

'I suppose it all depends on how much money the business needs. Would the money from me, Thierry and Sylvie be enough to turn things around?'

'We have discussed similar ideas before, but until now, we wouldn't have had enough money between us so we've dismissed it so far. I'll have to check the books again to see how we could make this work, but I think your money could make a big difference. I wouldn't want to be too pedantic about everyone investing in the business if it was too difficult for each of you to do it though.' He ran his hands through his hair. 'I don't even know if I have the courage to ask all of you to bail us out in this way. This is our problem, and we should be the ones solving it.'

'But your mum is making a contribution on your behalf, and everyone has a vested interest in making the vineyard work.'

'It's a good idea, Ellie. I would be happy to create a partnership with the four of you. If *Maman* agrees, I think I'd just have to put it to everyone and see what they say. And then it would be dependent on the state of the finances and the amount being put in, but if we could make all that work, then this plan could save us and help us turn things around.'

Ellie's face lit up. 'That's what we want, isn't it? When do you think you'll call the meeting?'

'Let's go for tomorrow morning. If you can let Henri know and

I'll catch Thierry, and I'll tell Fran and my mum, as well, to make sure everyone can be there. I think we'll meet at the café.'

'Excellent. I can't wait to hear what they all think.'

Henri

Henri had been amazed once again to see how many orders had come in via the online shop over the weekend. He was meeting with Lottie and Thierry this morning to discuss how they were going to deal with the orders over the coming weeks, especially with Christmas coming up when there should be gift orders being placed, as well as the usual orders. Bookings for tours and tastings were also growing, and while Henri was delighted about that, he was also worried about how Lottie and Thierry would manage with everything else they had to do.

'*Salut*, Lottie. How's things?' Henri asked as he walked into the Centre a few minutes later and met her at the reception desk. He took in the newly delivered Christmas tree in the corner and made a mental note to thank their supplier for getting it to them in time for the tasting.

'Busy, but brilliant,' Lottie's face glowed with enthusiasm. 'We've got a full schedule of tours and tastings today, so I'm going to be kept busy all day doing that. We've asked Sylvie to look after Marie today, otherwise we just wouldn't be able to manage everything.'

'Hmm. We're going to have to be careful about how we manage this. Did Thierry tell you how many new orders we've had in as well? He did say we might have to take someone on if the orders increased, but how can we do that when we hardly have any money to pay the staff as it is?'

'I was wondering whether Frédéric might be able to help out. He knows so much about wine, and we could employ him to do the tastings and to pack up the orders, as well, if he'd be interested in that. What do you think?'

'I think that sounds like a great solution as long as the bookings and orders continue. We'll just have to keep our fingers crossed that he's interested. Will you speak to him about it?'

'Sure. I might run it past Sylvie first and see what she thinks about it. I wouldn't like to upset her by asking him.'

'Hey, sorry to keep you waiting. I've only just finished the inspection,' Thierry said as he joined them then.

'No problem. We were just talking about how well everything's going,' Henri said with a smile. 'It's just as well because the finances really are so stretched at the moment. I came over to see if you need any help with planning the wine tasting for Wednesday evening. Fran said there'd been a lot of interest.'

'I think it helped because I posted something on the Facebook page as soon as Ellie set it up,' Lottie told him, 'and also I used the designer you met at the market after reading the interview with him on the blog. And then we delivered the leaflet around as much of the village as we could on one of our evening walks with Marie. We sold all thirty tickets in just a couple of days, which brought in some much-needed cash and left us feeling that we could probably run these monthly in the future.'

'Anyway, we've got all the wines ready, and some of the Christmas gifts have started arriving, as well, so that's all good. Didier will take the lead on the evening, but we'll need more help with serving food as well.'

'And I need to cook the food on the day too.' Lottie wiped a hand across her forehead, her stress clear to see.

'Well, Ellie and I can definitely help, and perhaps the next couple of days and that evening could be a trial run for Frédéric too.'

'That's a good idea. If you and Ellie could help, as well, we should be all sorted. Fran's going to stay at home and look after the children. I wouldn't be surprised if Sylvie comes, because she's already been quite involved in getting the event off the ground.' Lottie unpacked a box of baubles for the tree as they chatted.

The door to the Centre opened behind them, letting in a rush of cold air as a group of people came in for the next tasting.

'See you later, Henri,' Lottie said as she went off to greet them, abandoning the baubles for now.

'Are you going to be able to manage with just the two of you today?' Henri asked Thierry with a look of concern.

'I don't know, if I'm honest. The plan is for Lottie to cover the shop and the café while I do the tastings, but if we get busy in the shop, that could be quite difficult.'

'I could stay now and manage the shop. I'll message Fran to check that's okay with her. Then I'll ask Ellie if she could cover the afternoon.'

Thierry nodded his thanks and went off to take over from Lottie, leaving her free to go and prepare the drinks for after the tour.

Henri sent off messages to Fran and Ellie, and as expected, Fran had no problem with him helping out. Ellie also agreed to come and cover the shop in the afternoon after she'd finished updating the blog and doing her own admin. It was quiet in the shop while the tour was going on, so Henri took it upon himself to decorate the Christmas tree, which he just managed to finish in time. As soon as the tour had finished, things started to get busier. Thierry did a short wine tasting of three samples per person and then the visitors either made their way into the shop or the café, keeping all three of them busy right up until the next tour was due to begin.

It was clear that if this level of bookings continued, they would definitely need a third person in the shop all the time. It was going to be a fine balance over the next few months, Henri thought, to make sure that they had enough staff and enough money to pay them, as well as making a profit.

CHAPTER THIRTEEN

Ellie

Ellie had spent the rest of the morning after her meeting with Didier updating the vineyard blog with articles about the progress she was making on the château and their plans to rent out the rooms eventually and maybe even offer it as a wedding venue. She'd also written a post about their trip to London and included some wedding photos within the piece, highlighting elements she thought would work well at the château if they did go down that route.

She'd also received a lot of comments on posts she'd already published, especially Lottie's one about Paris and the interviews with local businesses. She was certain that the blog and their Facebook page were now encouraging people to come and visit the Centre and go on tours and tastings, and she was proud of what they were achieving. Still, they would need this to continue for quite a while for the estate's finances to be sorted out, and she was sure that her investment idea was the best way forward for the vineyard's future to be secure.

After receiving Henri's message asking if she could work in the shop that afternoon, she turned her attention to her emails, unable to put it off any longer. She'd received so many while they'd been away, and some were quite pressing now as she hadn't been able to get to them over the weekend either.

She read through the emails from the French vineyards first. They'd seen the blog and the Facebook page and wanted to know if she would talk through with them what she'd done to revive the Domaine's fortunes to help them do the same with their own businesses. Not only that, but they were prepared to pay for her time as a consultant. She couldn't wait to tell the others. She sent back a quick reply saying she'd be happy to help and would get back to them with more information soon.

She whizzed through most of the remaining emails until she reached the one from the travel company. After reading it through once, she read it again, almost unable to believe what they were offering.

We're so impressed with your writing on your blog, and we'd like to offer you sponsorship for your travel articles. There would be certain conditions – a set number of articles about different places you've visited each year – but other than that, you'd be able to write the articles at your own pace. Please get in touch to discuss this further with us if you'd be interested in doing this.

This was her dream come true – to be paid to travel and write about the places she'd visited – and she still couldn't quite believe that this company had got in touch with her based on her writing. She looked the company up on the internet to check they were legitimate and was pleased to see all the good reviews about them. She rested her elbows on the desk in front of her and let her face fall into her hands. A couple of months ago, she would have jumped at this opportunity without a second thought, but now everything had changed.

Since coming back from their travels, her love for Henri had deepened, and although the idea of travelling still appealed to her, she still couldn't see how to do that without hurting Henri. Not only that, but she was starting to feel like she belonged on the vineyard, that this was where her real family were. She wanted so much to have it all, but she still hadn't worked out how to do that without hurting all the people she loved. And as a result of all the interviews she'd done in the community, she now understood what a wrench it would be to leave that all behind.

But if she didn't find out more about this opportunity, would she always regret it and wonder what would have happened if she'd taken it? She took in a deep breath and released it gently as she pondered what to do. It couldn't hurt to ask for more information, could it? She wouldn't be committing herself just by doing that. She nodded to herself and composed a reply, redrafting it a few times before she was happy enough to send it. The minute it had gone, of course, she was filled with doubts again, but she had to put it to the back of her mind and get off to relieve Henri at the shop.

She was soon crunching along the path towards the estate and taking in the beauty of her surroundings, as well as calling out hellos to people she passed on her way. Even though it was winter, the village landscape was still eye-catching, from the bare branches of the trees lining the path, to the gravel sparkling with frost under her feet. There was no sign of the Christmas market now – only the Christmas tree had been left behind – but the memory of the lovely day they'd had would stay with her for a long time.

Ellie snuggled down into her coat, pushing her gloved hands deeper into her pockets, enjoying the fresh, cold air against her skin and the breeze in her hair. Maybe she had come to appreciate winter after all.

The warm rush of air as she opened the Visitors' Centre door a few minutes later was still welcome, though, and she was glad to be inside again. She stomped her boots off on the mat and looked around her, delighted to see so many visitors milling about in what was now a very nice Christmassy atmosphere. What a change from the first time she'd come, after their travels, when the Centre had been more like a ghost town. Henri gave her a little wave and she went to meet him.

'Isn't it wonderful to see so many people here?' he said, gesturing around him.

'It's fantastic. It shows that we've done the right thing in getting the blog and our social media up and running. Have you been run off your feet?'

'I have and it's been great. It all bodes well for the tasting on Wednesday, doesn't it?'

Ellie nodded. She had so much to tell Henri about the meeting with Didier and about all the emails she'd received, but now wasn't the right time. It would all have to wait till later. For now, she had a shop to run and customers to tend to, and she couldn't be happier about it.

Tuesday, 18 December 2018

Henri

Henri tapped his fingers lightly on the tasting room table, waiting for the meeting to get started. Didier had finally called them all together, but he wasn't sure if he was excited or nervous about what Didier was going to say. Ellie had delivered the message about the meeting to him, so she'd obviously spoken to Didier about it, but if she had any idea about the agenda, she was keeping it very close to her chest.

He sighed and looked at his watch for about the tenth time since they'd arrived. There were still five minutes to go and no sign yet of Sylvie or Lottie and Thierry. Ellie squeezed his arm and he looked at her for reassurance.

'Don't worry, it won't be long now,' she whispered to him.

He nodded and tried to keep calm. He wanted to support Didier and Fran, and the estate, in whatever way was needed. After all they'd done for him over the years, it was the least he owed them. But he genuinely loved them all, and he saw the vineyard as his home, so meant to do whatever he could for them.

Sylvie and Frédéric finally arrived, followed by Lottie, Thierry and Marie. Marie's little face was flushed, and Lottie and Thierry both looked stressed, so Henri forgave them all at once for being only a few minutes late after all. Once everyone had a drink and was settled, including Marie who was now on the brink of falling asleep, Didier began.

'Thank you all so much for coming. I appreciate you all taking time today to come and listen to me.' He paused and Henri thought he had never seen his friend look so nervous.

Didier cleared his throat. 'As you know, the estate has been in some financial difficulties since the poor harvest we had earlier this year. As always, we had a lot of things riding on pre-sales of that vintage, and when the end results were so poor, we suddenly found ourselves struggling with our cash flow. All of that, coupled with a lot of extra expense this year on building and restoration works, has left us in a precarious position. We're facing having to let people go unpaid, or worse still make staff redundant unless we get a hefty injection of cash soon. As you all know, *Maman* has already promised us some money from the sale of her house, for which we're very grateful, but I have to say that it did seem unfair to me for her to be offering that money to receive nothing in return.' He glanced at Sylvie and she nodded and smiled at him, encouraging him to carry on.

'Yesterday, I had a long conversation with Ellie, during which she suggested an idea to me that I think could work for everyone, and, after talking it over with Fran and *Maman* last night, it's that idea that I'd like to put to you today.'

Henri glanced at Ellie with surprise. Why hadn't she said anything to him about her idea last night after she'd met with Didier?

Didier looked round the room before speaking again. 'You all love the vineyard as much as we do,' he said, gesturing at Fran and his mother. 'So it makes sense for you all to have a stake in the business as well. Most of you are directly involved in the success of the vineyard anyway, and although we pay you, you all go above and beyond a salary for the business. So, my proposal is that you all take a financial stake in the business, by investing as much money as you're able and reaping a share of the profits when we return to that situation in the very near future. In return for that, you will all become partners in the business, along with me and Fran, *Maman* and Frédéric.'

There was silence as Didier finished speaking. For Henri's part, he was horrified. While he thought Didier's idea was a good one, Henri himself had no money that he could use to invest in the business, and he was immediately disappointed that he wouldn't be able to help in the way he would have liked or take a stake in the business that he loved.

'I've just found out, for example, that I've inherited a sum of money from my mum, and I'd like to use some of that to invest in the estate. Obviously, my focus would be on the château specifically so that the restoration can be finished and we can start letting out the rooms.' Ellie spoke first as if she wanted to get the ball rolling.

'And Didier is thinking about using the money Frédéric and I will give to buy a new parcel of vines on the other side of the village to supplement our future harvests with a more reliable crop,' Sylvie chipped in then.

'I do have some savings that Lottie and I could contribute, which we'd like to see invested in the Visitors' Centre and café so that we can start making them profitable as soon as possible.' Thierry smiled at Lottie as he finished speaking.

All eyes fell on Henri to see what he would say. He took a deep breath and swallowed his pride. 'It's a great idea, Didier, but I wouldn't be able to make any contribution as I have no savings. I don't think it would be fair for me to become a partner without some contribution on my part.' He shrugged, humiliation rising up inside him at the thought that he would be the only person unable to join in the plan to rescue the vineyard.

'Strictly speaking, I wouldn't be able to contribute anything either, Henri,' said Lottie. 'Thierry would be putting in his savings on behalf of the two of us, if I've understood correctly, so you shouldn't feel bad about this.'

'Exactly,' said Didier with a smile at Lottie, 'I don't want anyone to feel obliged to make a financial contribution. I'm just grateful that this could be a way out of this for us.'

'This idea has taken me by surprise,' said Henri, 'so I'll need some time to think about all this before I make a decision.'

Didier nodded. 'I understand that this is a big step, but I regard you all as family, and this is a family business – it always has been as you know. If we all had a stake in the business, no matter how small, we'd all be reaping the rewards together in the future. I'm going to leave you all to think about it, and we'll speak again soon. Thanks, everyone.'

Everyone drifted away until Ellie and Henri were left on their own again.

Henri struggled to contain his irritation with Ellie, but kept his voice low when he did finally speak. 'What I want to know is why you kept this from me when we've been completely honest with each other about it all up to now?' Henri looked around to make sure they weren't being overheard.

'I understand you're upset with me for not telling you about my idea, but I did have good reasons,' Ellie began. 'Please let me explain. I didn't know what Didier would say to the idea, first of all. If he'd said no, there would have been no point in telling you about it. And then when he agreed to put it to the meeting, I didn't want to steal his thunder, and I just wanted you to be able to make your own mind up without any influence from me. But I'm sorry, I should have talked it over with you first. I know that now.'

Henri turned away, still upset by what she'd said, but more understanding now that she'd explained her reasoning. 'I would have like to be forewarned, that's all. It was such a surprise. And now I feel that if I don't contribute, I won't be doing my bit for the business, and it may also mean that they don't have enough money coming in to turn things round.'

'We'll need to speak to Didier about how the finances look and what kind of investment the business will need, but my feeling is that with the money from me, Thierry and Sylvie, there would be enough to resolve the problem. As Lottie said, she won't be able to put any money in herself, so that money will come from the two of them, so my money could come from the two of us as well. Would you be happy to accept that?'

Henri pulled himself up, struggling to admit that it would be hard on his pride for him to accept her idea. 'I don't know... It would be hard for me, but at the same time, it would solve the problem around my lack of savings.'

'Look, we don't have to make a decision now, so why don't you think about it for a bit, at least until after the wine tasting tomorrow?'

Henri stood up. 'Okay, that's a good idea. I have to get back to the office now. There's so much to do still before tomorrow and I've got a meeting with Thierry scheduled in.'

Ellie

Ellie followed Henri out to the main shop area and watched him leave with Thierry for their meeting. She was still kicking herself for not telling him about her discussion with Didier before the meeting today. She'd thought she was doing the right thing, but she couldn't have been more wrong. In keeping Didier's confidence, she'd hurt Henri's pride and that was the last thing she wanted to do.

'Is everything okay between you two?' Lottie asked.

'Not really. He's upset because I didn't tell him what Didier and I discussed before the meeting, and it all just came as a bit of a shock to him when he realised that he wouldn't be able to put any money in. I hadn't thought that one through.' Ellie winced once again at the thought of Henri's bruised pride.

'What I said didn't make him feel any better then?' Lottie asked.

'Unfortunately not, but thanks for trying. I appreciated that.' She gave her friend a tired smile. 'I did suggest to him that my money could come from the two of us in the same way, but I'm not sure whether he'll go for that idea once he's thought it over.' Ellie took a seat behind the reception desk.

'I don't mean to poke my nose into your business, but I wonder if Henri would feel happier about the money coming from the two of you, if you had committed to him for the long term. You know, if you were getting married.'

Ellie was so surprised by that suggestion that she couldn't think of anything to say for a minute. 'I have no idea about that,' she said at last.

'I'm sorry, but I have to get over to the café because Frédéric will be back with the tour shortly. Try not to fret about it all too much. I'm sure it will all come good in the end.'

Thankfully, it was another busy day in the Centre so Ellie didn't have too much time to think about things, but whenever she did have a spare moment, Henri was always at the front of her mind. She was still keeping him waiting about what she was going to do in the longer term, and now she was committing to investing her money in the château. She could hardly do that and then set off on her travels again. That would make no sense at all. So was she gravitating towards staying here after all? And if she was, didn't she owe it to Henri to tell him that she'd made that decision so he knew where he stood?

And what would she do if the travel company came back and confirmed that this really was the opportunity of a lifetime for her? Would she take it? Could she do that to Henri and her friends after all the promises she was making to them? She wasn't sure she'd be able to live with herself if she let them down after all the plans they'd made together.

The latest tasting finished and the attendees spilled out into the Centre, some of them going straight to the café and the rest going into the shop to find wines they'd enjoyed after the tour. She brought up the details of the next tour for Frédéric and printed out the list of names so it was ready for him when he needed it.

She was kept busy with a queue of customers buying wines and Christmas gifts for the next fifteen minutes, at which point, Frédéric made his way over to pick up the list.

'Here you go. You've got another full tasting coming up,' she told him.

'Thank you, Ellie, that's great. I like to be busy,' he told her with a smile.

'Are you enjoying it?' she asked.

'I'm loving every minute. I have to admit that I was already getting bored with my retirement. Don't get me wrong, I love being with Sylvie and I enjoy the garden, but it's great to have something like this to focus on and to keep my brain cells ticking over.' He laughed, and Ellie joined in, glad of the chance to get to know Frédéric better.

'And you're happy to be a partner in the business as well?' Ellie asked, keen to hear his thoughts about the plan.

'I was delighted when Sylvie asked me. Incidentally, I won't be putting in any money of my own either. Our contribution is all coming directly from the sale of Sylvie's house, but she's happy for it to come from us both, and now I'm working for the estate, I feel glad to be doing my bit to help.' He gave her a broad smile before turning towards the door when it opened and then going to greet his next tour of people.

That was interesting, she thought. If she could persuade Henri to see that he was doing so much for the vineyard that it didn't matter if the money was his, hers or theirs, it could still come from the two of them. He was proud and she understood that, but he would need to get past that if this partnership plan was to succeed. But what if Lottie was right and there was more to this than just the money? She sighed as she tried to weigh up all her dilemmas and make the best decision for everyone.

Henri

'I think that's the final item on the wine inventory, then,' Henri told Thierry as they finished going through all the wines in the cellars. They'd spent all afternoon going through the wines and darkness had fallen while they'd been at it.

'It always surprises me just how many different wines we have, and also how many different vintages. Now we just need a better year for sales next year and things will start to pick up again,' Thierry replied.

'Yes. It's unfortunate that it only takes one poor vintage to knock cash flow, but we'll sort it out soon, one way or another.' They'd gone all afternoon without talking any more about the meeting that morning, and Henri had been glad to be distracted with something else.

'How are you feeling now about Didier's proposal this morning?' Thierry asked as they put their coats on before going back outside and making their way up to the office.

Henri shrugged. 'I've been trying not to think about it. I just wish I had some savings to put in so that I'd feel equal to the rest of you. I know that's my ego talking, but I can't help it. That's how I feel.'

'What about your house?' Thierry ventured.

'My house? What do you mean?' Henri looked confused.

'You could sell your house, if you were determined to contribute something.'

Henri's mouth dropped open. His house was his only possession, and it was his place of security. 'I couldn't sell my house, it's all I have. I bought it after my parents died, so it means a lot to me. And as much as I love the vineyard, I also like being able to get away sometimes.'

'I understand you not wanting to sell your house and put all your

166

money into the vineyard. That's a tough ask. I do like living here, as you know, but it's different for me when the vines dictate so much of my life. Since Lottie and Marie moved in, though, I've had much more of an incentive not to let the vineyard take over my life and to stick to that plan.'

'Yes, of course. But where would we live if I sold my house?'

'There's the cottage on the estate,' Thierry suggested.

Henri laughed out loud. 'The cottage is tiny. I couldn't imagine the two of us living there if I sold my house.'

Thierry nodded. 'It's possible that there'll be enough money with the investment from me and the others to give the vineyard the financial boost it needs right now, without you having to contribute anyway.'

Henri grimaced. 'Ellie suggested that her money could come from both of us, but I'd always feel like I wasn't a proper partner if I didn't contribute any money.'

'That's not true at all. Even though Lottie won't be putting in any of her own money, that doesn't make her contribution to the success of the estate any less important. You two are as integral to the business as any of the rest of us.'

'I appreciate that, thank you.' It was a fair point from his friend, and maybe that was how he would need to look at things.

'Anyway, not to bring up another bad subject, but how's it going between you and Ellie?'

'It was all going well until today. I had no idea about the plan she was discussing with Didier, and I don't know why she kept it from me, so that threw me a bit. But otherwise, we had a good trip to London, despite the revelations, and she seems to be enjoying the work she's doing here on the vineyard.'

'But still no decision on settling down here with you?'

'No, not yet.'

They reached the Centre and stepped out of the chill night air into the warmth indoors.

'Ooh, shut that door, it's freezing out there.' Lottie rubbed her arms up and down in protest at the cold air invading the warm space inside.

'Sorry,' said Thierry with a grin. 'The temperature really has dropped, even on our walk up from the cellars, and it was cold in there.'

'Did you finish the inventory though?' she asked.

'Yes, all done and up to date,' Thierry replied.

'Right, well, I think it's time we went home and enjoyed our evenings. It's been a long day and it will be another long one tomorrow. Ellie's already gone home.' Lottie stood up from behind the reception desk and went to put her coat on.

Thierry turned off the lights as they all went back outside.

'Will you be able to meet me at the cellars early tomorrow morning to bring the wines over to the Centre for the wine tasting in the evening?' Thierry asked Henri.

'Of course. Did you speak to Frédéric about helping out at the tasting as well?'

'Yes,' Lottie replied, 'and he was really keen. Sylvie said he should only work occasionally, though, so he doesn't get drawn into working all the time again, and that's exactly what we need really. But if he's going to be a partner, as well, now, it will be good for him to see the operations side of things too.'

'That's great news. He'll be really valuable at the Centre, especially when the vineyard is taking up more of your time, Thierry, during the growing season.'

'Exactly.'

'I'll get off home then and see you both tomorrow.'

Henri turned to carry on up the hill towards the car park and the office. The lights were off there, so Fran must have gone home as well. What a day it had been. He had been thinking about what to do on and off all afternoon, but had been unable to reach a definite conclusion. Still, he couldn't sell his house. That wasn't even up for discussion as far as he was concerned; even though he wanted to help the vineyard to recover from its financial issues, he was convinced that selling his house to put money in was not the answer. If he could get over his pride, the best he could do would be to share Ellie's money as she had suggested, as long as that would be enough. He would continue to work hard for the estate as he always had done and he hoped that would be enough for them to move forward.

CHAPTER FOURTEEN

Wednesday, 19 December 2018

Ellie

The next day, Ellie awoke to a message from her dad saying that he was free to come and visit her for the weekend. He apologised for the short notice but said it would be great to see her and Henri again before Christmas. As she stared at her phone, her fear of developing a relationship with him after all this time almost got the better of her. But that was at odds with her real need to see him and to get to know him better. If she rejected his attempts at reconciliation now, she might not get another chance with him.

She gave it some more thought while she was in the shower, trying to get over her irrational fears. Her dad had shown her nothing but remorse for not being in touch for so long, and she'd believed him when he'd apologised for that. And she'd liked him when they'd met at the wedding, as well as enjoyed talking to him a few times since. So, she was being irrational, although perhaps understandably after all that had gone before. But now it was time to try and put the past behind her and to move on, facing her fears one by one.

She rinsed her hair of shampoo and found herself humming by the time she'd finished in the bathroom. Henri appeared just as she was finishing getting dressed. She'd apologised again to him the night before, repeating that she'd wanted to hear Didier's views on them forming a partnership before telling Henri about it, and he'd accepted that. But things were still fragile between them.

'Morning. I'm just about to go and meet Thierry. Will you be along shortly?'

'I will, but I've had a text from my dad this morning to say he wants to come and visit on Friday for the weekend. I'm sorry it's such short notice, especially with everything else that's going on.' A flash of anxiety passed through her at the thought of it, but she tried to keep calm.

Henri came towards her and took her hands in his. 'And how do you feel about it?' he asked.

'Honestly?' Henri nodded at her question. 'Scared to death, but I'm dealing with it.'

'I'm glad he's followed through with his promise, for both your sakes.'

'So I'll go back to him and confirm then?'

'Definitely. And we can pick him up from the station once he gives us the details. Now, I must be off, but I'll see you soon.'

She kissed him goodbye and went into the kitchen to grab some breakfast. She texted her dad back shortly after sitting down, before she could change her mind about it, and he replied almost at once.

Fantastic! It will be so good to see you. I'll text you again once I know my arrival time. See you on Friday!

At least he was keen, she thought as she read his reply. She was glad that he'd be coming on his own – it would be too much right now to have to get to know Annie, his wife, as well. That made her think that maybe she should see him on his own without Henri, at first, so that they could get to know each other one-on-one. Then they could

171

meet Henri after that. She would have to tread carefully if she was going to put this suggestion to Henri, though, after already upsetting him at the meeting.

The more she thought about it, the more she liked the idea of staying in Strasbourg to start with, which would give them a chance to visit the city together, as well as giving her more material for the blog. She had no real idea what he liked to do and started to fret about what it might feel like to spend concentrated time with her dad after all these years apart. She willed herself not to overthink things, deciding that she should just keep things simple.

She had a quick look at her blog to see if there were any new comments and answered the ones needing a reply. There were also some positive comments on her post about their trip to London already. Finally, she got round to checking her emails again. There was a reply from the travel company. She let her hand hover over the email for a good few seconds before taking the plunge and clicking on it. They reiterated their requirement for a certain number of posts about different places she'd visited, but then went on to say that ideally, they would like to receive a new post every month. She really couldn't commit to those conditions – if she did, she would have no choice but to leave the vineyard for good and to always be travelling, and that wasn't what she wanted at all. With a sigh, she sent back her reply, knowing that was the end of that idea.

Once she'd sent back her reply, she was surprised at how easily she put it behind her and turned her attention to the busy day ahead on the vineyard. She threw her coat on and rushed out the door to make her way to the Visitors' Centre shortly afterwards. It was freezing, but she hoped that wouldn't put people off from visiting the Centre or from attending the wine tasting that evening.

'Hello, you,' she said to Lottie as she approached the welcome desk at the Centre a few minutes later.

Lottie glanced up in surprise at the sound of her voice. 'Ellie, hi! Gosh, I didn't even hear the door open, I was so engrossed in this paperwork. Thanks so much for coming to help. We've got another busy day on, and what with planning for the event this evening, as well, it's all a bit overwhelming.' She stood up to come round the desk and give her friend a hug.

'Tell me where you need me then and you can get on with what you have to do.'

Lottie's shoulders sagged. 'What a relief to have you here. If you could watch the shop and fill up the shelves so that we're fully stocked for this evening, then I can get these invoices out of the way before setting up the café for when the first tour ends. The food's all ready for this evening; it just needs cooking later on. Frédéric's running the tours again for us today so that's all in hand. Thierry, Henri and Didier should start arriving with the wines for the tasting soon, and can you look out for the delivery of glasses, please? The chairs and tables are all set up already.'

'Of course. You take yourself off to the café and get your work done. If I need you, I know where you are.'

Lottie gave her a grateful smile. 'You know where the coffee machine is and everything. And don't hesitate to come and get me if you get stuck with anything.'

'I'll be fine.'

Lottie nodded and went off to the café. At the sound of the door opening, Ellie turned her attention to a new customer.

Henri

Henri made one last check around the tasting room, satisfied that it looked professional and smart. They'd hired the tables, chairs, tablecloths and glasses locally, and it had made a big difference to the look of the room. They'd set it up for the thirty people attending the event to be seated at five tables of six, and Didier and Thierry had chosen eight wines for them to taste, so each place had eight glasses laid out in two rows of four. It had been a challenge to fit that many glasses out neatly, but he was pleased with what he and Ellie had been able to do. They had dedicated one staff member to each table – Lottie, Thierry, Ellie, Henri and Frédéric – and they would be kept busy all evening serving the wines between them while Didier took the attendees through the tasting.

'Henri, I've printed out the tasting notes,' Ellie said as she entered the room and surveyed the tables once again. 'It looks amazing in here.' She smiled.

'It really does. Thank you for thinking about the notes. That will be the final touch.' He took a pile of sheets from her and they set about squeezing them into the middle of each table.

'It's just about time for us to go out and get ready to greet people with the others now. Lottie and Sylvie are going to serve the canapés and Frédéric's going to serve the *crémant*, while I check people in, which leaves you three to greet people and direct them to the tasting room when they're ready.'

'Great. Let's get to it then.' Henri experienced a flutter of nerves but his overriding feeling was one of excitement. He loved social events like this and it was a great opportunity to show off the vineyard's wines.

They went back outside to the main shop area just as people started to arrive. The next half an hour passed in a flash as everyone arrived and mingled together. Ellie had the foresight to take some photos once everyone had been checked in. This would be such great promotion for the vineyard, and she was using the blog and social media to such good effect now.

Didier appeared at his side. 'It's time to get everyone into the tasting room now. Shall I make an announcement or shall we just go round and guide them?'

'An announcement would be quicker,' Henri advised.

Didier made a brief announcement and then people gradually began to make their way into the tasting room. While he started his introduction, Henri and the others began pouring the first wine for their respective tables. They were starting with the Pinot Blanc from last year's vintage. Didier brought everyone's attention to the tasting notes and then told them a little about the grape variety and how the vintage had been perfect for it last year. The tasting notes also detailed foods that would go with the wine, recommending it as a perfect aperitif for Christmas, alongside the *crémant* they'd just tasted.

They went on to taste a Riesling next, followed by a Pinot Gris and then finished the white wines with a Gewurztraminer. As the tasting progressed, more and more people started to ask questions, and Didier relaxed into the evening, confidently talking about the estate's wines to his audience. When he was unsure about something, he introduced Thierry and deferred to him for his expertise, but the look on Thierry's face afterwards when he glanced over at Henri showed that he was happy to leave the main presentation to Didier.

Next they went on to taste the 2014 Pinot Noir, which was just beginning to come into its own. Henri loved this wine and had no trouble extolling its virtues as he went round his table pouring it. Didier also recommended this wine for Christmas dinner, and Henri was glad that they'd brought a good few cases up from the cellar because he was expecting a lot of sales after the tasting.

Finally, they were on to the sweet wines – another Gewurztraminer and Pinot Gris first of all, which were both medium sweet, and the perfect match for a slice of festive *kugelhopf* cake. And last of all, they finished with a dessert sweet Riesling. Henri's mouth was watering by the time he'd finished pouring, and he could tell from the comments around his table that the tasting had been a success.

'Our tasting is now at an end,' Didier said not long afterwards, and a sad groan went round the room at the thought of the lovely evening finishing. 'However, our shop will remain open for you to browse your favourite wines from the tasting,' he said with a smile. 'And please do come and talk to us if you have any questions.' His speech was finished by a large round of applause, and then people slowly made their way outside.

'Frédéric and I will clear the glasses away, Henri, and then we'll come and join you. Ellie's going to go on the till but she might need your help if it gets busy,' Lottie told him.

Henri nodded and made his way out to the shop where Ellie was already busy serving someone. The atmosphere was buzzing and Henri had never felt so proud of all they'd managed to achieve. He spoke to several people on his way over to Ellie, all of whom were full of praise for the way the evening had gone.

'Do you need some help?' he asked Ellie when he finally reached her.

'Yes, please. You could pack while I put things through the till. We're so busy, it's wonderful. I've had nothing but compliments from people as they've come up to buy wine and gifts.'

'This evening has been a huge success, and we've all worked so well together. We should definitely do this more often.'

It was ten o'clock by the time the last person left, and everyone was exhausted. Didier had sent his mum and Frédéric home earlier, and between the rest of them, they had got everything tidied up so the Centre could reopen on time the next day.

'Thanks so much everyone for making this evening such a great success. We sold out of all the wines we brought up from the cellars, so we've had to take back orders from some people, which is so wonderful after the difficult few months we've had. You've all had your part to play in bringing this about, and I really am so grateful to you all. It's not long till Christmas now, and Fran and I would like you all to come to us in the château for Christmas Day so we can celebrate together and thank you all personally for all your help.'

Friday, 21 December 2018

Ellie

'I'm only going to be gone for a couple of days, you know,' Ellie said to Henri once they were on their way to Strasbourg to meet her dad on the Friday morning. 'You'll hardly even notice I'm not here.' They'd got over their bump from earlier in the week, and things were easier between her and Henri now.

He glanced over at her from the driver's seat. 'Of course I will, and you know it. I always miss you when we're not together, but it's fine. I know how important this time is to you.'

'It's just... that there'll be personal things we want to discuss as this is our first time together for many years, and I wouldn't be able to raise them if we were at home at the vineyard with everyone popping in all the time.'

Ellie had told Henri her plan of spending the first couple of days alone with her dad in Strasbourg, and then meeting up with him for lunch on the Sunday before bringing her dad back to the vineyard. To his credit, Henri had understood her feelings, and this plan would at least allow him to spend some time with Bill again, which she knew he'd be looking forward to.

They arrived at the station car park a few minutes later and Henri parked up smoothly before taking Ellie's case out of the boot and following her inside the station. Ellie was first to spot her dad, who was waiting in the Arrivals area, and she waved at him to get his attention. She ran to greet him and they shared a hug, before she turned round to let him say hello to Henri.

'Henri, it's great to see you again.' Bill extended his hand and Henri shook it firmly.

'You too. Did you have a good journey over, Bill?'

'It was excellent. So quick and easy. I hope I'll be able to do it more often now.'

Henri passed over her suitcase and she leaned forward to kiss him on both cheeks. 'Enjoy yourselves,' he said, 'and I'll see you on Sunday.'

They took a taxi from the station, and after checking in at their hotel, Ellie set out with her dad to show him the main sights of Strasbourg. Their hotel was right in the centre of the old town, not far from the *cathédrale*, so she decided they should make their way there first.

As they walked, her dad took her hand and tucked it into his arm. She was touched by the affection he was showing her already and happy that they were getting on so well.

'I hope you don't mind me asking,' she began as they wandered along the narrow cobbled streets, 'but did you feel any resentment towards Mum after she made you leave?'

'I have to be honest, Ellie, and say that I was very bitter for a long time after I left. I felt tricked into giving up my children and my life, and then I felt stupid for having given in so easily.'

'How did you get past all those feelings then?'

'Meeting Annie was what really helped me. She helped me see that it wasn't my fault, and she gave me hope that I would see you and Chris again in the future. In the meantime, I became a father to her children, which also helped me to heal.'

'And what about now? Do you still feel resentful towards Mum?'

He patted her hand. 'No, there's no point now she's gone. I've missed you and Chris terribly, but I've managed to have a good life, despite everything that's happened, and I never lost hope that I would see you both again. Hopefully, we can all put the past behind us now.'

'That's proving to be hard for me, Dad. I was never close to Mum after you left, and now I feel so angry with her for what she did. I don't know how to let those feelings go.'

'It will be hard for you, Ellie. I can't deny that. But with Henri's help, and mine, as well, you'll get there eventually.'

Ellie took in a deep breath, knowing that it was time for her to admit the truth she had finally understood about herself. 'My big problem is that I've spent my whole adult life running away from commitment because of what happened between you and Mum. I've never let anyone get close before, and when they do, I just up sticks and run away to somewhere, and someone, new. But there's more at stake this time.'

'Do you love Henri?' her dad asked simply.

'I do. I love him very much but I'm so afraid of hurting him.'

They reached the Place de la Cathédrale and for a moment, they were both transfixed by the wondrous site of the Gothic building in front of them.

'Shall we have a drink first and then go and visit the cathedral afterwards?' Ellie suggested, and her dad nodded his agreement.

They found a cosy little café down one of the side streets and settled down at a table in the window with a view of the cathedral to their left. They both ordered hot chocolate and people-watched while they waited for their drinks to come.

'Why do you think you'll hurt Henri?' her dad asked after taking a sip of the cream-laden drink in front of him a minute later.

Ellie considered her answer for a moment. 'If I stay, I'm worried that I'll get itchy feet down the line and want to go travelling again to get away, which will hurt him. If I leave now, he'll be equally upset, so I don't know what to do.'

'The only reason you should be choosing to stay is if you love him. So let me ask you again – do you love Henri? If you're saying yes but not meaning it, then that's the worst thing you could do to him.'

Ellie sucked in a breath. 'I do love him. That's the one thing I know for sure.'

'What makes you think you love him?' her dad asked after another sip of hot chocolate.

'I care about him and how he feels. I think about him when I'm not with him. I could see myself settling here with him because he's made it feel like home to me. Even though the very idea of having children scares me, I think I could have them with Henri. And although I go on all the time about loving to travel, he has tried to understand that need in me, despite not feeling that way himself about it. He even came travelling with me for five months when it's not his thing at all.' She shrugged as she came to a stop. She could have gone on longer, but she didn't need to.

'I think you've just made it very clear how much you love Henri and why. And when he's around you, I can see how much he loves you, too. I liked him very much when I met him in London, and even though I could see he was disappointed not to be seeing much of me this weekend, he put your needs first. That's a man you can trust, Ellie, if you want my opinion.'

'I trust him completely.'

'Enough to marry him?' her dad asked with a smile.

Ellie's eyes widened. 'I haven't even thought about marriage.'

'Perhaps you should. Now, shall we go and visit this lovely cathedral?'

Her dad went over to pay the bill, leaving Ellie reeling from their conversation. Was Henri thinking about getting married to her? And what would her answer be if he proposed? The very thought of it frightened her, and maybe that gave her the answer as to what she would say. There were always so many questions to think about, but never any definite answers. She wished she could just be sure about the right thing to do both for herself and for Henri.

Henri

While Ellie had been away with her dad, Henri had given further thought to whether he should sell his house so that he could make a contribution to the estate in exchange for becoming a partner. After the success of the wine tasting the other night, he wanted more than anything to be part of shaping the estate's future. So he'd decided to get his house valued so he could get an idea of what it might be worth to the business before he finally made up his mind.

The valuation had arrived that morning and now that he'd looked at it, he couldn't stop thinking about it. It was for a much higher amount than he'd been expecting, but the high valuation didn't leave him feeling as pleased as he might have expected. In his heart, he still didn't want to have to sell his house just so that he could contribute to the vineyard's finances, even though he wanted to help Didier and Fran if he could. He wished he had some other funds that he could put in so that he could still help with the vineyard's future.

As it was Saturday, he decided to walk into the village to visit the market as he would normally do. He felt at a loose end with Ellie away, and the day ahead stretched long and uninviting without her. Their first stop was always the *boulangerie*'s pop-up shop, and he was delighted to see how busy they were when he arrived. There were lots of Christmas-themed treats on offer today, which had only added to the stall's usual popularity. He waved at Liliane's daughter, Madeleine, from the back of the crowd queuing in front of her stall. She mouthed '*Bonjour*' at him before turning her attention back to her customers. He decided to return later in the hope that she was less busy.

He turned to leave and almost walked straight into Sylvie and Frédéric.

'*Salut*, Henri. How are you? And where's Ellie?' Sylvie looked around her, expecting Ellie to materialise at the sound of her name.

'I'm fine, thanks,' Henri replied with a grin. 'Ellie's spending some time in Strasbourg with her dad.'

'Oh, well, that's lovely, but that means you're on your own. I thought you looked a bit forlorn.' Sylvie gave one of her wise nods.

'It does feel strange, I must admit, but I'm not sure I'd describe it as being forlorn.' He laughed, not sure who he was kidding with his denial. He missed her and there was no doubt about it.

'Have you got any plans for the day ahead?' Sylvie asked. 'Because you know you're always welcome to come and join us for the day.'

Henri glanced at Frédéric, wondering if he felt the same. 'I don't want to spoil your plans. I'll be fine on my own. I've got lots of things I can be getting on with.'

'At least join us for lunch. It would be great to catch up.'

'Yes, do,' said Frédéric. 'It would be good to spend more time with you than usual.'

'Thank you both. I have some shopping to do, so shall I see you at your house in say, half an hour?'

'Perfect,' agreed Sylvie, and off they went to get their shopping.

Henri wandered around the stalls, picking up a whole chicken for dinner the following day, as well as some other bits and pieces for the coming week. He also managed to pop back to the *boulangerie* stall and pick up a delicious-looking apple tart to take to Sylvie's by way of a thank you for inviting him round.

'How are you, Henri?' Madeleine asked. 'I haven't seen you for ages. And where's Ellie today? I loved her blog interview with my mum. I was going to ask her whether I could do one next time about our new venture.'

'I'm fine, thanks. Ellie's in Strasbourg visiting with family, but I'm sure she'd love to do an interview with you. I'll ask her to get in touch with you after Christmas. How are you, apart from being rushed off your feet?'

'I'm filling in for Mum today and she's babysitting for me. It gives us both a break from routine. I suppose that's why I haven't seen you for a while. Anyway, take care and say hello to Ellie.' She smiled and turned to her next customer.

As he made his way out of the market, he popped into the florist's and bought a bouquet of winter flowers for Sylvie as well. The only thing he wouldn't have, was a bottle of wine, ironically. Still, he reasoned that Sylvie would be well-stocked up in that department and set off for their house.

Frédéric let him in a few minutes later at their home on the other side of the village square, and they sat down to an impromptu lunch shortly afterwards.

'Thanks so much for inviting me. I appreciate it.'

Sylvie waved away his thanks and concentrated on serving herself some bread and pâté. 'Have you thought any more about Didier's partnership idea?'

'I have thought about it a lot. And I've realised that if I do want to invest money of my own, the only asset I have is my house. So I've had it valued, even though I don't really want to sell it.'

A worried look crossed Sylvie's face. 'I'm very surprised about that, Henri, when I know how much it means to you. What do you think you're going to do? You know you don't have to put any money in, don't you?'

'I do know that, but I feel so bad about it. Still, I've pretty much made up my mind not to sell my house.'

'You're already a part of our team, just as Lottie is, just as Frédéric is now.' Sylvie smiled at him and Frédéric nodded his agreement.

Henri was surprised to hear that Frédéric was also in the same position as him and seemed perfectly happy with it. 'Ellie has suggested that her money could be a joint contribution, as well, but I'm struggling to agree to that. All I know is that I want to feel I'm doing my bit along with everyone else to turn the vineyard's fortunes round.'

'You've been doing your bit for years, Henri. And things are already getting better, aren't they?' Sylvie turned to Frédéric for backup.

'Yes, we're already starting to see a change, what with the success of the wine tasting the other night,' agreed Frédéric. 'I must admit I'm really enjoying running the tours and tastings, and helping out with events will also be good in the future.'

Henri was surprised to hear Frédéric speak so enthusiastically about the vineyard when he was usually so quiet. Maybe it would be good for him to have his own interest in the future.

'You must get over your pride about this, Henri,' Sylvie said. 'You already do enough for us as it is, and you will be as much a partner as everyone else, regardless of whether you put any money in or not.'

But for Henri, if he wasn't going to be risking his own money, then he would never be equal to everyone else, and that would gnaw away at him no matter what they all said.

CHAPTER FIFTEEN

Ellie

It was another crisp, sunny day in Strasbourg and Ellie was looking forward to spending more time with her dad. Even though it was their last full day together, she wanted to make the most of every moment, and move on from the past.

'I thought we might walk in the other direction today towards Petite France. Is that okay with you? There should be some Christmas markets for us to look at on the way there and back.'

'I'm happy to do whatever you suggest as you know the city better than I do,' her dad replied with a smile. 'You seem to have settled very well into life in France. Do you miss London at all?'

'I do miss it, although not as much as I was expecting to, but it was great to pop back for the wedding, and I know I can do that easily in the future, so I'm not too worried about that. I have come to like living here, and I didn't expect that to happen, especially when we were travelling.'

They strolled through the old quarter until they were alongside the river where the railings were festooned with garlands and baubles instead of the usual flower boxes. There were Christmas trees everywhere, and the markets were in full swing selling the now expected Christmas trinkets, toys and traditional Alsatian *vin chaud*. It was just like at home but on a much bigger scale.

'Is it too early for some mulled wine?' her dad asked, a twinkle in his eye as the spicy, citrussy flavour floated out from a nearby stall.

'It's never too early, and it is quite cold today,' Ellie replied with a chuckle.

They wandered across the cobbled street to the stall and Ellie suppressed a laugh at her dad's French accent as he ordered them two cups of wine. At least he was trying. He handed her a cup, and they gently bumped the paper cups together before continuing on their way.

'I hope we can continue to meet regularly like this from now on,' her dad said a few minutes later. 'It's been wonderful getting to spend time with you after wasting all these years. I'm so sorry about that.'

'I'd like that, Dad. We've got a lot of catching up to do.'

'Perhaps you can come and visit us next time, if you'd like. Annie would really like to meet you.'

'I'd like that, too, and so would Henri.'

'And is the vineyard far from here?'

'No, it's only about half an hour away.'

'I'm looking forward to spending this afternoon there with Henri before I leave tomorrow morning.'

'It will be lovely to be able to show you the vineyard and the village where we live.'

Ellie made a quick call to Henri about their plans to meet for lunch while her dad went to look at a stall selling traditional Christmas gifts. 'He'll be with us in about an hour,' she told her dad when she rejoined him.

'That's great, so we have some more time to wander around until he gets here.' He tucked her arm inside his and they continued their walk around Petite France, enjoying the hustle and bustle of Christmas shoppers and jolly stallholders as they progressed along the river. Ellie had plenty of material for her next blog post and found herself looking forward to writing it up when she got home again.

'Henri was delighted when I rang him. He always takes everything in his stride and hardly ever loses his temper. He's nothing like me.' Ellie laughed at the thought of how different they were.

'You know what they say about opposites attracting. But he does strike me as a very easy-going chap, and he seems to be good for you. He clearly loves you, and I think he would do anything for you as well. That all bodes well for your future together.'

'I know he's a good man, and I do love him, but I find it so hard to have faith in love lasting forever. I don't know how you've managed to have the faith to believe in love again after Mum betrayed you in the way she did.'

'But Annie's not your mum. She's her own person and so very different to your mum in every way. She brings out the best in me, as well, and when you love someone, you just know. I mean, I don't know for sure that Annie and I will be together forever, but because we love each other so much, I'm prepared to put my faith in that love we share to bind us together for years to come. I feel sad about your mum, but I don't think about her much these days. I'll always be grateful to her for giving me two wonderful children, but I've let go of all the rest.'

Ellie shook her head, amazed at his ability to move on. They were just a short walk away from the restaurant Henri had suggested they meet at for lunch now. Ellie guided her dad round an excited bunch of children eating traditional *bredele* biscuits, and then she spotted Henri waiting for them outside.

'Hey, it's good to see you,' she said, giving him a hug and a kiss.

'You too,' he replied. His face was warm and reassuring, despite the chill in the air. He took her hand and reached out with his other one to shake hands with Bill.

'This place looks amazing,' Bill said, taking in the wooden beams and the leaded windows on the façade of the restaurant.

'Wait till you see the menu.' Henri laughed. 'It's to die for.'

Ellie smiled, pleased that her dad and Henri got on so well together. It had been a great weekend so far and good to talk things over with her dad. She couldn't put off making decisions about her life for much longer, though, but she didn't feel any closer to knowing how, despite all the advice she'd received.

Henri

Henri watched the interaction between Ellie and her dad throughout their lunch together, noting how at ease they were with one another after just a short time spent together on their own. He'd been longing to see her himself, but now he could see the benefits of her getting to spend some time alone with her dad, and he had taken the opportunity to reflect on his own situation.

At the end of the meal, Bill got up to visit the bathroom and Henri took his chance to speak to Ellie about how everything had gone. 'Are you feeling better after spending some time with your dad? You seem so comfortable with each other.'

'I feel so much more relaxed about everything. We've had some good chats and had some fun together, too.' She smiled at him. 'Thank you for being so patient with me.'

'I bought a roast chicken at the market yesterday, so we're all set for dinner. And maybe we could take him on a tour of the vineyard beforehand.'

'That's just what I was thinking.'

When Bill returned, he had his coat on and had brought Henri's and Ellie's coats with him as well. 'I've paid the bill, so we're all set to go.' He raised his hand at their protests. 'Come on, let me pay this once.'

They gave in gracefully and made their way outside to walk back to the car. Henri had been lucky to find an on-street car parking space not far away, so it didn't take them long to get there.

'How long have you worked at the vineyard, Henri?' Bill asked as they drove home.

'For about ten years now. I first came to the village after my parents died, and Sylvie, who managed the vineyard with her husband back then, took me under her wing. They gave me a job and I've stayed ever since.'

'Do you live in the village or on the vineyard estate?'

'I have a house in the village.'

They were approaching the village now, and soon, Henri was pulling up outside the house.

'This is a real beauty, isn't it? I love these traditional Alsatian houses,' Bill said as they got out of the car.

Henri lifted the cases out of the boot and took them both to the front door while Ellie and her dad followed behind. He put the bags in the hallway and went on to the kitchen to make some drinks. Ellie took Bill upstairs to show him to the spare room before appearing in the kitchen a few minutes later. He turned towards her and she stepped into his arms for a hug.

'It's good to be home. I missed you and this place.' She leaned her head against his chest and his heart warmed at her words.

'Do you want to go out on your own with your dad for the tour? I don't mind.'

'No, I want you to come, too. You know more about the history and everything than I do, and it will be nice for us all to spend the afternoon together anyway.'

He kissed the top of her hair, glad that she wanted him to come along. 'I'll send a quick text to Didier to let him know we'll be there and walking around.'

They set off shortly afterwards, pointing out the local sights on the route before wending their way along the footpath to the estate. When they reached the courtyard, Henri stopped for a moment.

'So, this is where I work with Fran, Didier's partner. We run the office together and deal with all the admin and the marketing.'

'And so much more besides,' Ellie prompted. 'The place wouldn't run without you.'

Henri felt his face flush, embarrassed and pleased at her praise.

'And how did Fran and Didier get together?' Bill asked. 'Has she worked here as long as you, Henri?'

Henri deferred to Ellie to explain as they made their way down past the closed Visitors' Centre and on to the château. 'Fran met Didier at university, but things didn't quite work out for them first time round. Then she came to London to work and that's where we met. She'd been dating someone and was supposed to be getting married, until she found out he was cheating on her, and she decided to move back home to Alsace. She came for a job here, not knowing it was Didier's family vineyard, and she's been here ever since.'

'And you moved here when you were made redundant. Is that right?'

Ellie smiled at her dad. 'Yes, that's right. I'd already met Henri before then when I was visiting Fran, and he'd been to stay with me in London, so it seemed like a good plan to come here to be with friends when I lost my job.'

Bill whistled as the château came into view. 'And this has been your restoration project. What an amazing building. Can we go inside?'

'Didier and Fran live there, but I'm sure they won't mind if we pop in.' Henri sent off a quick text to Didier and a few minutes later, the front door opened.

'Come on in, you guys. Don't hang about in the cold.' Didier waved them over and soon they were all gathered together in the hallway of the old building. Ellie made the introductions.

'It's great to meet you, Bill. Would you like a look around so you can see how much Ellie has achieved?'

Ellie and Bill disappeared upstairs first and Henri followed Didier down to the kitchen where he found Fran and Chlöe doing some baking.

'Henri!' Chlöe cried. 'I haven't seen you for ages.' She jumped

189

down from her chair and threw herself and copious quantities of flour at her friend amid a flurry of giggles.

'Let Henri come in, Chlöe,' Fran said. 'Shall we make some hot chocolate?'

Chlöe nodded and Henri took a seat at the kitchen table.

'How are you?' Didier asked as he joined him at the table.

'I'm okay. I'm still wrestling with the partnership idea. Well, not the idea, which is a great one, but just the fact that I'd like to make a contribution, and unless I sell my house, I won't be able to.'

Didier paled. 'I would never ask you to do that, Henri. I hope you're not seriously considering doing that when it means so much to you.'

'I did think about it, but it's not really what I want to do.'

Didier blew out a breath. 'I'm glad about that. But you think the partnership idea is a good one?'

'I definitely do. You could see what a great team we are together from the wine tasting the other night. I'm sorry you missed it, Fran, but Ellie took some great photos.'

'There'll be plenty more from what I hear.' Fran smiled at Henri over Chlöe's head.

Ellie and her dad joined them then, and Henri found himself relaxing about the whole idea of the partnership and the role he would have to play in it.

Christmas Eve, 2018

Ellie

Ellie let herself back into the house, slipped off her shoes and collapsed onto the sofa. She'd just finished her last shift working in the Visitors' Centre shop and now she could relax and get ready for Christmas. Christmas Eve was always one of her favourite days of the holiday and she and Henri had the rest of the day to themselves once he got home. It had been such a busy week and they were both exhausted, but she was looking forward to Christmas together and with their friends.

She hauled herself off the sofa just as Henri was coming back in with their lunch from the *boulangerie*.

'Hey, sweetheart. Merry Christmas,' she said as Henri came in the door.

'*Joyeux Noël* to you, too.' He smiled and they kissed. 'It's good to be home.'

They went down to the kitchen to make their lunch together. Ellie put the oven on after peeking in the bag that Henri had deposited on the table and finding one of the *boulangerie*'s delicious quiches.

'So, I still have a few presents to wrap up, and I'd like to do a last sweep of the blog and my emails before we close for Christmas if that's all right with you,' she told Henri as he prepared a salad to go with their quiche.

'I have presents to wrap, too, but all my work is done now. Any orders will have to wait till Thursday. I don't mind you doing some work as long as you're not going to take too long. We both need a break,' he said firmly.

'I know, and I agree. I won't be long, I promise.'

Ellie made them both a drink and they sat down at the table to wait for the quiche to be ready.

'By the way, Didier confirmed to me this morning that there will be enough money from you, Thierry and Sylvie to sort out the vineyard's finances without any more needed from me, Lottie or Frédéric, so he's going to push ahead after Christmas and contact his lawyers about setting up a partnership between the eight of us.'

'That's fantastic news, and the best Christmas present of all.' Ellie beamed at Henri.

'And the finances are already looking so much better after the tasting, as well as the advertising revenue trickling in.'

'The other new thing I've been meaning to tell you about is that a couple of French vineyards, one near Bordeaux, and one down in Provence, have contacted me asking if I would be prepared to be a consultant for them and help them reverse their own fortunes based on our experience here. They said they'd be happy to pay me.'

Henri sat up. 'That's great news. Have you told Didier?'

'No, I just haven't had a chance, but I will.'

'What a great compliment for them to ask you for your help. Would you like to do it?'

'I would, but I'd have to talk more with them about what they'd be after. I'd probably have to go and visit them both for a couple of days to start with. How would you feel about me doing that?'

'That would be fine, I think. I could manage without you for a couple of days at a time.' He laughed and she joined him, pleased that he thought this idea could work. She liked the idea of travelling around the country to other vineyards as a way of fulfilling her need to travel to new places.

The timer went off then and Henri jumped up to retrieve the quiche from the oven. He cut two slices and served one on each plate, next to his salad, before delivering the plates to the table.

After lunch, Ellie settled in the living room while Henri went upstairs to wrap his presents. She checked over her blog, delighted by the number of comments she was receiving on all her posts now. The Christmas market one had gone down really well, as had the one about Strasbourg, and she had a number of interviews scheduled in for the New Year as well. She was getting regular advertising revenue coming in from both village-based companies and from the companies who'd done work on the château. Now that they'd used the wine-tasting revenue to pay all their other suppliers what they owed them, they had a fresh slate to move forward from after the celebrations were over. She released a sigh of relief.

She worked through her emails next. As she'd expected, there was nothing more from the travel company after she'd had to say she couldn't commit to writing a new piece for them every month, and she was still fine with that. But there were two new emails from other vineyards, and these ones were in northern Italy and Spain, and again, they were asking for her help. One of them was even asking her if she could come and stay for a month.

She was sure that Henri would have more to say about that. She groaned inwardly. No sooner had she dealt with one dilemma than another one presented itself. She would have to reply immediately, what with Christmas being upon them and her wanting to take a break from her computer. So she let them know that she could help but that she couldn't be absent from her own vineyard for that length of time. Surely they would understand that?

She closed her computer at last and readied herself to go and wrap her presents, very pleased to put the whole business to bed for a few days and get some respite from all the decision-making. She was looking forward to exchanging presents with Henri later and enjoying a quiet evening meal together.

Christmas Day, 2018

Henri

Henri woke early on Christmas Day despite his longing to stay asleep a little bit longer. He rolled over onto his side to watch Ellie as she slept, her red curls all around her face, and thanked God once again for the beautiful woman lying beside him. He glanced at the clock, surprised to see that it wasn't early at all, but it was actually eight o'clock. He listened for a moment, expecting to hear the birds tweeting or some children outside, but it was curiously still.

He sat up and turned to swing his legs over the side of the bed. He padded across to the window and his face lit up. Outside, it was snowing, and everywhere he looked was a winter wonderland. He loved the snow and it had been a long time since they'd last had snow at Christmas. His thoughts went immediately to Chlöe and Marie – it would be their first time, and they would be ecstatic. Turning round to tell Ellie, he found her getting out of bed.

'Morning,' she said, rubbing her eyes. 'I can't believe I slept in till this time. Why's it so quiet?'

He grinned at her and beckoned her over.

'Oh no, don't tell me it's snowed?' she groaned.

'Don't be so grumpy. It's lovely!'

Ellie was still grumbling about the snow an hour later when they set off for Fran and Didier's house.

'It's going to be so cold and my feet will probably get wet,' she said as they walked outside.

'You've got boots on so your feet won't get wet, and anyway, you've got spare clothes and shoes if they do. Try to enjoy it,' he coaxed her. He grabbed their bag of presents for everyone and followed her along the path into the village.

The market square was full of families building snowmen and teenagers throwing snowballs at each other. And the snow on the timber beams of the houses was just magical.

'Ooh, wait a minute, Henri. I have to get some photos.'

Henri laughed. 'You've changed your tune. How are your feet?' he asked as Ellie stepped gingerly across the street.

'They're fine, but we've still got a long walk down to the château.'

After Ellie had taken some photos, they continued slowly on towards the vineyard, stopping several times on the way to admire the beauty of the landscape around them. They met Thierry, Lottie and Marie halfway down as they were coming out of their house.

Marie's face was a picture and Henri couldn't stop looking at her expressions as she took in the changes around her. Her laughter filled the air as Thierry stomped along in the snow and brought her up close to the hedges so she could see the snow on the branches inside them. A group of birds flew across the sky and she pointed to them with delight.

'Did you have a good Christmas Eve?' Ellie asked Lottie then. 'I bet Marie loved it.'

'It was such a wonderful time with it being her first Christmas. We spoilt her too much, but it was lovely. How about you?'

They soon arrived at the château as they chatted and played with Marie, and Henri noticed that Ellie had stopped complaining about the snow once she got used to it.

'Look at the château,' she said as they arrived. 'Doesn't it look beautiful?' She took another couple of photos and then Fran and Didier were at the door with Chlöe to welcome them in.

'Come on in, everyone,' Didier cried. '*Maman* and Frédéric are already here. Make your way down to the kitchen when you're ready.'

Frédéric passed hot drinks to the adults and gave Chlöe a glass of juice before they all sat down around the farmhouse table for a snack. The air smelled of roasting turkey and vegetables, and Henri felt his mouth water. He loved Christmas Day roast dinners most of all. He was envious not to be cooking himself for such a great crowd, but he and Ellie would have their own smaller version tomorrow, just the two of them, so he could put his culinary skills to good use then.

They spent the next hour unwrapping presents and the children had great fun testing out all their new toys.

'Will you do my puzzle with me, please, Ellie?' Chlöe asked straight after opening her present, and Ellie happily obliged. She padded into the living room in her socks following Chlöe and sat down with her in a quiet spot. Henri watched Ellie with the little girl and thought to himself what a good mother she would make.

Henri wandered back out to the hallway, where Thierry was helping Marie to play with her new toy dog. Ruby looked on, unsure whether the toy dog was a threat to her status or not.

'This is a lovely present, thank you,' Thierry said. 'She's a bit obsessed with dogs at the moment so this is perfect.' He laughed as Marie woof-woofed up and down the corridor.

'*A table, tout le monde*,' Sylvie cried a short while later, and they all returned to the kitchen to take their seats.

Didier remained standing and waited for them all to be ready. He lifted his glass of *crémant*. 'Thank you all so much for your support this year. It's been a challenging one in some ways, but so good in many other ways.' He smiled at Fran and then at Chlöe. 'I look forward to next year when we will have a new member of our family, and when we will become a partnership all together, my friends. *Joyeux Noël à tous. Santé!*'

'*Santé!*' they all replied before settling down to enjoy the feast before them.

Henri filled his plate with a little of everything that was handed to him: roast turkey, chestnuts, roast potatoes, a whole host of different vegetables, cranberry sauce and gravy.

'This is a superb meal, everyone. Well done and thank you for cooking for us,' Ellie said.

'And the Pinot Noir is a perfect match,' Frédéric said.

'Goodness knows where we'll be having Christmas this time next year,' Didier said. 'We'll have to vacate as soon as work starts again on the château, won't we?'

'It's probably for the best,' Ellie agreed. 'Could you use the cottage for a while, at least when the baby's first born?'

'To start with, yes, but it's nowhere near big enough for four people to live in long-term.'

'Will you extend it then?' Thierry asked.

'That could be the way to go, but the thought of even more building work and the costs involved fills me with horror right now.'

'You don't need to worry about it now,' Sylvie reassured him. 'And when the time comes, we'll all muck in and help you manage.'

Henri smiled at Sylvie. She was right, of course, because they were one big family and they pulled together when they needed to. The rest of the meal passed smoothly and mostly in silence as everyone enjoyed their food and the company.

'I'm about ready to fall asleep,' Henri told Ellie mid-afternoon as they sat on the sofa together watching the children play after lunch.

'It really was a wonderful meal. I'm glad we have another day off to rest and relax tomorrow, as well, before everything picks up again for New Year.'

Shortly afterwards Sylvie started passing round the *kugelhopf*, but even as Henri took a small piece, he wasn't sure he'd be able to fit it in.

'Go on.' Sylvie laughed. 'There's always room for a piece of cake.'

Henri duly obliged even though he thought he might pop, and for a brief moment, he closed his eyes, safe in the knowledge that he was among friends and family and they wouldn't mind.

CHAPTER SIXTEEN

Ellie

'Hello, little sis, how are you? Did you have a good Christmas? Thanks for your presents by the way. Dad dropped them round on Christmas Eve.'

Ellie ignored her brother's jibe at her and concentrated on the main reason for her call. 'I'm fine, and yes, it was lovely, thanks. But most importantly, how was the honeymoon? Did you have an amazing time?'

'We did. We travelled to so many different places – we drove from Santiago to Buenos Aires, and then we flew up to see the waterfall at Iguazú. It was fantastic, and such a wonderful way to spend our honeymoon. We're both exhausted now, though, but so glad that we have some time off over Christmas before we have to go back to work.' Chris groaned but she could tell he was happy.

'I'm so envious, but I'm pleased you had a great time. How's Michelle?'

'She's fine, although we both feel a bit deflated to be home again. But we'll get back to normal soon.'

Ellie understood that feeling. She made a mental note to remind

Michelle to write her a blog post about their trip. 'It was lovely to see Dad last weekend.'

'I'm so happy you've seen each other again since the wedding. He said you had a great time together.'

'We really did. I find him so easy to talk to, and I managed to spend some time with him on my own in Strasbourg, and then Henri came and joined us, and we brought him back here to the vineyard. Hopefully, I'll go and visit him and Annie with Henri next time.'

'You sound really happy, sis.'

'I feel much more settled than I did, but I still get that yearning to travel sometimes.'

'But that's normal, and it means you can look forward to your next trip away.' He paused for a moment. 'Is that all it is, though, or is there something else you're still not telling me?'

He knew her so well. 'I'm still struggling with the whole idea of commitment to one person, you know, the 2.4 kids and house with a picket fence thing. I just don't know if I'm cut out for that kind of life, and I don't want to let Henri down by agreeing to stay and then changing my mind further down the line.'

Chris sucked in air between his teeth. 'I felt like that, too, until I met Michelle, and then settling down with one person for the rest of my life seemed like the most natural thing in the world.'

'So why don't I feel like that, even though I know I love Henri?'

'I don't know, only you can know that really, but if it's fear that's holding you back, you're just going to have to make a decision at some point and take that leap of faith.' He paused after delivering his wisdom. 'Changing the subject, what have you decided to do about Mum's money?'

'I've decided to keep it, and to put some of it towards finishing the restoration of the château here. Didier's agreed to form a partnership with us all.'

'That will keep you busy for a while, and forgive me for saying, but that does sound like you've made a commitment to stay on the vineyard at least. I'll get on to sorting the transfer out for you with the solicitors. Look, I'd better go, but let's speak again soon and sort out getting together again.'

Her brother rang off and she pondered their conversation for some time. Was her wanderlust just a normal longing that everyone who enjoyed travelling had from time to time? Had she just been using that as an excuse not to settle down with Henri? Maybe now that her dad had come back into her life and told her the truth of what had happened, it was time to put the past to bed, to move on as Chris had done. She had plenty of evidence all around her of people who had found love, often against all the odds, and were managing to make it work. Could she dare to hope for that for herself?

She sighed at all the thoughts whirling round her head. She'd just settled down to do some work on the blog when a knock at the door brought her back to reality.

'Hello, Sylvie. This is a nice surprise, come on in.'

She held the door open to let the older woman in and then exchanged kisses with her.

'I thought I'd pop in as I was in the village, and I know Henri was going into the office today. Did you have a nice day together yesterday?'

Ellie led the way into the living room and then disappeared to put the kettle on. She returned a moment later and sat down opposite Sylvie.

'We did, thank you. It was very relaxing and we needed that after the busy couple of weeks we've all had.'

Sylvie accepted the coffee Ellie handed her. 'Yes, it was a great run-up to Christmas, and now with the plans for the partnership, next year is looking much brighter. Will you be seeing your family again soon?'

'We don't have any plans in place at the moment, but hopefully, we'll see them all again fairly soon. I spoke to my brother this morning. He's just got back from his honeymoon in South America. It sounded fantastic.'

'And now we have a double wedding at the vineyard to look

forward to. I love the idea of holding the ceremonies at the château, and I'm so grateful that you've started work on the restoration again. It will be wonderful to see it restored to its former glory.'

Ellie took a sip of her drink. 'Do you know anyone that might be able to help tidy up the gardens? It all looks a bit of a mess at the moment and it would be good to neaten it all up before the event.'

Sylvie frowned. 'We always used to have gardeners, but now I come to think of it, I haven't seen anyone doing any maintenance for some time. I wonder if we had to stop because of lack of money to pay them. I'll ask Didier about it and then I'll sort something out. You can leave that job to me.'

Ellie smiled at Sylvie as another piece of the puzzle clicked into place. She wanted to make the weddings a wonderful celebration for them all, but especially for her friends, and to finish the job she'd started on the château. She was happy here with Henri and with the life they had built together. All she had to do now was to let herself enjoy it.

Henri

After a couple of days off, Henri was eager to get back to work and check whether any online orders had come in while he'd been away. Lottie and Thierry were opening up the Centre today, although there would be no more tours or tastings until the New Year now. So this was the perfect opportunity to get everything tidy before the new season started. Then he could take New Year's Eve off without any concerns about loose ends.

The office was chilly when he first arrived as they'd turned the heating down while they were off to save on costs. He was glad Fran wasn't coming in today – she wouldn't have appreciated the chill in their working environment at all. After opening up and turning on the coffee machine, he boosted the heating and switched on his computer.

He went straight to the online shop dashboard and was staggered to see at least a dozen orders at a quick count, which would have come in since lunchtime on Christmas Eve. When he considered it, he supposed that people were buying wines for New Year celebrations, and when he looked more closely at the orders, he could see that a lot of them were for bottles and some cases of their *crémant*. Thierry should have seen these orders by now, but he fired off a quick email to him to make sure and to ask if he needed any help.

The New Year was now looking a lot more hopeful for the vineyard estate, which was a great relief to them all. Henri was still disappointed that he couldn't contribute any money of his own to the business, but he was trying to come to terms with that and to accept that he already did a lot to help the estate. Thanks to the ideas they'd put in place over the past month, as well as the plan to form a partnership between them all, the future was now much more secure.

All he wanted to do now was to sort out his personal life. He pondered the current situation as he drank his second cup of coffee. Ellie had thrown herself into the vineyard blog and had helped him set up the online shop so that they could help with the vineyard's finances. She'd also made a start on the second phase of the château restoration, persuading Didier to let her use the advertising revenue from the blog as soon as it started coming in. While she'd been floored by all the revelations when they'd gone to London, she went on to offer to invest her own money in the vineyard after they came back. She was also happy for that money to come from the two of them, which was generous beyond belief. And he thought that the consultancy work she'd been offered by other French vineyards might fulfil her need to travel to new places as well. He couldn't remember the last time she'd talked about travelling further afield. So everything pointed to her being ready to settle on the vineyard for the future.

And that meant that it was time for him to ask the most important question of all. Despite all the evidence that she was ready, though, he still had his doubts about what she would say if he proposed. She loved him, he knew that, but was she ready for marriage and children? Should he ask her first to test the waters? He'd still be devastated if she said she wasn't ready, but would it be worse to just propose with no idea of what she might reply?

He heaved a big sigh, hating the fact that the first option was really just the lesser of two evils. He glanced at the clock on his computer. It was nearly lunchtime. He would talk to Ellie over lunch, he decided, about how she was feeling, and then at least he would know how to proceed.

When he arrived home about fifteen minutes later, Ellie was on the phone. He stood in the hallway for a minute listening to her side of the conversation, wondering who she was talking to. Feeling like he was spying, he popped his head round the corner of the living room door and gave her a little wave to let her know he was there. She faltered for a moment before regaining her composure and bringing her conversation to an end. He went ahead to the kitchen to prepare some eggs for lunch.

'Hey, sweetheart,' she said a moment later when she joined him. 'How was your morning?'

'All good. Lots of orders, though, so I'm going to check in with Thierry on my way back to make sure they're not swamped. How about you?' He hoped she would tell him about her call.

'That's great news about the orders. I've been updating the blog and dealing with emails, although Sylvie popped in, as well, so it took me a while to get going.' She smiled at him, but didn't say anything about the call.

Once they were eating their lunch, Henri decided to take the plunge. 'I wanted to ask you something,' he began, putting down his knife and fork for a moment.

'That sounds ominous,' she said, giving him her attention.

'It's not, honestly. It's just that, I wondered, with everything going so well here now, well, I wondered if you'd made up your mind to stay, with me, I mean.' Henri suppressed a wince at his disjointed question and went back to eating his lunch.

'I was just thinking about everything this morning after Sylvie came round, and I do feel a lot more settled, but there have been some temptations.'

Henri's eyes widened, and he dreaded what she was going to say next. 'That phone call I was on when you came in was from a travel company that had offered me sponsorship for the blog in exchange for a monthly travel article about a different place each time. I didn't tell you about it because I couldn't commit to that. I just wouldn't want to be away from you or the vineyard on that sort of basis.'

Henri grinned at that. 'It makes me really happy to hear you say that.' He paused. 'But why were they calling you?'

'They came back to say they'd be happy for me to write ad hoc pieces instead because of the quality of my writing. But they still want me to commit to a certain number of articles a year.'

'So what did you say?' Henri held his breath.

'I didn't really even have to think about it. I don't want to be away that often, and I have enough going on here to keep me busy.'

'That's fantastic. I'm so glad that you're ready to settle down.'

'There is something else I need to tell you about, though, which only came up the other day. I've been contacted by more vineyards, but these ones are in Italy and Spain, and they'd like me to visit them for longer.'

Henri pushed his plate away. 'And how do you feel about that?' He knew how he felt, but he willed himself to let her make her own mind up.

'I've already told them that I couldn't come for a month because I couldn't afford to be away that long.'

Henri sucked in a breath. 'A month? That would be a long time. The other ones had only asked you to come for a couple of days, hadn't they?'

Ellie nodded. 'How would you feel about me being away for a week at a time, say?'

Henri shrugged, annoyed with himself for not wanting her to go away at all, but knowing this was something she needed to do. 'I'm not mad about the idea. But we can only give it a try, can't we? And then see how it goes.'

She reached out and took his hand. 'A week isn't that long in the grand scheme of things, but I would love to do this. And maybe you could even come with me sometimes.'

Henri nodded, trying to get over his pride. Ellie wanted to go, and he had to show that he understood that and that he supported her in this new development. At least she didn't want to go for a month or to be travelling all the time any more, and that meant a lot to him.

Ellie

As much as Ellie was looking forward to celebrating Fran and Lottie's upcoming weddings, she was feeling a little unsettled still following her talk with Henri the previous day. His reaction when she'd told him about going away for a week at a time had left her feeling unsure about his expectations of their relationship in the future. He'd been so shocked when she'd said that the vineyards had asked her to go for a month, but he didn't seem any happier with the idea of her being away for a much shorter time either. He hadn't even seemed pleased that she'd rejected the travel company's idea. He'd struggled with the whole idea, even though he'd done his best to hide it from her.

She would have liked to discuss it with Fran and Lottie to get their take on what Henri's reaction meant, and today was the perfect opportunity as they were having their final wedding planning get-together before the toned-down hen party. But the minute she arrived at Fran's, all thoughts of doing that went out the window. Today wasn't the day for that sort of discussion, not when her friends were both high on their forthcoming nuptials.

'Come on, we're supposed to be having fun today, and you look as miserable as sin,' Lottie told her.

Ellie snapped out of her reverie and plastered a smile on her face.

'Sorry, I was miles away. I've got the checklist with me so that we can make sure we've finally done everything.'

'Let's do that first so that if there is anything left to do, we can get onto it before we spend the rest of the day having fun,' Fran said.

'First of all, I spoke to Sylvie about the gardens. She's going to sort all that out, she said. I contacted the priest at the village church and asked if she would be prepared to come here and perform the blessing, which she said she would. I managed to find a photographer and a local band for you, and the hairdresser is now on board to come here on the morning, and to do your make-up as well. Your mum has been a star and cancelled the arrangements we'd already made near your house – it turned out that the restaurant was still going to be closed anyway, so it seems like this was fate.'

Fran ran her hand gently over her tummy with a smile. 'Thanks so much, Ellie. You've been so good sorting all this out for us. And you're right, Mum really has been a star. We couldn't have done all this without her. I'm going down there this weekend for my final dress fitting and to see them before the big day. I want to see *Papi*, too. He hasn't been that well recently, and I want to make sure he'll be well enough to come to the wedding.'

'And I've got someone booked to do the catering for us here,' Lottie confirmed. 'Thierry was adamant that I wasn't going to do that for my own wedding day, and secretly, I agree.' She laughed.

'What about your wedding dress, Lottie?' Ellie asked, tapping her pen against her chin.

'That's all fine. I'm not into a big, frilly number. I've probably got an outfit that's right for the day.'

Fran clapped her hands together. 'Thank you both so much for all your help. I'm so grateful to you both and pleased that we're going to be able to hold the weddings here.'

'What about the cake?' Ellie asked, running her finger down her checklist. 'We didn't speak about that before, did we?' Ellie looked up at last to see Fran and Lottie exchanging shocked glances.

'I hadn't even thought about it. God, how can I have been so stupid?' Fran looked distraught.

'Liliane and her daughter Madeleine at the *boulangerie* are branching out into celebration cakes now,' Ellie said. 'I did an interview with Madeleine recently when she asked me if we could promote it on the blog from the New Year. I bet she'd jump at the chance. Leave that one with me.'

Fran reached out for her sister's hand. 'Is that everything now?'

'Yes, I think it is, and it'll be fine. Don't worry.' Lottie gave her a reassuring smile.

'It sounds like we're pretty much all set then. Shall we decamp for some lunch?' Ellie asked.

They all piled into Ellie's car, with Fran moving to take the passenger seat so she didn't get travel sickness in the back. She stopped for a moment on the way and Ellie watched her as she took some slow, deep breaths.

'Everything okay?' she asked with a frown as Fran eased herself in.

'Yes, I'm sure it's nothing. I'm just so tired from not being able to get comfortable at night, and it's wearing me out.'

Ellie had to take Fran at her word because she'd booked the bistro in the village and she didn't want to be late. She glanced at her watch before they set off, knowing that their surprise guests would already be there if everything had gone according to plan.

They arrived at the bistro a few minutes later, and Ellie waited for Lottie to help Fran out of the car before leading the way inside the restaurant.

'Hello!' The greeting echoed across the tables and Fran's face was a picture of delight when she saw her mum and Sylvie already waiting for them.

'Oh, this is lovely,' she cried, her hands flying to her face. 'Mum, how are you? Sylvie?' She kissed both mums and wiped her eyes. 'Did you organise this?' she asked, glancing at Lottie and Ellie.

'We did. We couldn't have a party without the mums, could we?'

Lottie winked at her sister before taking a seat at the round table they'd booked in the corner.

The waiter brought over a selection of drinks and left menus for everyone.

Ellie took the last seat between Sylvie and Lottie and reached out for a glass of *crémant d'Alsace*.

'It's time for a toast to the brides-to-be, isn't it?' she asked, raising her glass.

Everyone clinked glasses and wished Fran and Lottie lots of luck for their big day.

'Thank you all for celebrating with us today,' Fran said. 'It means so much to me to have you all here together.'

'Thank you all for all your help in organising the weddings, as well,' Lottie added.

'*Santé!*' they cheered.

Ellie found tears springing to her eyes. She loved these women so much, and they had become a family to her in such a short time. She thought about her dad, and about Chris and Michelle, too, delighted at how everything had turned out there as well.

The only fly in the ointment was Henri. Just when she'd made up her mind to settling down here, and accepting that she would have to compromise if she wanted to travel as well as start a new life with him, he had made her feel as though she was still asking too much. And that had led to the old doubts creeping back in about whether she really was ready to commit to him after all. She shook her head, trying to move on from her negative thoughts.

'Penny for them,' Sylvie whispered to her, cutting into her worries.

'Oh, I'm sorry, it's nothing,' she said. 'I'm just distracted today.'

Sylvie studied her face as if she could see right through Ellie's words, but she couldn't reveal what was on her mind. This was for her to sort out with Henri, and sooner rather than later.

New Year's Eve, 2018

Henri

At last it was New Year's Eve and time for Henri to put his plan into action. He'd been thinking about it all weekend, while Ellie was working at the Centre on Saturday and while he'd gone out with Thierry and Didier for their pre-wedding get-together on Sunday. Didier hadn't wanted to have a big do, so they just went for a drive out to the country and enjoyed a nice meal and walk together.

He hadn't seen much of Ellie as a result, but for what he had in mind for today, he needed to make the occasion as special as it could be. He wanted her to be absolutely sure of just how much he loved her and how glad he was that she'd decided to stay. He'd got over his wobble about her going to the vineyards for a week at a time, accepting that he had to be prepared to compromise as much as she did.

As Ellie had volunteered to work in the shop again today because they were so busy, Henri had spent all afternoon, after he finished in the office, preparing dinner for the two of them. He had a joint of beef cooking in the slow cooker with a delicious red wine sauce around it made with wine from the vineyard, of course. All he had to do now was get the vegetables ready. He'd cheated by buying dessert from the *boulangerie*, but it had saved him some time.

He just had enough time to remove his apron and get changed before Ellie would be returning from the Visitors' Centre. As he changed, he went over in his mind once again what he wanted to say to Ellie, despite having done it several times already that day. His stomach was tied in a knot, but it wouldn't be for much longer. The door opened and then banged closed as Ellie returned home just as he was leaving the bedroom.

'Ooh, something smells delicious. What have you been up to?' she asked, smiling, looking up the stairs at him as she removed her coat.

'I've made roast beef. You won't have to lift a finger tonight,' Henri replied as he met her at the bottom of the stairs.

She stepped into his arms and kissed him lightly on the lips. 'Thank you. It's been an exhausting day, and this is just what I need, plus a good night's sleep.'

'Come on into the kitchen then, and I'll get you a drink.' He'd been chilling a bottle of *crémant* in the fridge, which was just right for the occasion.

He poured two glasses and handed one to Ellie. 'Happy *Saint-Sylvestre*, I hope you enjoy our special feast to celebrate.'

They clinked glasses and she sank onto one of the dining chairs while he carried on prepping the potatoes before putting them in the oven.

'Have you been doing this all afternoon?' Ellie asked after taking a sip of her drink.

'I have, and I've had a great time cooking and getting everything ready for you.'

He transferred the pre-boiled potatoes into the heated roasting pan and put it back in the oven, before joining Ellie at the table.

'I'm sorry we haven't seen much of each other this weekend,' she said.

'Me too, but now we can spend a great evening together knowing we have the day off tomorrow as well.'

He served up dinner for them both shortly afterwards and served them each a glass of Pinot Noir before tucking into his meal.

'Oh, Henri. This is divine. The potatoes are so soft and the meat so tender. You really do know how to make a fantastic roast dinner.'

'I have to agree. I know it's not modest, but the food is delicious, even if I say so myself.'

When they'd finished eating, Henri cleared his throat in preparation for what he was about to say.

'There was another reason why I wanted to make you this meal tonight.' He waited until she looked up at him to make sure he had her full attention. 'Now that you've decided to stay here with me, I can ask you what I've been waiting to ask for months.' He paused, then rushed on. 'Ellie, will you marry me?'

To Henri's dismay, Ellie put down her glass and didn't say a word. He couldn't help but think the worst.

'Ellie?'

She swiped her hand across her face. 'Henri... I...' Her hesitation didn't do anything to reassure him either.

'Please tell me that I'm reading this all wrong. Has everything changed?'

Ellie finally found her voice. 'Some things have, yes.'

'What things?' Henri asked, his heart in his mouth.

'I was upset after I talked to you about visiting the vineyards the other day. It doesn't seem to matter how much I compromise about travelling, you just don't understand my need to get away sometimes and explore.'

Henri looked shamefaced. 'I know I reacted badly, and I'm sorry about that. I was just having a panic, and then I realised that I needed to compromise, as well, if we're going to make this work between us. I've got past that now.'

'But you're only just telling me that now. I've been really worried over the past few days.'

'But are your feelings for me still the same?'

Her face softened as she looked at him. 'My feelings for you haven't changed at all. I love you very much, Henri. But I wasn't expecting this and I can't give you an answer right now. I'm sorry. I'm going to need some time to think.' She put her cutlery on her plate and pushed it away, then stood up from the table.

Henri watched her leave the kitchen and go upstairs before putting his head in his hands. He couldn't believe the way the evening had turned out. If only they'd had the chance to talk again before he made his proposal and they could have cleared the air. Now he had embarrassed himself by jumping the gun and proposing too soon. And he had no idea how to get things back on track between them.

CHAPTER SEVENTEEN

Ellie

As Ellie plodded slowly upstairs, her phone began to ring. She wondered who on earth could be calling right now when their whole life was in such turmoil. She pulled her phone out of her pocket. Lottie's name flashed on the screen. She was probably ringing to wish them Happy New Year before going to bed. Ellie hesitated for a moment, not feeling much like celebrating with anyone after all that had happened, but then accepted the call from her friend.

'Hello, have you had a good New Year's Eve?' she asked, trying not to let her voice wobble under the weight of emotion she was feeling.

Lottie sobbed. 'Ellie, it's Fran, they're taking her into hospital for observation. She's okay but they want to do some tests. Can you both come here to be with Thierry while we go with Didier?'

'Oh my God, Lottie, I'm so sorry. Of course. We'll get there as soon as we can. Give Fran and Didier our love and let us know as soon as you hear anything.'

Ellie rang off, by which time Henri was by her side. 'Is everything okay?' he asked.

She relayed to him what Lottie had told her as they put on warm clothes and went back downstairs to get their boots. They left for the walk to the office a few minutes later, taking care along the now icy footpath. The temperature had dropped significantly and ice crystals had already started to form on the plants and hedges lining the path.

They weren't far from the courtyard when they saw vehicles and people gathered outside the office. They both sped up to find out the latest from Thierry, who was holding Marie in his arms and bouncing her gently up and down.

'What's happening?' Henri asked as they drew closer.

'Didier's gone with Fran in the ambulance. They couldn't get down as far as the château because of the ice and snow, so they had to bring her up here on a stretcher,' Thierry told them. 'Frédéric's driving Lottie there, and Sylvie's looking after Chlöe. Fran's parents are on their way up from Colmar.'

Ellie's hands flew to her face at the thought of the pain her friend must be in. 'At least she's got everyone there, and she's in the right place if there are any problems. How did this all come about though? Do you know?' Ellie asked.

'When Didier got back yesterday, she said she hadn't been feeling well, so they called the doctor, who came out to see her and said that everything was as it should be. But she carried on feeling sick all day today, so they eventually rang for an ambulance.'

'God, I hope she's okay. It's far too early for the baby to come yet, isn't it?' Henri asked.

'Yes, she's only coming up to six months gone, but she was experiencing contractions, which does sometimes happen,' Thierry said. 'Look, it's late now and I need to get Marie to bed. Have you both eaten?'

Ellie shot a guilty glance at Henri. 'Sort of,' she said.

'Well, why don't you both come back with me? I can put Marie to bed, and we can wait for news together.'

'That's a good idea, thank you,' said Henri, taking Ellie's hand.

They followed Thierry back down the hill towards his house.

The château was mostly in darkness and Ellie worried about Sylvie being on her own.

'Do you think one of us should go and keep Sylvie company until Frédéric gets back?' Ellie suggested to Henri as they approached the house.

'Oh yes, she'll be very worried. I'll go. Will you let me know straight away if you hear anything?' Henri asked.

'Of course. Be careful on that ice.'

He took her face gently in his gloved hands. 'I love you, you know.'

'I know,' she said before kissing him goodbye. She watched as he made his way down the hill, her worries from earlier that evening fading as she realised just how much she did love him.

'Come on in, Ellie. I'll take Marie upstairs for her bath and put her to bed now. Help yourself to a drink. I won't be long.'

Ellie removed her coat and gloves, but then Marie began to cry at the thought of being separated from her. She gently lifted her from Thierry's arms to distract her. 'Shall I read to you after your bath?' she asked.

The little girl nodded wide-eyed and Thierry smiled at Ellie. 'Come on then, sweetheart,' he said to Marie as they went upstairs. She made herself a coffee while she waited, then nervously paced up and down the living room as she thought about Fran.

Soon Thierry was calling downstairs and Ellie disappeared to fulfil her promise to Marie, glad of something to do. She snuggled up with Marie on her lap in the armchair in her bedroom and read through one of her picture books with her. Then she lifted her carefully into her cot, pulled up the side rail and watched as her little eyes closed.

'Oh, she is so adorable,' Ellie said when she'd put Marie to bed. 'She's such a chatty little thing and so responsive to stories, isn't she?'

'She really is. When I think how scared I was of starting a family with Nicole, and now I'm so lucky to have met Lottie and to be dad to

Marie. It just makes me so happy. I can't wait for us to have another one now.'

'I've always been worried about starting a family, as well,' Ellie found herself admitting then. 'It's not that I don't want children; I just don't want to be a bad parent.'

'No-one knows whether they'll be good at it until they do it, but the fact that you already think about it and want to do the best you can suggests that you will be a good parent. From what I've seen, you're very good with children. Perhaps you're better at it than you think,' Thierry told Ellie with a smile.

Ellie frowned then. 'For Fran, it's all she's wanted for so long. I really hope and pray that both she and the baby will be okay.'

Thierry checked his phone as they moved to sit down in the living room. 'There's still no word from Lottie or any of the others. I'm quite worried now about what's happening.'

'Do you think you should message her and ask?'

'I'm tempted to. I don't want to bother her, but it's hard for us being here and apart from them.' He composed a quick message and sent it.

There was a knock on the door at the same time as his phone pinged with a message. He jumped up to go and answer the door. Ellie heard Henri's voice a minute later and stood up to go and find out the latest.

'Frédéric's with Sylvie at the château now. He said that Fran is still under observation. They're keeping her in because she's dehydrated and she's not been getting much sleep. They also want to be sure that she's not going to go into early labour.'

'That sounds quite worrying, but at least they can take proper care of her there. What a terrible way to be starting the new year though. Didier must be worried sick.'

'We'll let you get off to bed now, Thierry,' Henri said. 'I'm sure Marie will be up early tomorrow.'

They said goodbye to Thierry and made their way back home

before it got too cold again and the walk became treacherous. Henri held on to Ellie's hand tightly all the way home.

'I'm so sorry about spoiling the evening earlier,' Ellie said after they'd reached the courtyard car park.

'What? You didn't spoil it. I misjudged it. I should have discussed things with you again beforehand. But look, let's not worry about it now when there's so much else going on.'

Try as she might, though, Ellie couldn't put Henri's proposal out of her mind and she spent a restless night thinking over everything that had happened that day.

New Year's Day, 2019

<u>Henri</u>

Henri was up early on New Year's Day, desperate to check in with Thierry to see whether there was any more news about Fran. He'd tossed and turned all night and sensed that Ellie hadn't slept very well either. He slipped quietly out of bed to go and make breakfast, leaving Ellie to lie in. He had hoped to be waking up engaged to Ellie today, and instead everything was in a mess, and Fran was in the hospital.

He reached the kitchen, put the coffee on and picked up his phone to send a quick text to Thierry to see if there had been any more news about Fran overnight.

No more news yet. Lottie stayed there with her mum and dad, and Didier, of course. I'll let you know when I hear anything.

The shower went on upstairs so Henri delayed making breakfast until Ellie came downstairs shortly afterwards. Her hair was bundled up in a towel, and although she looked as beautiful as always, there were bags under her eyes.

'Morning, sweetheart. Did you get any sleep?'

'Not much. I don't think you did either. Is there any news?' she asked as she poured out some juice for them both.

'Not yet, no.'

They worked side by side to prepare a breakfast of French toast, their unspoken concern about Fran uniting them. Henri piled the toast onto a serving plate and they sat down at the table together to eat.

'Mmm, this is delicious,' Ellie said, her love for the food pushing her to speak at last.

As they finished eating, Henri's phone pinged with a message.

'It's from Thierry. He says Didier's been in touch and that Fran is still being monitored, but that they think she's going to be okay.'

'That is a relief. They'll keep her in for the rest of the day, though, won't they?'

'At least,' Henri agreed. 'But, yes, what a relief. Now she can concentrate on getting better and coming home again.'

Ellie looked up at him. 'Now we know Fran's going to be okay, perhaps we can talk about yesterday.'

Henri nodded, but he was nervous about what Ellie would say. He stood up to clear the plates before turning towards her and leaning back against the kitchen counter.

'I want you to know that there was no need for you to feel embarrassed about your proposal. I can see how you might have put things together in your mind when you saw the signs from me. It's just that I wasn't expecting you to propose, and that caught me off guard, I'm sorry.'

'But you still don't want to marry me?' he asked, unable to hide the hint of bitterness in his voice.

'I didn't say that,' she pointed out. 'If you could put that to one side for a minute, I want to talk to you about something else.'

Henri was at a loss but there was obviously something on her mind. 'Go on.'

'I want to talk to you about the house and the money again, if you can bear it.' She held up her hands when he tried to interrupt. 'It's all right, I know your feelings haven't changed, but I also know that this house is worth a lot of money, as well as being of great value to you emotionally. And I know that you're very proud.'

'Where's all this going, Ellie?'

'What if I bought into the house with you, by which I mean, giving you half the value? As I live in your house for free at the moment, that would seem like the fair thing to do. It would also show you, I hope, just how committed I am to staying with you, even if I do go away for a few days from time to time.'

Henri was speechless for a long minute. 'You know you don't have to do this, don't you? I've already told Didier that I won't be putting any money in and he's accepted that.' He paused for a moment but she didn't say anything. 'Have you really thought about this, Ellie? It would be a big step for us to take, so you must be certain about it before you sign any paperwork. And there would be paper-work to sign because I'd want to do it properly.'

'I know you would.' She laughed. 'I feel sure about it, Henri. It would be an important step for us to take together into our future. I want you to be sure that I mean it when I say I'm committed to you and to staying here. And I want us to see the château as our joint project. I'll oversee the restoration, I know, but you would bring all your experience of the day-to-day work of running the estate, and when the château is ready to receive guests and to hold weddings, you'll be brilliant at setting up the website and the booking system, especially after your experience of setting up the online shop.'

'I would be really happy to do that, but I think you should think about this for a few days before making up your mind. We don't need to rush into anything.'

She shrugged. 'I can do that if you like, but I don't think I'll change my mind now. I want this to be our house and our future.'

'And can you forgive me for not wanting you to go away for too long? That's all it is. I don't want to stop you from having a great career. I just want to be with you as much as I can. But this is a good compromise and will allow you to spread your wings.'

'There's nothing to forgive, I understand that now. I just wished we'd had the chance to talk sooner about it before things got confused. I want to be clear now that if we do this, it will be a fresh start for us both.'

'Agreed. I'm happy with that.' He kissed her then, long and slow, happier than he'd been for a while, and looking forward to a long future with Ellie on the vineyard.

Ellie

When Lottie had offered to drive Ellie to the hospital the next day, Ellie had gratefully accepted. She still wasn't that familiar with the route to Strasbourg, let alone driving on the other side of the road, but today, her stomach was in knots at the thought of going to the hospital. She'd hardly said a word to Lottie on the drive over, and now they were almost there.

Lottie pulled deftly into a space in the hospital car park before turning the engine off.

'You've been very quiet the whole way. Are you okay?'

'I'm nervous about going into a maternity ward.'

'Have you never been to one before?' Lottie sounded incredulous.

'Nope. And I have no idea what to expect.' Ellie gave a shaky laugh.

'It'll be fine.'

Ellie wasn't quite convinced of this, given her fear of having children, but she went along because she wanted to see Fran. They made their way inside the modern hospital building, Lottie guiding Ellie to the right lift, floor and finally the ward where Fran was being monitored.

'Has it felt strange for you to be back here again?' she asked Lottie as they arrived in the maternity unit.

'At first it was odd, but then you just get used to it all over again.

It has been quite nice to be here without actually having to give birth though.'

Ellie managed a laugh. 'Don't tell me anything about it. I don't want to know.'

When they reached the corridor outside the ward, Fran's parents, Christine and Joseph, were deep in conversation with Sylvie. Fran's mum came over to her at once. Her face was drawn, but she put on a bright smile for Ellie.

'It's so good to see you, Ellie. Thanks for coming. Fran will be so pleased you came.'

'*Salut*, Christine. How is Fran today?'

'She's better, and much more relaxed, I think. We'll see if we can get you in to see her soon. Didier is understandably being very protective, but I'm sure he'll let you go in for at least a few minutes.'

Ellie kissed Joseph, Fran's dad, and then Sylvie, before taking a seat next to her.

'How are you, Sylvie?' Ellie noted the dark circles under Didier's mum's eyes and could only imagine the worry she'd experienced for the last couple of days.

'I'm better now. Poor old Fran and Didier. They've really been through it these past few days. It will cheer Fran up to see you.'

Ellie worried at her lip, but didn't say anything about her fears, not wanting to cause Sylvie any more concern than she was already experiencing. Fran was much more important than her fear of hospitals and maternity wards in particular. She steeled herself for what was about to come.

A door squeaked open down the corridor and Didier appeared a minute later, striding along towards his family and friends. The rigid look of his back showed the strain that he was under, and Ellie could tell that he was working hard to contain all his emotions.

Ellie wanted so desperately to see Fran, but if Didier wasn't prepared to let her see her friend, then she would have to accept his decision. Lottie had warned her that he was being protective but still she'd decided to try.

'Didier, how are you and how's Fran?' she asked, as she stood up and went to him.

'She's better, but she's still vulnerable. I know you want to see her, Ellie, but I can only let you in for a few minutes. I don't want to take the risk of her getting overtired.'

Didier had his arms folded protectively across his body and she could see the toll this had all taken on him as well.

'I understand that, of course. But she's my dearest friend, Didier, and I love her almost as much as you do. I just want to see for myself that she's okay. I promise I only need a couple of minutes.'

Didier stared at her for a long moment, his gruff exterior almost persuading her to flee, but she maintained eye contact with him and crossed her fingers behind her back, willing him to agree.

He turned away and drew in a deep breath, his shoulders relaxing as he did so. 'I'll go in and ask Fran how she's feeling. It will be up to her, and whatever she says, I'll stick by that.'

Ellie nodded and watched as he disappeared into Fran's room just down the corridor. She waited with bated breath for him to reappear, which he did a couple of moments later. He gave her a quick nod and held open the door for her.

'Don't be in there too long, please. She's still very fragile.'

Ellie went in and waited for Didier to shut the door. She stared at her friend in the hospital bed, a pale, weakened version of her normal self, attached to all kinds of machines, and she struggled to hold herself together.

'I'm so sorry that you've not been well, Fran, we all are. But we're all looking forward to the weddings and to your baby's birth and for everything from here on in. We're a team and a family, and we all want you to get better.'

Fran cleared her throat, wincing at the effort. 'Thank you, Ellie. I'm so sorry to have worried you all.'

A tear escaped and rolled down Ellie's cheek then. Fran smiled at her and extended her arms, and Ellie had never been more grateful for a hug in her whole life. There was strength in it, and it reassured her that Fran would come back from this.

'How are you feeling now?' she asked.

'Better now that I don't feel sick all the time, but I do feel so weak. I haven't been able to eat much for the past few days, and I'm just so tired. They won't let me go while I'm feeling like that.' Fran's eyes closed briefly and Ellie had to stop herself from shedding more tears.

She took Fran's hand instead and squeezed it gently. 'Just try to take it one step at a time, and you'll get there.' She had no idea if that was true, but she would give anything for Fran to be okay and back home again, including making promises she had no control over.

Henri

It had been a long day, during which Henri had manned the office, and Thierry and Frédéric had managed the Centre between them. They weren't going back to their normal schedule across the business until next week, so at least things were manageable for the time being. Now he was looking forward to cooking dinner and spending time with Ellie. He made his way down the hallway to the kitchen where he found Ellie chopping vegetables for a stir fry.

'How was Fran? Did you get to see her?' he asked as he joined her.

Ellie put down her chopping knife and turned to face him for a kiss. 'Oh, Henri, she looked like a shadow of herself. It was so hard not to let her see how worried I was. I really think she's so brave having a baby.'

'Fran's a strong person, though, and she wants this baby so much. She'll get through it; I know she will.'

Ellie resumed chopping. 'I have to be honest, Henri, and say that as much as I love children and want to have my own, the thought of giving birth to one does frighten me, let alone being a good parent after they're born. The others all seem so naturally good at it, whereas I have no experience at all.'

'I can't help on the giving birth front, but when we're in that position, I will support you every step of the way. I hope you know that.' Henri paused to give Ellie a reassuring smile. 'And I'm sure no-one knows how to be a good parent when they do it for the first time. We'll learn it along the way together. And the more time you spend around Fran and Lottie, the more experience you'll gain. Look how much you've come to love Chlöe in the past couple of years and Marie since she was born.'

Ellie smiled. 'I do love them, that's very true.' She was quiet for a moment and Henri waited patiently while she worked out what it was she wanted to say. 'What if we start a family, Henri, and I get called away somewhere? How would you feel about that? Would you be happy to stay here on your own with our children while I went off on trips?'

It was a fair question, and an important one. 'I'd be happy to stay here, as I know you would, if I ever got called away for some reason. The thing is that what children need is stability. That's what I wanted most as a child, and I found constantly moving around hard, but my parents were devoted to one another and that kept us together as a family. I think stability was lacking in your life, too, and so that would be the most important thing for me, to make sure our children had that security.'

'You're right,' Ellie replied. 'Chris was the only constant in my life when I was growing up. When I look back now, I can see that I depended on him so much. He was a mum and a dad to me in the face of all we had to deal with. That's what got me through it all really. I couldn't bear to fail at everything in the way my parents did.'

Henri stopped what he was doing and washed his hands. 'Oh, Ellie, we have to be brave and take a leap of faith here. Neither of us knows what's going to happen in our future, but we do know that we love each other, and we've been together long enough now to know that we belong with each other. Now it's up to us to decide whether we can take the next step. I want to take that step with you, and I think we've got a strong chance of finding our own happy ever after.'

Ellie shook her head. 'I want that, too. I honestly can't believe how much you love me, Henri.'

'We'll be fine, I promise. I'll be there with you every step of the way, and we'll face everything together.'

Henri abandoned making dinner and drew Ellie closer, slipping his fingers into her hair.

'I love you, Henri,' she whispered.

He lowered his lips to hers, and as the kiss deepened, she put her arms around his waist so that their two bodies were almost like one. Their heartbeats thudded together confirming that this was where they belonged. Henri dotted kisses along her jaw and down to her neck, and she arched her body into his as the pleasure built within them. He broke off then to take her hand and lead her upstairs.

As they undressed each other, their eyes remained locked together, each of them communicating their love to the other without the need for words. Henri guided them to the bed and Ellie trembled as he continued to worship her body, his fingers gliding over her skin. When they joined together, it was as if they were making love for the first time, as all the barriers between them finally came down, and Henri sensed Ellie no longer felt the need to hold anything back.

'I love you, Ellie, so much,' Henri told her as a tear rolled slowly down her cheek. He hoped she knew how much he meant it.

They held each other for a long time afterwards as if they both recognised that their relationship had now moved to a different level.

'Are you okay?' Henri asked as he lay back down beside her. 'You were crying at the end there.'

'I'm fine. It was just the emotion of it all. I don't think I've ever felt like that before.' She rolled onto her side so she could look at him. 'I want to spend the rest of my life with you, Henri,' she told him.

'Thank God.' He chuckled. 'My heart would have broken if you'd left.'

CHAPTER EIGHTEEN

Friday, 4 January 2019

<u>Ellie</u>

'You look one hundred times better than when I saw you the other day,' Ellie told Fran after Didier had showed her up to their bedroom. She reached out to pat Ruby, who was lying underneath the bed, happy to be looking after her mistress once again.

'It just feels so good to be home again,' Fran replied, sinking back against the pillows after kissing Ellie hello.

'I bet it does. You're going to have to take it easy over the next few days, though, to make sure you're fully better. Henri can manage on his own in the office and I can cover wherever I'm needed.'

Fran smiled at her. 'You've changed so much since you came back from your travels, you know. Back then, you couldn't wait to be off again, and now you've really become a part of the family here.'

'Thank you. You've all been so good to me, and I really do feel like a member of the family. I love working on the château, and I'm delighted that we've now got the money to finish the job properly.

And I love my work on the website and blog, too. I haven't even had a chance to tell you that some other vineyards have been in touch asking for my advice to help them revive their own estates.'

'That's amazing. Your reputation is already spreading far and wide, and that will reflect well on Domaine des Montagnes, too. And where are those vineyards?' Fran's eyes twinkled and Ellie smiled at the way her friend understood her so well.

'Two in France, one in northern Italy and the other in Spain so far.'

'How does Henri feel about you travelling to see them?'

'We've agreed that I won't go for longer than a week at a time, and that suits me, too. I don't want to be away for long periods, but I think it will do me good to travel every now and then.'

'So everything's good with you and Henri?' Fran asked.

Ellie hesitated for a moment. Should she tell Fran everything that had happened? 'Yes, mostly.'

'Well, go on, what else has happened while I've been away?'

'He asked me to marry him.' Ellie grinned as Fran gasped.

'And what did you say?'

'I haven't really given him an answer yet, because at that point, we hadn't sorted out the issue of me travelling to those vineyards, and then you went into hospital. We have talked since then, though, so if he were to ask me again, well, anything could happen.' Ellie shrugged and laughed.

'He will, I'm sure of it. He loves you so much, I don't think he could live without you now. I've always known you were right for each other, from that very first day you met.'

Ellie remembered that day fondly, when she'd travelled from London to see Fran in Alsace for the first time, and on their first night out, she'd met Henri at the bar. They'd come a long way since then.

'We've even talked about starting a family now.'

'Oh, Ellie, I'm so pleased. I know that's always been one of your biggest worries. So, how do you feel about it?'

'Since we spoke about it, I've realised that I've spent a lot of my life being frightened of one thing or another. Frightened to be in a relationship in case it turned out like my parents' one did; frightened to stay in one place in case I feel trapped by it; frightened to have children in case I'm a rubbish parent like my mum was. And now I think maybe it's time for me to stop being frightened and to try being brave, with Henri's help.'

Fran took Ellie's hands in hers. 'You're one of the bravest people I know, but you've had a lot to deal with in your life, and recently, as well, and you needed time to come to terms with that, to build your trust. And Henri has shown that he's worthy of your trust. He'll always be there for you.'

'I know, just like Didier's been there for you. Changing the subject slightly, I wanted to ask you about the wedding date – not to put any pressure on you, but to take it off. We can postpone everything if you don't feel up to it. It's only three weeks to go, and I'm worried that it will be too much for you to try to get better if you're constantly worrying about things to do with your wedding day. Are you sure you're up to the wedding on that date?'

'Oh, I will be, I promise. Nothing's going to stop me marrying Didier after all this time. We've both waited long enough for it. And now it's all going to happen here, it couldn't be easier for me.'

'Does Didier agree? Because he can be fierce when he wants to be, and I don't want to go against his wishes.' Ellie held up her hands, remembering just how protective Didier had been of Fran at the hospital.

Fran laughed. 'He does, but I know he's worried about it. I think he'd just like me to stay in bed for the next few months until the baby's born, but I can't do that. I want to get back out there–' she gestured out the window '–and to be a part of this new partnership we're going to form together.'

Didier appeared at the door then, knocking softly before coming in.

'I think you need to get some rest now,' he said, interrupting them. 'I'm sorry, but I just don't want you to get too tired, otherwise you never will get back out there.'

'I hope you haven't been eavesdropping, Monsieur Le Roy,' Fran said, wagging her finger at her husband-to-be.

Didier feigned innocence but looked pointedly at Ellie.

'Okay, okay, I'm on my way. I'll see you both again soon. Let us know if you want us to look after Chlöe any time, won't you? Or pick her up from school when they go back.'

She blew Fran a kiss and then made her way back downstairs, glad to see her friend back at home and in good spirits.

Henri

Henri had covered the office without Fran again today, and while he had no problem doing that, he was starting to miss her company.

'How was Fran when you went to see her today?' Henri asked Ellie when they were sitting down before dinner that evening. 'I was hoping she might be well enough to come back to the office some of the time next week.'

'She was much better, but I wouldn't say she was strong enough to be coming into the office again yet. And I think Didier would have something to say if she even suggested it.'

'Yes, he was adamant that she wouldn't be coming in when he popped in after his inspection, and I understand that, but knowing Fran, I think she might have other ideas.'

He leaned back on the sofa and put his feet up on the stool in front of him, before slipping his arm round Ellie to draw her closer to him.

'I asked her whether she still wants to go ahead with the same date for the wedding, given all that's happened, and she was determined that they would still be getting married then.'

Henri chuckled. 'She knows her own mind, doesn't she? I wonder what Didier thinks about that.'

'She must have talked it over with him, but she's told me to press on. I didn't talk about any specifics today. I don't want to tire her out when she's trying to get better.' She paused for a moment and Henri sensed there was something else on her mind. 'There is something I want to talk to you about, though,' Ellie said a moment later.

'What's that?' He forced himself to keep calm and ignore the nerves he experienced every time she said something like that. Maybe it would be good news, he said to himself.

'A few days ago now, you asked me a question and I still haven't given you my reply.'

He sat up then and stared into her green eyes, trying to remember what it was he'd asked her. Then all of a sudden, it came back to him. The proposal.

'Oh, that's fine,' he said, wanting to put her at ease. 'We don't have to talk about that now.'

'What if I want to talk about it?' she asked.

He gasped, unsure of the right thing to say. 'Go on,' he said, once they were sitting face to face on the sofa.

'Would you mind terribly if I asked you to propose to me again?' She looked nervously at him and his love for her almost overwhelmed him.

'Not at all. Hang on though. There's something I need to get from upstairs.'

He dashed up the stairs, taking them two at a time, coming to a stop in front of his chest of drawers. He opened the top drawer and took out the little velvet box he'd stored there since the first time round. He hadn't expected to need it for quite some time. He opened the lid of the box quickly, just to check it was still there, before turning and bounding back downstairs again.

He stood before Ellie, the only woman he had ever loved, catching his breath.

'Ellie... would you...?'

'Hang on. I want you to do it properly, please.' She gestured to him to get down on one knee, and he laughed at her bossiness.

He cleared his throat and took a deep breath. 'Ellie, I love you. Will you do me the honour of becoming my wife?' It had never been so hard to say so few words, but he preferred the words he'd used this time to what he'd said before.

Ellie beamed at him before leaning forward to kiss him. 'Yes, I will. Thank you.'

Henri slipped the ring on to her finger and then they were whooping together and kissing and hugging. 'I don't think I've ever been happier than I am now, hearing you say those three words. I love you so much and I can't wait to spend the rest of my life with you.'

'Me too. I'm sorry it took me so long to get round to saying yes.'

'Don't be sorry for one minute. It's better that you're sure now.'

'I think we should celebrate tonight then so that I can make up for ruining the lovely meal you cooked for me the other day.'

They spent the next hour gathering together the ingredients for a *tarte flambée* and then preparing the thin dough before sprinkling on the toppings. Once it was in the oven, Henri fetched the bottle of Domaine des Montagnes *crémant d'Alsace* he'd put in the fridge earlier. He popped the cork and poured out two glasses, handing one to Ellie.

'To us. *Monsieur et Madame* Weiss.' He clinked his glass against Ellie's and tried not to think about his parents, the last couple with that name.

'To us,' Ellie echoed. 'I can hardly believe that Chris has got married, and now I'm going to be getting married too.'

'And we still have Fran and Didier's wedding, as well as Lottie and Thierry's to come.'

'That's given me an idea.' Ellie's eyes gleamed and he wondered what plan she was hatching now.

'What about?' he asked.

'What if we got married at the same time?'

'A triple wedding? I like the idea but I wouldn't want to steal their thunder, and I wouldn't like to add any more stress.'

'I don't think it would, but I know what you mean. Still, it would be wonderful if we could all get married together.' Ellie looked wistful and Henri wanted so much to make this dream come true for her.

'We'll have to ask them and see what they think. We can only ask.'

The timer went off in the kitchen and Henri grabbed the oven gloves before removing the *tarte* from the oven.

'That looks fabulous,' Ellie said as Henri brought it over to the table. 'I can't wait to taste it.'

'I hate to say it, but if we do go for the original date, it might be short notice, you know, for Chris and your dad to come over for the wedding.'

Ellie's face fell. 'That's true. I hadn't even thought of that. I'll have to ring them over the weekend and let them know it's a possibility. I definitely want them both to come. And I'll be able to have my dad give me away.' Ellie's eyes sparkled and, at last, Henri felt at peace.

Ellie

'Hello, how are you both?' Ellie was delighted to see her dad and Chris appear on the screen before her at the same time. Modern technology was such a marvellous thing when it worked.

'Michelle and I are both fine. We're just about getting used to having to be back at work now.'

'You look very happy. Married life obviously suits you.'

'It does, sis. Maybe you should try it.' He laughed, not realising that this was the perfect cue for what she wanted to say.

'Well, that's why I'm getting in touch actually.'

Both men were rendered speechless for a second, and it was her turn to laugh at their reaction. Then they both started speaking at once. She held up her hands and waited for them to fall quiet.

'Yes, I have good news. Henri's proposed and I've said yes.'

'Well, congratulations first of all. I'm so pleased for you both. When did it happen?' her dad asked.

'We had a false start on New Year's Eve, but then he asked me again yesterday, and well, here we are.'

'So when's the date? Michelle will be delighted to hear about this,' Chris said.

'I'm here,' Michelle said, suddenly joining the conversation. 'I could hear all the whooping and hoped it was for the obvious reason.' She leaned against Chris and waited for Ellie to reply.

'Henri and I are getting married,' Ellie confirmed, 'and if everything works out, the wedding will be three weeks today. Is that enough time for you all to make it?' She nibbled at her lip, hoping they'd all be able to come.

'That's fine for me and Annie, I'm sure,' her dad replied. 'I'll look forward to it.'

'We'll have to check at work and maybe just come for the weekend, but you can count on us being there,' Chris said. 'I'm so happy for you both.'

'The only issue with the date is that Fran's been unwell in her pregnancy so we're hoping she'll be well enough to go ahead with that date. She says she will, but Didier's worried about her having too much on when she's trying to get better.'

'Well, you can keep us in the loop about that. Send her our love, though, won't you?' asked her dad.

'And Dad... Would you be prepared to give me away on the day?' Ellie asked tentatively.

Her dad cleared his throat. 'It would be an honour.'

'You two, honestly,' Chris joked, but Ellie could see he was touched, too. 'I have news about Mum's money, as well,' Chris continued. 'That should be through within the next week so you can get started on the château soon.'

'That's great news.' She told them all about the partnership then, and that they would be transforming the château into a wedding venue in due course.

'It's been lovely to chat but I'd better get off. We've got a triple wedding to plan,' Ellie said.

'Who else is getting married?' her dad asked, looking perplexed.

'It must be Lottie and Thierry! There's something in the water at that vineyard, I reckon,' Chris cried, and they were still laughing when they rang off.

Henri was coming back in from the market as she hung up, and she went to help him with the shopping.

'Hey,' she said. 'How did you get on?'

'All fine. I saw Sylvie and Frédéric, and she's looking much better now that Fran is at home. I told them our news and they were delighted. How about your dad and Chris?'

'Oh, the same,' Ellie replied, taking one of the bags of shopping down to the kitchen. 'They all think they'll be able to come on that date, but I said I'll let them know.'

'What time did you say we'd pick Chlöe up?' Henri asked as they unpacked the shopping.

'After lunch, so we've still got plenty of time.'

They made their way back to the château an hour later, enjoying the walk through the village and along the footpath. Ellie was glad that things would be returning to normal next week. She'd just about managed to keep on top of her emails and blog post comments, but she was itching to write new articles and do new interviews. She would have to let the vineyards who had contacted her know that she might not be able to come for a while, what with Fran being ill and every pair of hands being needed on the estate once work started up again next week. But she was sure they'd be able to work something out that suited everyone.

They were level now with the cottage where Fran and Didier had lived with Chlöe when they'd first got together.

'Do you really think Fran and Didier will be okay to live here when work starts on the upstairs of the château again?' Ellie asked. 'That cottage really is tiny and won't be good enough for them in the longer term.'

'Thierry seemed to think it would be an easy job to extend it. There's plenty of room around it. They'd have to move out while that happened, but it could work. It would just all be a bit disruptive for them, and there is the cost, of course, which is what Didier would be most worried about.'

'I think we can get round that, and maybe they can alternate between the château and the cottage while the different works are being done. When the baby's first born, it would be in with Fran and Didier anyway, wouldn't it?'

'That's true. I think that could work. It would be nice for them to have a home of their own on their estate at the end of it as well.'

Ellie turned her focus to the château and smiled at the thought of finishing the restoration work at last. Everything was finally working out and she couldn't be happier.

Henri

Henri was hoping that today would be the day when finally everything would be sorted out. He already felt so much lighter knowing that Ellie had accepted his proposal and that everyone was pleased for them. They'd told Fran and Didier at the weekend, as well, and Ellie had called Lottie so that she didn't hear it from anyone else first.

Henri was just finishing a phone call to one of their suppliers when Didier came in. Henri gave him a quick wave, taking in his friend's more relaxed demeanour, before concentrating on his call.

'Morning, Didier. How are things?' he asked when he finally rang off from the call.

'Things are better, but we're still very tired. Still, it's so good to have Fran home again. Thanks for looking after Chlöe on Saturday. She had a lovely time with you two. And we were so pleased about your news.'

'No problem at all about Chlöe. We're always happy to look after her. And thank you.'

'Now all I need to do is to make sure that Fran takes it easy until the wedding. Three weeks isn't a very long time for her to get herself completely well again. And I know how tempted she'll be to get back to normal, but she really does need to rest.'

'Has she said she wants to postpone?' Henri asked.

'No, no, but I don't want it to stress her out.'

'Of course. I think Ellie and Lottie have been working hard to make sure that they only speak to Fran about the crucial things, and I'm managing okay on my own here.'

'I know, and I appreciate that.'

'There is something I wanted to talk to you about concerning the wedding. I hope it's not bad timing to mention it now.'

'Don't tell me something else has gone wrong. I don't know how much more I can take.'

'No, no, nothing's gone wrong.' He paused for a moment, hoping this wasn't a bad idea. 'It's just that Ellie and I wondered if we might join you on your wedding day and turn it into a triple wedding.'

'A triple wedding?' Didier's expression suggested he'd never heard of such a thing.

The door opened then and Thierry came in.

'*Salut, tout le monde. Ça va?*' He stamped his boots off on the mat before walking over to the coffee machine.

'Henri was just telling me that he thinks we should have a triple wedding.'

'Ah yes, congratulations! So glad I can now say it in person,' Thierry said, reaching out to shake Henri's hand. 'I think a triple wedding sounds like a fabulous idea.'

Henri and Thierry both turned their attention back to Didier, waiting for his answer.

'I like the idea, but I'd have to talk to Fran about it first.'

'Do you think we could pull it off in the short time left before the date?' Thierry asked.

'It was Ellie's idea, and she and Lottie have been planning the wedding with Fran, so they know better than anyone if it's a goer. I don't think Ellie would have suggested it if she didn't think it would be possible. But if you're upset by the idea, we'll understand. We don't want to steal anyone's thunder.' Henri shuffled some papers around on his desk.

'I'm definitely not upset. I'm just exhausted and I think my brain has been turned to mush after the past few days. Let me talk to Fran and then we'll take it from there.' Didier stood up from his desk and stretched his arms above his head.

'You're going to need to get some sleep in before this baby comes, you know,' Thierry told him as he went to put on his coat.

'Ha! Listen to the expert.' Didier laughed. 'I know. You're right. Given the opportunity, I would sleep for a day, I tell you. I'll see you both later.'

'So do you think Lottie would go for a triple wedding?' Henri asked Thierry.

Thierry shrugged. 'I don't think she'd mind at all. She's just happy we're getting married.'

'She loves you more than anything.'

'I'm glad everything's worked out for you and Ellie as well.'

'Me too. It's a relief not to have to worry about the future any more,' Henri told his friend.

'Do you really think we could pull off a triple wedding though? You weren't just saying that for Didier's benefit?'

'Why not? Everything's in place for the first two. All this means is adding in a few more guests, more food, more drink, more flowers... Just more. It will be amazing.'

'It's been such a difficult year, but everything's coming together now, and this will be a great way to celebrate our new venture all together.'

'Exactly. It will be a great celebration all round with all our friends and family.'

Thierry left then to make his way up to the Visitors' Centre, and

Henri took a moment to reflect on the absence of his parents on his wedding day. He would miss them on the most important day of his life, but he also had a new family now. Not just his friends from the vineyard but also Ellie's family, who had welcomed him in as one of their own without any hesitation. So as much as he would always miss his parents, he could also start to look forward now to the new family he would form with Ellie and the new life they would lead together.

CHAPTER NINETEEN

Ellie

Ellie arrived at the château to start work again the following morning, having spent the previous day catching up on emails and blog comments. She'd booked in some more interviews with village traders and some more of their suppliers as well. There were going to be a few busy weeks ahead.

She made her way quietly upstairs, careful not to disturb Fran as she passed by her bedroom.

'Ellie, is that you?' Fran called out, causing Ellie to jump in the otherwise silent house.

She went in to find Fran sitting up in bed looking much better. 'Hello,' she said. 'I'm sorry if I disturbed you. I was trying to be quiet.'

'You didn't disturb me at all. Come and sit with me for a minute before I die of boredom.'

Ellie hesitated, not wanting to go against Didier's wishes and overload Fran, but also desperate to ask her the question she most wanted the answer to. 'How are you feeling?'

Fran threw her hands up. 'I feel much better and I want to get back to work. I'm so bored.' She rolled her eyes and Ellie laughed.

'You have to take it easy though. You can't just go straight back to how things were before. What does Didier have to say?'

'He just wants me to stay in bed and rest, and I know I need to, but I'm determined to start going into the office again soon. Anyway, talk to me. Tell me exciting things.'

'Has Didier mentioned my idea to you?'

Fran frowned for a moment as if trying to remember. 'Ah, yes, the triple wedding idea.' Ellie nodded and held her breath. 'I definitely like the idea, but that's another thing that Didier's worried about me getting stressed out about.'

'It's fine if you don't want us to join you,' Ellie said, trying not to sound disappointed.

'Of course I want you to join us. It's the best idea ever.'

Ellie's hands flew to her face. 'You don't mean...?'

'Yes, I do. I'll be fine, and I know I can rely on you and Lottie to bring the last few remaining jobs together.' Fran laughed in delight.

Ellie sank onto the chair at the side of Fran's bed. 'Are you sure you wouldn't mind us gatecrashing your big day?'

'Of course not. What could be better than the three of us all getting married together? It will be fantastic.'

'I put my dad and Chris on standby in the hope that you and Didier would agree, so I can confirm now. And everything else is pretty much sorted.'

'But what will you wear? You won't have had time to get a dress.'

'I have a dark green velvet dress that I bought for Christmas, so I'm going to go with that. It will be a break with tradition, but I'm not worried about that anyway. You know me.'

Fran laughed. 'I do know you and that sounds perfect.' Fran clapped her hands together. 'It will be so wonderful. Can you imagine my mum's face if we all get married on the same day?'

'Christine might be speechless for once,' Ellie said with a wink.

There was a quiet tap at the door and Ellie stood up to answer it.

'Surprise!' Lottie cried.

'Lottie, remember what I said,' Didier's voice called up from below.

'Come on in,' Ellie said, giving her friend a hug.

Lottie went over to give Fran a hug and a kiss as well.

'I just had to come and see you. I want to know whether we're going for a triple wedding or not,' Lottie asked.

'We most definitely are,' Fran confirmed to her sister.

'That's amazing. All three of us, really?'

'I know,' Fran said. 'It's going to be such a wonderful occasion.'

'Why aren't you wearing your ring? I was looking forward to seeing it,' Lottie asked Ellie.

'It had to be resized. It was Henri's mother's wedding ring and it was a bit too big, but it will be ready in time.'

'And have you got something sorted to wear, Lottie?' Ellie asked this time.

'I haven't had a moment to look, but I'm sure I can find something.'

'All we need to do now then is get there and say yes at the appropriate moment,' Ellie said.

'In just over two weeks' time, we will all be married. Can you believe it? I never would have thought that this year would begin with me getting married and then becoming a mum,' Fran said.

'It's been a bit of a rollercoaster this past year, but we've made it and it's all going to end fabulously.' Ellie beamed at her friends, delighted that everything had worked out for them all at last.

Ellie left Lottie to chat with her sister so that she could go and do some more preparation work in the small bedroom. She stood for a moment surveying her handiwork. She'd done a good job, but she had to admit that she would be glad when she could employ the plasterer to pick up the task. She could hardly wait for her inheritance money to come through so that work on the château could start again and she could finish the job she'd started over a year ago. That would be a fitting way to spend her mum's money and a good legacy after all that had gone before.

Thursday, 24 January 2019

Henri

The only thing left to sort out before the wedding was the honeymoon, and it had been weighing on Henri's mind as he and Ellie had had no time to discuss it. Tonight was their only chance to make their final decision, and he wanted Ellie to be happy with whatever conclusion they reached, knowing how important travel was to her.

He finished washing up and went to join her in the living room, where she was busy packing her things neatly into her suitcase. They'd all talked about the difficulties of them taking honeymoons at the same time with things now being so busy at the estate, and it had been agreed that he and Ellie would go away for a week before coming back to allow Lottie and Thierry to get away. Fran and Didier were going to delay their break until after the new baby was born.

'So, apart from choosing to go back to Italy, we still haven't decided on where we're going to go for our honeymoon yet,' he said as he collapsed onto the sofa.

'I know,' she said, glancing up at him before continuing with her packing, 'but I have given it a lot of thought. Have you had any ideas?'

'I have, but I want you to be happy. I don't mind where we go.'

'If we had more time, I'd like it if we could combine the trip with some research for when we start work again on getting the château ready to receive guests. I've seen quite a few vineyards in Italy that have accommodation for paying guests, and I'd like to find out more about how they've done it. And we loved Italy so much when we went there earlier in the year, so it would be great if we could go back but this time visit the places we didn't get to last time. And as a bonus, I'd have lots of new material for my blog.'

'That sounds interesting, but I wouldn't want it to turn into a work trip when we're supposed to be relaxing. And as you said, we do only have a week.'

She stopped packing and looked at him properly this time. 'I know that, and I promise it wouldn't. It just makes sense if we're going anyway to combine the two, I think. Where would you like to visit?'

'I'm happy to go wherever you want to go. As long as we're together, that's all that matters to me.'

'You're such an old romantic,' she teased.

'Are you mocking me, Miss Robinson?'

'I wouldn't dare,' she joked, a look of false innocence on her face.

'So, back to the matter in hand,' Henri said, trying to regain his focus when all he wanted to do was make an early night of it with his wife-to-be. 'Shall we plan it all out or just choose our first destination and go from there?'

Ellie zipped up her suitcase and came to sit next to him. 'You know how much I love the sense of adventure we'll get by not planning it out. Let's just get our train ticket to our first destination and then go where the fancy takes us.'

'Done. Are you all packed and ready?'

'I am, which reminds me that you still have to do all your packing too.'

Henri groaned. 'I hate packing.'

'Why? All your stuff's ready. All you have to do is put it into your suitcase. It's not that hard.'

'Will you help me?' He gave her his best 'sad puppy' look and she rolled her eyes at him in return.

'Go and get everything and then I'll direct you,' she told him.

They spent the next hour sorting out all his things and discussing where they might start their honeymoon.

'Have you ever been to Venice?' Henri asked. 'We should definitely make time to go and visit.'

'I haven't been to Venice or Verona which is also nearby. And then there are the lakes as well. I think we might have to draw up a shortlist. There are so many beautiful places in Italy and we won't be able to see them all, even though we made a good start last time.'

'Maybe we should focus on one area this time, as we had a good go at the south last time. What do you think?'

'I like that idea. I'd like to get down as far as Tuscany though if we can. There will be some lovely estates we can visit there.'

By the time they went upstairs to bed, Henri was buzzing with excitement at the thought of it all. He loved planning his future out with Ellie and couldn't wait to get married to her at long last.

He lay awake long after she'd fallen asleep next to him, thinking how far they'd come together since they'd first met just over a year ago. His only regret was that his parents wouldn't be there on his wedding day. They would have loved Ellie. He was sure of that, and he hoped that wherever they were, they were looking down on him and able to see just how happy he was to have met her.

He started going over his checklist for the wedding day on Saturday in the hope that it would calm his busy mind and help him to fall asleep. They'd organised cars to bring Fran, Lottie and Ellie from Thierry's house where they'd be getting ready, to the château where Didier, Thierry and Henri would be waiting. Ellie had sorted out the flowers and the cake, and Lottie had taken charge of the rest of the catering. Thierry and Didier had sorted out the wine, while Joseph and Frédéric had made sure that the band and photographer were organised. Even though he'd been over this list a thousand times in his mind, he was still worried that they might have forgotten something.

But first, tomorrow was the day of the civil ceremonies. He had the ring and that was the main thing. He had collected Ellie's engagement ring just yesterday, and the wedding ring he'd chosen matched it perfectly. He was sure she would like it, and as he began to dream of putting the ring on her finger and making Ellie his wife, he finally began to fall asleep.

———

Saturday, 26 January 2019

Ellie

Ellie studied herself in the dressing table mirror as she considered the significance of the day ahead. Although they'd held the civil ceremonies the day before, the blessing that was taking place today at the château was more important to her. She'd never imagined herself trusting anyone enough to get married to them, and yet here she was. Henri had transformed her life by believing in her, and giving her his commitment, and she loved him more than she would have thought possible.

She turned her head from side to side, marvelling at the flattering updo Sylvie had created with her hair. The light caught all the different shades of red as she moved, and for once, she was proud of her curls. The emerald stones in her earrings matched her resized engagement ring, and together with her green velvet dress, they finished off her look. Her heart was full, and she didn't have any doubts about what she was about to do.

As she stood and smoothed out her dress, there was a quick knock at the door. It must be time, she thought to herself.

'Come in,' she called.

'Oh Ellie, love. You look stunning,' her dad told her. 'I'm so proud of you.'

'Thanks, Dad. And thanks so much for agreeing to give me away. It means the world to me that you're here.'

'There's no other place I'd rather be than here today. Shall we go? It's time.'

They made their way downstairs where Lottie and Fran were waiting in the hallway, together with their parents, Chlöe and Annie.

Ellie hugged her friends one last time and gave Chlöe a kiss. 'You all look amazing,' she told them.

'Just as well I went for the bigger size on this dress. I can only just about breathe as it is.' Fran laughed.

'It looks so beautiful,' Lottie said with a smile.

'So does yours,' Ellie said. 'Sylvie did a wonderful job transforming her wedding dress to fit you. Isn't it amazing that she got married in wintertime, too?'

'It's perfect, and I feel so lucky,' Lottie agreed.

'Right then everyone,' Joseph called. 'It's time to go. Can we start getting everyone into their cars, please?'

Ellie was travelling with her dad and Annie, leaving Lottie, Fran and Chlöe to travel to the château with their parents. It wasn't far, but she was glad of a few moments to think before everything got going. Her dad helped her into the back of the car and then he and Annie sat on either side of her.

'How are you feeling?' Annie asked as the car pulled away from the house for the short journey.

'I feel fine. I'm not nervous at all, and I expected to be.' She smiled at Annie. Even though they'd only just met, they'd hit it off at once, and that had added to Ellie's sense of contentment.

They were soon pulling up in front of the château, which looked smart with its newly tended gardens, and saying goodbye to Christine and Annie, who made their way inside together. Chlöe was going to lead the way with her basket of flowers in her hand, followed by Joseph, with Fran on one side and Lottie on the other. Ellie and her dad would bring up the rear.

'Are we all ready?' Fran asked, looking first at Lottie and then at Ellie.

'Let's do this,' said Ellie.

Her dad tucked her arm into his and they readied themselves to follow the others inside, where Didier, Thierry and Henri would be waiting. When the music began playing, they recognised their cue, and Fran, Lottie and Joseph stepped inside the building that had come to mean so much to all of them. Ellie held on tight to her dad's arm as they followed the others down the hallway, and as she progressed, one gasp after another rang out as all their guests reacted to their appearance inside the transformed living room.

She spotted Chris with Michelle and Annie and chuckled as he gave her a thumbs up. Sylvie was sitting next to Christine and her father, *Papi*, and she was already dabbing at her eyes. Marie was on Frédéric's lap, her little face full of wonder at the spectacle before her. As they neared the front of the room, Ellie's heartbeat sped up at the prospect of seeing Henri in his wedding suit, and knowing that very soon she would become his wife.

The others came to a stop, and Joseph kissed his daughters before taking Chlöe's hand and joining the rest of the family on the seats. Fran moved to join Didier, Lottie went to Thierry's side, and finally, Ellie saw Henri patiently waiting for her. His smile told her all she needed to know. She kissed her dad goodbye and went to join the man she loved for the most important day of her life.

Henri took her hand in his and leaned in to kiss her. 'You look gorgeous. I can't believe how lucky I am.'

They both turned to face the front and Ellie listened to the priest's words as if she was in a dream. The six of them all getting married together was the most wonderful thing, and she looked forward to celebrating with them all at the Visitors' Centre long into the night.

When it came to their turn to say the words to each other, it was all over and done with so quickly that Ellie thought she must have imagined it. Then Henri was taking her hand to slip the wedding ring on to her finger, and she was doing the same for him.

'You may now kiss the brides!'

No-one needed telling twice and cheers rang out throughout the room at the traditional end to the saying of the marriage vows.

'Congratulations, my darling,' Henri said, before kissing her firmly on the lips. 'I love you.'

'Oh, Henri, I love you so much,' she replied, hugging him to her.

Then it was time to make their way back outside as husband and wife, following behind Fran and Didier, and Lottie and Thierry, and looking forward to the biggest party any of them had ever had.

Monday, 28 January 2019

Henri

Henri dropped the last bag for their trip in the hallway and made his way through to the kitchen to start on breakfast. He wanted to make sure they wouldn't be hungry for a while, as the first leg of their journey was going to take quite a few hours.

As he whisked eggs together for an omelette, he could hear Ellie singing in the shower upstairs and he smiled at the thought of her strutting her stuff up there. He couldn't wait to set off on their honeymoon with her, but first they would be meeting up with everyone one last time for a big send-off.

'Hey, husband of mine, what are you cooking? It smells delicious.' Ellie slipped her arms around his waist and pressed her warm body against his.

'Nothing at all if you keep distracting me with your luscious body.' He laughed as she kissed his neck before turning to lay the table.

'I'm starving, though, come on. Feed me, please.'

He set two plates down on the table with a flourish. 'Ham and *Gruyère* omelette to send us on our way.'

Ellie took her first mouthful and groaned. 'You are a saint. Thank you.'

'Have you managed to finish all your packing now?'

'Yes, all done. I put my bag in the hallway on my way down. So just last-minute checks to do now. I've got the paperwork to give Didier, as well, for the château so that he can get started with moving the funds around while we're away.'

Henri breathed a sigh of relief knowing that they'd now managed to sort out the final job before their departure. Ellie's mum's money had come through at last and she would be able to pass it on to Didier for the benefit of the vineyard before they left today. They'd also contacted a solicitor about adding Ellie's name to the title deeds of his house.

'It feels good to have got it all organised before we go, so we don't have to even think about it while we're away.'

Half an hour later, they were ready to say goodbye to the house for a week and to load their bags into the car for the short journey to the vineyard. Henri locked the front door and gave the house one last glance before jumping into the car next to Ellie.

'Okay?' she asked with a grin.

He nodded. 'You?'

'More than okay. Let's go and say goodbye to everyone so we can get on our way.'

He pulled up in the car park outside the office a few minutes later. Didier and Thierry were both outside chatting, and Ruby, the dog, was chasing round after Chlöe and little Marie, who was just about stable on her feet now.

'*Bonjour, tout le monde,*' Henri said as he climbed out of the car.

The children came over to join them, and soon, Fran and Lottie emerged from the office, too.

'Here's the paperwork you need, Didier, before I forget,' Ellie said after kissing him hello.

'That's great, Ellie. Thank you both so much.' Henri nodded and smiled at his friend.

'Are you all set then?' Thierry asked, picking Marie up to give her a rest from Ruby's playful attentions.

'We are, and keen to get on our way now. It won't be long before you and Lottie are off too.'

'Yes, we've only got last-minute stuff to do this week. As we're driving, though, it makes it easier on us. We're going to leave early next Monday morning for Paris.'

'You'll have a wonderful time, I'm sure. And Sylvie's looking after Marie still?'

'Yes, that's right. She should be here in a minute to see you off.'

Lottie joined them then and Henri kissed her, too. 'I hope you both have a wonderful time, Henri. I know you will.'

'Thank you, and the two of you. It will be funny for you without Marie, won't it?'

'Yes, but she'll be happy with Sylvie. Oh, look, there she is now.'

Sylvie and Frédéric pulled in to the car park, and soon they were fussing over the children, and greeting everyone like long-lost friends.

Henri went to join Ellie and Fran. 'How are you feeling, Fran?'

'I'm fine, thanks, Henri. Now that the wedding's over and the finances are more under control, I feel so much more relaxed about everything. I don't even mind that you're all getting to go on honeymoon and I'm not.' She laughed.

'Ah, you'll have a wonderful time without us getting under your feet.' This time they all laughed.

'Now then, you two, you make sure you take care on these travels of yours, but have a wonderful time,' Sylvie said, coming up alongside Ellie and Henri.

'Oh, we will, Sylvie, we promise,' Ellie said, giving her a kiss and a hug.

'I think it's probably time for us to get our bags out of the car. The cab will be coming soon.' Henri looked at Ellie and she nodded.

He put the bags onto the gravel just as the taxi pulled in, and then braced himself to say goodbye again to these friends who had become his family.

'Wishing you lots of luck and good times on your honeymoon, both of you,' Didier said, shaking Henri's hand.

One by one they all came to say goodbye, and finally, the two of them were in the car waving as they set off for Strasbourg and then Italy.

Ellie wiped tears away from her eyes. 'That was much more emotional than I was expecting. They all mean so much to us, don't they?'

'They really do. They've become my family now, and you're part of that, too. Now we're going to have the time of our lives and bring back some wonderful memories to treasure.'

'Absolutely. I can't wait to make more memories with you, Henri.'

He leaned over to kiss his new wife and thanked his lucky stars for bringing her into his life.

The End

Because reviews are vital in spreading the word, please leave a brief review on **Amazon** if you enjoyed reading *A Leap of Faith at the Vineyard in Alsace*. Thank you!

ALSO BY JULIE STOCK

From Here to You series

Before You - Prequel - From Here to You

From Here to Nashville - Book 1 - From Here to You

Over You - Book 2 - From Here to You

Finding You - Book 3 - From Here to You

From Here to You series

Domaine des Montagnes series

First Chance - Prequel - Domaine des Montagnes

The Vineyard in Alsace - Book 1 - Domaine des Montagnes

Starting Over at the Vineyard in Alsace - Book 2 - Domaine des Montagnes

Standalone

The Bistro by Watersmeet Bridge

Bittersweet - 12 Short Stories for Modern Life

ABOUT THE AUTHOR

Julie Stock writes contemporary feel-good romance from around the world: novels, novellas and short stories.

She published her début novel, *From Here to Nashville*, in 2015, after starting to write as an escape from the demands of her day job as a teacher. *A Leap of Faith at the Vineyard in Alsace* is her latest book, and the third in the Domaine des Montagnes series set on a vineyard.

Julie is now a full-time author, and loves every minute of her writing life. When not writing, she can be found reading, her favourite past-time, running, a new hobby, or cooking up a storm in the kitchen, glass of wine in hand.

Julie is a member of The Society of Authors.

Julie is married and lives with her family in Cambridgeshire in the UK.

Sign up for Julie's free author newsletter at **www.julie-stock.co.uk.**

ACKNOWLEDGMENTS

I would like to thank my husband for his support during the writing of this book, which took place while we put our family home on the market for the first time in seventeen years! This meant that there were long periods of time when I couldn't write at all because we were so busy packing, and then finally moving to our new home.

Once we moved though, I set up my new office as soon as I could, and got back to writing and rewriting with a vengeance, to make sure the book would be finished and published in summer 2021. And even though I'll be doing it by the skin of my teeth, I am pleased and proud to be reaching the milestone of publishing another book.

Thank you for purchasing this book. I really hope you enjoy reading it. Technically, this book brings the trilogy to an end, unless of course, I have another idea for a book set on The Vineyard in Alsace...

Printed in Great Britain
by Amazon

18510748R00150